Praise for Susan Union and *Rode to Death*

"Readers will thoroughly enjoy Susan Union's debut mystery, *Rode to Death*, a skillfully crafted modern day western of greed, lust, treachery and revenge."

—Michael Murphy, author of *Goodbye Emily*

"*Rode to Death* offers noble animals, smart (and smartass) women, and an intriguing mystery. Lovers of all three will find much to enjoy in Susan Union's charming book."

—Marianne Wesson, author of *Render Up the Body*

"Susan Union combines a naive heroine, fancy horses, Southern California wealth, several hunks and no shortage of good guys in a tale of threats and murder that keeps the reader turning pages until the last unexpected reveal at the end."

—Betsy Ashton, author of *Mad Max: Unintended Consequences*

"Susan Union writes with a crisp voice that makes *Rode To Death* a compelling read and an engaging debut novel."

—Mary Billiter, author of *Not My Kid...* and *The XYZ Affair*

"Susan Union's characters will clench your heart. In *Rode To Death*, she has written a suspenseful tale that will keep you reading late into the night."

—Shelley K. Wall, author of *Chloe's Secret*

Rode to Death

by Susan Union

© Copyright 2014 by Susan Union

ISBN 978-1-938467-84-4

Published by

◤ köehlerbooks™

210 60th Street
Virginia Beach, VA 23451
212-574-7939
www.koehlerbooks.com

Publisher
John Köehler

Executive Editor
Joe Coccaro

Visit the Author's website

www.susanunion.com

For my family, with love.

Rode
to Death

A Randi Sterling Mystery

Susan Union

VIRGINIA BEACH
CAPE CHARLES

Men are generally more careful of the breed of their horses and dogs than of their children.

—William Penn

One

RANDI STERLING STEPPED OUT of the sunlight into the breeding barn. She breathed deep. Some people thought horses stunk or considered them large, frightening beasts to be avoided, but to Randi, a life without the scent of hay and horse would be colorless and flat.

Forget a shrink's couch. A horse beneath you, a beckoning trail and the squeak of saddle leather was far better therapy than trying to resolve if it was your mother's infidelities or your father's alcoholism—or, perhaps, both—that made you screwy.

In the center of the breeding room, six-figure Quarter Horse stallion Hesa Rebel Man, Rebel for short, pranced sideways until he hit the end of his rope, neck arched, ears up.

Randi's friend Kira came through the double doors and gave her a hug. "I'm here for you, but we're shorthanded at the restaurant so I can't stay long. Besides, you know Houston likes to keep these breedings private. I mean, I get that it's his ranch and all, but it's not like there's a bunch of equine voyeurs out there."

Kira's white-blonde hair and St. Pauli Girl curves were hardly inconspicuous. Randi handed her a notebook and camera.

"Take these. If Houston gives you a hard time, I'll say you're here as my assistant. He can't argue with that."

Kira waved the notepad. "Journalists hardly need a Sherpa to schlep their stuff around."

"Don't sell yourself short. You're helping me carry my emotional baggage, and we all know how much that weighs."

Kira swiveled her head. "I don't see *her*. So far so good."

"She'll be here. Rebel's her stallion, and you know how possessive she is. The good news is this is probably the last time I'll have to watch her hang all over my ex. I'm starting to pack as soon as I'm done here."

"That's what you think. I know you've only been in San Diego six months, but it feels like I've known you forever. Which is why I'm not letting you leave."

"That's sweet, Kira, but there's nothing worse than being a third wheel and watching the guy you thought you'd marry make out with his new wife."

"It's February. Why would anyone in their right mind leave Southern California for Colorado in the dead of winter?"

"Who says I'm in my right mind? Anyway, Colorado's home."

Kira clucked her tongue. "Forget about skipping town and focus on the horse. He's the reason you're here right now, remember?"

"How could I forget? *HorseWorld* magazine is my shot at the big time. Let's go stand near the wash rack where we can get a better view."

The breeding manager of Lucky Jack Performance Horses, gave the two of them a cursory nod before she handed Rebel's lead rope over to his groom.

Randi leaned in. "Piper didn't even do a double take on you, and there's nothing she likes better than snitching to Houston. I think you're in the clear."

Kira tucked the notebook under her arm and applied a coat of her trademark red lipstick. The combination of bright red lips on milky-white skin made her look like a porcelain doll or an Austrian farmer's daughter. She dropped the lipstick into her bag. "Piper doesn't notice anything unless it has four legs and a tail. Come to think of it, I've never seen her with a guy, only with stallions."

"Hey, at least a horse will sometimes give you a warning snort before he bucks you off. Men are far harder to read."

Houston Hill, the ranch's owner, leaned against the wall, an unlit cigarette dangling from his lip. A stranger might think him relaxed, but anytime a stallion was present, Houston had his guard up. Most stable owners put maximum effort into absolving themselves of culpability, but Houston refused to shy away from duty—making him a guy Randi would have been proud to call her father-in-law, if things had turned out the way they were supposed to.

Houston's eyes skimmed the room, landed on Kira, registered a question mark followed by a look of resignation when he saw Randi. He removed a fleck of tobacco from his tongue and pushed himself away from the wall.

Kira nodded at the group of strangers gathered in the breeding room. "Look at them. If I sold my restaurant and everything I own along with it, I wouldn't come close to having the kind of money they do. Check out the hat. The silverbelly Stetson that guy has on. I bet it's at least a five X. Why are they here, anyway?"

"Looking to breed their mares to Rebel, if they can convince Houston they're worthy. How about the belt buckle on the tall one! Salad plate, anyone?"

The women wore True Religion jeans paired with tight Swarovski crystal-studded tops. Louis Vuitton bags swung heavy from their elbows, while waves of expensive perfume clashed with Rebel's musky sweat. The couples conversed in church-like whispers, eyes glued to the stallion who danced in place, hooves tapping the floor, snorting and pawing and wanting to get on with the business at hand. The temperature in the room had to have gone up a good ten degrees.

Rebel's mahogany coat gleamed. He sported a thick white blaze that zigzagged from underneath his forelock before splitting in two above his nostrils. Randi clicked her pen, hoping to capture the stallion's legendary charisma in a way that would differentiate her from the other journalists out there. When it came to horses, God *was* in the details. "His face marking reminds me of a Flying V."

"You mean the guitar?" Kira asked.

"Yep. Gibson. Electric."

Rebel bugled a whinny and all conversation stopped. Piper left Houston's side and crossed the room to take the lead rope from Rebel's groom.

Kira scratched her nose. "You're right about one thing. He's clearly ready to rock."

"That's clever. Mind if I steal it?"

"No charge. I'd be honored. What's your angle?"

"Business. Quarter Horse breeding is a high-priced, elite enterprise, but the horse is just doing what his hormones tell him to do, then we come along to manage and control it. People pay a lot of money to obtain the fastest and most athletic horses to annihilate the competition with style and grace, and it all starts here, in the breeding barn with the lust coming off Rebel's hide and the vibrations of his hooves galloping right up the readers' spines."

Kira snickered. "What are you writing? *General Horsepital?*"

"Whatever it takes. My job is to gather every relevant fact I can get my hands on, pick some brains, add colorful quotes and tidbits of human interest, put everything together in a cohesive format and deliver the polished article to *HorseWorld* by the deadline."

"Kind of like having Wolfgang Puck, Emeril and Gordon Ramsay all dining at my place on the same night."

Kira's restaurant, The Surf & Stirrup, was one of North San Diego County's most happening spots, known for its young and beautiful crowd, the best steaks in town and Kira's signature drinks, with beach and Western themes that went down easy to send you flying high.

"You're a culinary star, Kira. If your rib eye doesn't float their boats, your tequila sunsets will. If I can pull this off with half your grace and confidence, I'll be in tight with *HorseWorld*."

"You'll do fine. 'Fake it 'til you make it,' remember?"

"I remember. Now, be a good assistant and hand me my camera."

Randi reeled off shots: the fullness of Rebel's shoulders and the sturdiness of his haunches, muscles made to start like a jackrabbit and stop on a dime—the epitome of the All-American Quarter Horse. Finished, she exchanged camera for pen and paper.

All parts of Rebel's conformation have been bred for generations to allow the breed to work long, hard days over rough terrain yet still have the stamina and agility necessary to catch, corner and cut a cow from the herd. She lifted her pen, listened for a few seconds, kept writing. *From the rows of stables adjoining the breeding barn, horses kick the wooden panels of their stalls, the resounding thuds alternating with the stallion's primal—*

A clatter of hoofbeats broke her thoughts. She looked up to see Rebel twist his neck, pin his ears and rear. His hooves paddled the air, barely missing the side of Piper's head. Seconds later, he came crashing down. The rope, having slipped through Piper's hands, had too much slack to hold him and Rebel hurled himself toward the spectators. The men grabbed their hats and the women clutched their purses, stumbling backward and flattening themselves against the wall.

Piper braced her legs and reeled in the lead, tightening the links laced through the halter. She had a body like a whippet, but she was tough as a Rottweiler. The stud shank bit the tender skin of Rebel's nose and he skidded to a stop so fast it seemed he'd go down, yet somehow he managed to unscramble his legs and stay upright. He shook himself like a dog, then let loose an earsplitting neigh that rippled in waves down his neck and along his topline, slick with lather.

Houston wore a wide grin; everyone else looked like they'd

just wet their pants. "Damn horse reminds me of me." He tugged on the belt loops of his Wranglers, hitching them over his narrow hips. "Rowdy and ready."

"You think?" Piper's tone made it clear she was not amused.

"Sure. Ask the wife. She'll tell ya."

"No thanks. I'll take your word for it."

Randi scribbled fast so as not to miss any more action: *A chain linked through the noseband helps control the stallion, protecting against injuries to horse and human.*

Houston took Rebel's lead rope from Piper. "Where's Stacey? We can't wait all day for her to show up."

Randi froze. Stacey wouldn't come alone. Jaydee'd be tagging behind her like a lovesick puppy, calling her "sweet cheeks" and grabbing her butt every chance he got. Watching them frolic made Randi want to throw up.

Piper snapped a pair of rubber gloves over her fingers. She shrugged. "It's not like she checks in with me. If I had to guess, I'd say she's out getting her nails done."

Houston led Rebel forward, giving the gathering a clear view of the stallion's equipment.

"Wow!" Kira's eyes went wide. "They don't say 'hung like a horse' for nothin'."

"Shh!" Randi looked around to see if anybody had overheard. "You're supposed to be cool. Act like you see this sort of thing every day."

Kira jerked her thumb. "Yeah? Look at *them.*"

One of the bejeweled women stood with her mouth hanging open. She elbowed another, who dropped her purse on the floor. The men sat poker-faced. No doubt it took some effort.

Houston held out a plastic tumbler filled with soapy water. As Piper took it from him, the stallion bared his teeth and went for her back. Houston's fist slammed into his muzzle with a loud *smack.* Rebel jerked his head away with a grunt, giving Houston a look of surprise and newfound respect.

Houston wasn't one to lose his temper. His movements were smooth and purposeful. Enough... yet not too much. Let a twelve-hundred pound animal get the best of you and you wouldn't be in this business long.

Piper returned to her task, seemingly unfazed she'd almost lost a couple ribs. Pouring the water along the length of the horse's shaft she hummed as she rubbed the suds, as normally as if she was washing dinner dishes.

Care is taken to make sure all necessary parts are free of dirt and debris that might contaminate the sample.

The groom passed Houston a leather tube, about two feet long with a suitcase handle on the top.

"Okay," Houston said, "let's do this."

"You got it, Boss." Piper relaxed her grip on the rope and the stallion surged forward to straddle his conquest with an eye-opening squeal. The mare didn't protest, didn't move, didn't kick. "She" was a dummy, a phantom-breeding mount, a slanted pole wrapped in padding with a life-sized plastic horse head attached.

Houston grabbed hold of Rebel, guiding him into the handheld tube. Houston widened his stance and braced himself against the dummy to hold the container in place.

Doesn't seem to bother the stallion that what's on the receiving end isn't alive.

Kira peered over Randi's shoulder. "Reminds me of a football player I knew in college," Kira said. "Now I understand why they don't use a real mare."

Randi smiled. "You're right. This way is cheaper and easier. No trailering costs or risk of injury to the mom-to-be. UPS delivery and the vet's turkey baster and you're in business."

Seconds later, it was over. Rebel's muscles went slack and he hung on top of the dummy mount, front legs dangling. He shook his head and backed off, landing with a thud on a thick rubber mat beneath his feet.

Fire in the stallion's eyes dims. No more stamping of hooves or commanding calls. Day's work done and over in mere seconds.

Kira broke the spell. "I need a cigarette."

"You don't smoke."

Kira opened her purse and Randi half expected her to pull out a pack of Marlboros, but her lipstick appeared instead and she applied a fresh coat. "What's Rebel's liquid gold go for these days?"

One of the Stetson men cocked an ear and turned to look at them. He took off his hat, ran his finger along the brim. "We came a long way to convince Houston our mare is deserving of his stud. I'd do just about whatever it took to get a colt by Rebel, but Houston's already turned my nephew's horse down." The man cleared his throat and shifted his weight to the other foot. "Said her conformation wasn't up to par. The boy was itchin' to wring his neck."

Randi tapped her pen against her shoulder. "Are you telling me Rebel's sperm is worth killing for?"

"Could be." He grimaced. "Don't quote me."

The door to the breeding barn rumbled open. Stacey Hill stood framed inside the doorway, sunlight glinting off her hair. Conversation stopped and the back of Randi's neck prickled. Of course Stacey'd shown up. She was the type of owner who stuck her nose into every move her horse made. What he ate, how much he ate. Was he getting enough? Did he get his fly spray? Who left a sweat mark on his back?

"Speak of the devil," Kira said. "A day late, but never a dollar short."

The groom led Rebel down the barn aisle. Stacey stepped inside and held up her hands like she was checking for rain. "Houston? Why is Roberto taking my horse away?" She marched, stomping to a halt in front of the lab, a separate room housed inside the breeding barn, used to prepare the semen for shipment. Across the way, Houston faced the prospective clients, his back to Stacey. She raised her voice but didn't approach Houston's group. "You were supposed to wait for me. You seem to forget that stallion is *my* goddamn horse."

Randi kept one eye on the developing drama and the other on the door, sure any second now Jaydee would arrive to rescue his damsel—definitely in distress.

Kira touched Randi's arm. "It's getting late. I'd love to stay and watch the fireworks, and I promised to be here for you if Jaydee showed up, but I've gotta get back."

"Go. I'm fine. I'll fill you in later."

"Okay. Sorry. Call me." Kira waggled her fingers and slipped out the side door.

Houston excused himself and spun on his heels, rolling down the sleeves of his plaid flannel shirt as he strode toward Stacey while Randi moved in for a close-up of the woman who swiped Jaydee right out from under her naïve little nose.

Six months ago, after her then-boyfriend had begged her to move to California, she'd unknowingly bought herself a one-way ticket to a broken heart and rejection she'd never known the likes of. Kira would say the words sounded like a cheesy country song, but she didn't care. Cheesy country had its place.

A stack of bangles slid down Stacey's arm, tinkling like silver bells before they crashed into her Rolex. She plucked a stray curl from her mouth with a shellacked fingernail and glared at Houston. "I won't be treated this way."

What was it about Stacey that Jaydee found attractive? Randi imagined him stroking the goatee he could never quite grow, checking off items on a clipboard. Stacey's assets: Long shiny strawberry-blonde hair—check, overflowing C cup—check, a teensy waist—check, enough discretionary dough to shell out seven hundred bucks on the custom-made cowboy boots on her feet—check. Was it a combination of attributes or just one big thing? Perhaps it was her two big things.

Houston flung his arm to the side. "You see these people? Two of them came in from Tucson. Got up at four and drove seven, eight hours. Another couple flew in late last night from Miami. They made an effort to get here. We had a schedule. Not my fault if there was someplace else you wanted to be."

Stacey put her hands on her hips. "You were in control, Houston, not them. It was inexcusable for you to go ahead and collect from Rebel without me here. I told you I wanted to be a hands-on owner, not just the chick who writes the checks."

The door to the lab swung open. Piper stepped out, holding a small plastic cup with some milky liquid at the bottom. Her eyes narrowed at the sight of Stacey.

"How's the motility?" Houston directed his question to Piper, lifting his chin to gaze over the top of Stacey's head.

Stacey lengthened herself and squared her shoulders. "I'd appreciate it if you two didn't act like I'm not standing right between you."

Piper held up the container. "I checked them under the scope—suckers are swimming like Michael Phelps."

Houston cracked his knuckles. "The shipment's going to Johnny Collier up at the Double R, east of Santa Barbara. Address is in the computer. You've got about an hour before UPS comes."

Piper smiled. "I'm all over it."

Stacey's lips quivered, and for a half a second Randi actually felt sorry for her. "You'll regret you treated me this way, Houston. You've backed me into a corner. You'll pay for this. Father-in-law or no father-in-law."

Two

DAYBREAK THE NEXT MORNING, Randi stopped her F150 halfway up the road she shared with her landlord, Luke Andersen, who stood at the edge of the gravel driveway. Randi's husky-shepherd mix thumped his tail against the back of the seat as Randi leaned over and lowered the passenger window, bracing herself for a blast of cold air.

Thankfully, despite the early hour, Luke was fully dressed. Rancho del Zorro's most eligible bachelor was easy on the eyes, but that didn't mean Randi wanted to catch him in his robe retrieving his morning paper. From the guesthouse she rented, she'd spied him through the window one night, dancing in his living room in his tighty-whiteys like Tom Cruise in *Risky Business*. She'd watched for longer than she should have.

At thirty-six, seven years her senior, Luke had a body that wouldn't quit. He was also the local veterinarian and she worked for him part-time as a vet-tech.

Luke leaned inside the cab of the truck, filling it with the smell of his spicy soap. A thick band of silver ringed his wrist, with a hunk of turquoise centered in it. Half Zuni Indian, Luke's face had a sculpted quality, with smooth skin and prominent cheekbones, and when he fixed his hazel eyes on her for more than a few seconds, the heat rose in her cheeks, which made everything worse. A vicious cycle. The only flaw in the doctor's appearance was a crooked nose, broken in a hockey game, he'd said, when he was eight. She thought it defining of his character but kept that to herself.

"Morning, Ms. Sterling, Mr. Shane."

Shane took the sound of his name as an invitation to shove his nose under Luke's hand. Luke, in turn, buried his fingers in Shane's thick fur, massaging him in his favorite spot behind the ears. If the dog were a cat, he would have purred.

Randi pointed to the dashboard. "Thirty degrees? Are you kidding me? When I decided to move here, I had visions of basking on the beach holding a drink with a frilly little umbrella inside."

Luke grinned. "Not at six a.m. in February. Especially in this valley."

She rubbed her arms. Shouldn't complain. She'd be in *real* cold soon enough. "It's not like Colorado, of course, but throw in some humidity and a stiff ocean breeze and brrr."

Her boss made her nervous, and when she got jumpy she tended to ramble. She was far more relaxed around cold-blooded reptilian types like her ex.

Luke tucked the morning paper under his arm, seeming to find her complaints about the cold amusing. "You on your way to the ranch?"

She nodded, blowing into her fists.

"Where are your gloves?"

She shrugged. She didn't want to admit she'd forgotten them on her kitchen counter after blathering on about the weather. "My goal is to finish the horses early, then come home and work on my article."

Luke smiled. "I forgot you were going to be at Rebel's collection yesterday. Houston doesn't hand out invites to just anybody. You must be pretty special."

She put the truck in park but left the engine running since the heater was finally blowing warm air. "Special or not, I think Houston feels bad because of what happened with Jaydee."

"Jaydee's a putz, no argument there, but there's more to it. Houston likes knowing you're in the trenches every day, in spite of the way his son treated you. It takes a village to run that ranch, you know."

Now would be a perfect time to slide in the fact she was quitting. "You might be right. When I told Houston about my piece for *HorseWorld*, he said he'd help me any way he could."

"*HorseWorld?* That's a big magazine. Congratulations."

"Thanks. I'm more pleased about the doors it will open than the money."

Luke frowned and stopped scratching Shane. "They *are* paying you, aren't they?"

Randi fingered the silver Pegasus charm she wore around her neck for good luck, like a rosary or worry bead, and considered the sum she'd been promised upon completion. Luke lived in a mansion purchased with the proceeds from his father's estate. Not only had he owned a sizeable chunk of Montana, his father, Luke's grandfather, had possessed concession rights at Yellowstone. Big money.

Though Luke enjoyed the plentiful amenities of his house, he was humble and often mentioned it was lonely being there by himself. She and Shane occupied a little place at the back of his three-acre lot with a bunk bed and a view of the orange grove. The bungalow was perfect for her, but a certain dollar amount could mean one thing to one person and something entirely different to another. She settled on what she felt was an appropriate answer. "Enough to buy me a new pair of boots or pay my gas and electric bill."

"Or?" Luke gestured toward the floorboards. "No offense, but your boots have about had it, and I'd hate to think of you freezing your butt off in my guesthouse. Let me handle your bill this month."

She shook her head. Her boots were scuffed and worn, but

they'd practically molded to her feet over the years. Not to mention she owed Luke enough as it was. "I appreciate the offer, but I can't let you do that."

"Then I have a better idea. Come work for me full-time. That way you won't have to decide between heat and feet."

This wasn't the first time they'd danced around the issue, and she had the feeling it wouldn't be the last. She'd gotten her vet-tech AA degree at Denver Technology a week before Jaydee had called to invite her back into his life. He'd even arranged for her job with Luke, squelching her "I don't have a job in San Diego" excuse.

Trouble was, being a tech was crucial to her pocketbook, but journalism was her calling, plain and simple. "Working full-time for you wouldn't leave time for my writing, and you'd have to fire me on the grounds of constant bitchiness."

"I've dealt with far worse, believe me." Luke gave Shane a pat on the neck, signaling the conversation was over. "Speaking of your job, check on the newborn when you get to Lucky Jack, will you? I don't expect you'll find any problems, but take his vitals and make sure he's nursing. The mare was a bit of a pill about it yesterday and we can't take any chances with Rebel's colt."

Luke withdrew from the window and gave the side of the door a slap with the newspaper. "Now get to work or I'll fire you for loitering."

Lucky Jack's workers called to each other in Spanish, loading the feed truck with the last of the morning hay. Randi collected her untamed chestnut waves into an elastic band, then zipped her jacket. The property held about a hundred and fifty head of horses and was one of the few remaining equestrian facilities on the Southern California coast, the rest consumed by suburban sprawl and its relentless hunger for open land. Rancho del Zorro, where the ranch was located, was an affluent community north of San Diego and about three miles from the ocean, where the average resident could easily afford the cost of owning a horse or two. About a third of Lucky Jack's equines belonged to the Hill family; the remainder were split between trail horse boarders and serious horse-show clients with monthly training bills that rivaled a middle-class house payment.

Randi glanced at the ridge where the Hills' compound overlooked the property. The enormous home was actually two residences. Houston and his wife, Helen, lived in one, Jaydee and Stacey the other.

How would things be this morning between Houston and his daughter-in-law? Would they avoid each other, or would they act like their breeding barn spat hadn't happened yesterday? What about Jaydee? His wife and his father were feuding. If forced to pick sides, which one would he choose? The answer was easy where Jaydee was concerned. Bed over blood, for sure.

Shane trotted away from the truck, glancing over his shoulder every couple of strides to make sure she followed. She waved him on. The jangling noise her spurs made when she walked, and the way Shane wagged his tail with unadulterated joy, never failed to cheer her up, no matter what her mood.

The moment Randi had first laid eyes on her dog through the bars at the Larimer County Humane Society, she'd felt an instant connection. A lot of people thought she was nuts—her mother came first to mind—for losing her heart to something with four legs and questionable breath, but she couldn't fathom life without him. When Shane got old and it came time for the green needle, she'd likely offer herself up right along beside him.

At the paddock of an Appaloosa gelding, Randi ducked through the rails. All the horses she treated since coming to work for Luke were special, but Zany, short for Zane Grey, was her favorite. The smartest and most beautiful horse she'd ever seen.

Zany's head gleamed reddish-bronze, and when the sun hit it just right, his forelock reflected flecks of gold. His mane sprouted black between his ears and stayed that way until halfway down his neck, where strands of light hair began to lace their way through like frosty icicles. Inkblot markings dominated his rump. And his tail, typically sparse on Appaloosas, was full and black, as shiny as wet sealskin. Looks aside, her favorite thing about Zany was his personality. Patient, brave and as clever as hell, the horse must have been a Nez Percé warrior in a previous life.

His nose went straight for her pocket. Gently, she pushed him away. "You know the drill, boy. Meds first, peppermints second." After removing his fly mask, she applied topical steroid ointment to his eyes. He stood still while she worked, almost as if he knew her purpose in showing up twice a day, besides doling out mints, was to keep his debilitating eye condition from stealing his sight. Zany possessed a Zen-like peace, something she'd love to achieve one day, or die trying, which was a bit of an oxymoron. She finished Zany's treatment, put the fly mask on and left him munching a handful of peppermints.

Horse heads went up one by one, followed by a domino ripple of nickering, as she walked the path lining the paddocks. Her heart swelled. Who cared if the attention she got was tied to treats? She loved these horses unconditionally. Leaving them to go back to Colorado wouldn't be easy. Maybe that was why her boxes still sat empty on her floor.

At the end of the row was Kira's mare. A sturdy palomino with a feisty sense of independence, not unlike her owner. The Surf & Stirrup kept Kira busy enough to afford her board bill but left her without time to ride, so Randi was fortunate enough to be able to pick up the slack.

The mare stuck her head over the top rail and lipped a molasses horse cookie from Randi's palm. A flurry of footsteps running up from behind spooked them both. Oro jumped and Randi whirled around. Half the cookie fell to the dirt outside the corral. She pushed it under the fence with her toe so the mare could finish it. "Damn, Piper. You scared me. Where's the fire?"

"Have you seen Roberto?" Piper's shirt clung to her skin, making dark patches where sweat had soaked through. "I'm going to wring that scrawny Mexican's neck."

Randi shoved her hands into her jacket pocket. She liked Roberto. "What's going on?"

"Houston left for the show in Burbank and Roberto neglected to put Aztec's blanket in the trailer." Piper looked around like she expected to find the groom cowering behind a tree. "He managed to get all of the blankets packed except for the one belonging to the horse owned by our most demanding client. What the hell am I supposed to do?"

"When did Houston leave? Maybe he can turn around. Call him on his cell."

"Right. Call him on the phone that he keeps off and in the glove compartment. Great idea."

"Take a deep breath, Piper. It's not the end of the world."

"Yeah? Easy for you to say. Picture this: Houston Hill, owner of Lucky Jack Performance Horses, shuffling around the showgrounds trying to bum a blanket off the competition because his barn manager hired an incompetent groom who can't remember a goddamn simple thing like making sure the number of blankets in the trailer matches the number of horses."

"I think you're overreacting." Piper usually seemed to take great pride in keeping her cool in situations where most would lose it. "Roberto's a good groom."

Piper blinked like she had something in her eye. "You don't understand how bad it feels when I let Houston down."

"No, but he will."

"Of course he will. That makes it worse." Piper pulled out a Kleenex and blew her nose. She tucked the tissue in the back pocket of her jeans. "Do you have an extra jacket in your truck? I'm freezing."

"Here. Take mine. I'm warm now." A lie, but Piper was shivering. Her sweat must have dried cold. A little meat on her bones would help. If Randi had any chips or a granola bar in her truck, she would have offered it up.

"Thanks." Piper shrugged the jacket over her shoulders. "Houston and my father were good friends growing up, you know."

Randi shook her head. "I didn't."

"Three years ago, I was living with my dad in Phoenix. One morning I woke up and found him dead on the floor. His coffee cup was full and already cold."

"Oh. I'm sorry." Her words sounded woefully inadequate. "That must have been terrible."

Piper plucked a leaf from a tree outside the corrals. "After that, I didn't care whether I was coming or going. One day when I was seriously contemplating packing it in, I found Houston's number on the back of an old photo. I remembered my dad saying Houston was a guy he could always count on when things got bad, so I took a chance and called.

"Houston and Helen took me in, showed me the ropes, let me stay until I'd saved up enough money to rent my own place. Houston sent me to classes and seminars to learn everything there is to know about artificial insemination, then he made me his breeding manager."

"Houston's good that way." How his son turned out to be such a cretin was a complete mystery.

"Here's the thing," Piper pulled the jacket tight around her stick-like body. "Nobody knows this, but if it weren't for Houston, I'd be either dead or whoring myself in a back alley for my next hit of crack." She wiped her nose with the back of her hand. "I owe him my life."

The sky had turned pinkish-orange by the time Randi made her way to the foaling pen. Piper's story made her think. How long had it been since she'd spoken to her own father? A week? Two? A month? She couldn't remember. Why not? Fear of catching a slur in his voice? If she heard it, would she fret and stew and feel obligated, once again, to become her father's caretaker?

She'd be moving back to Colorado anyway, soon as she found the right time to break the news to Luke. This morning on the driveway would have been perfect if she hadn't wimped out. Regardless, going home didn't mean she wanted to be back in her father's townhome with its cat-pee carpet, paper-thin walls and kitchen window overlooking a poultry processing plant. It had less to do with aesthetics than it did living in constant fear that an offhand comment, or an imagined slight, would rub her father the wrong way and he'd fall headfirst back into the bottle.

She trudged down the path, thinking guilt was a worthless emotion and far too easy to come by, when a horse neighed in the distance. Not a greeting or a "hurry up with my hay," but urgent. She picked up a jog. The broodmares in the pasture had their heads turned and ears pricked in the direction of the foaling pen. It was her next stop anyway to check on Rebel's colt, per Luke's instructions.

After climbing a short rise to the left of the pregnant mares, the enclosure came into view. The newborn colt's mother paced the length of the fence, stopping every few seconds to toss her neck and paw the ground. Where was the foal?

Randi put Shane in a sit-stay and went inside the pen, fingers tracing the wings on her Pegasus charm. The mare continued her march, pivoting on her hind legs each time she reached a corner, head stretched high over the top rail searching for something. Had Piper moved the colt to a different enclosure? No, not without his mother. He was too young to be separated.

Seconds later she spotted the foal stretched on his side, but her relief was short-lived. Goose bumps prickled her scalp at the sight of a lifeless eye and parted mouth. She fell to her knees and pressed her fingers under the foal's jawbone. No pulse. His ribcage didn't move. Frantic, she pushed on it, willing him to breathe, but it did no good. Rocking back on her heels, she shoved the stray hair from her face. This was impossible. Had to be a mistake. A cruel joke. Yesterday the little guy was perfectly healthy. *He can't be dead. He just can't.*

Scrambling to her feet, she walked the perimeter of the pen in a daze. No telltale rattlesnake tracks, no sharp objects, no indication of anything that could have hurt Rebel's colt, much less killed him. Her brain raced and her heart followed, thudding against her ribs. If she hadn't had a second cup of coffee this morning, had skipped the driveway chitchat with Luke and had come straight to the foaling pen instead of listening to Piper rant and rave, would the foal still be alive?

A plastic bag picked up by the breeze skittered along the rail. The mare stopped pacing. She snorted, showing the whites of her eyes. Her sides heaved. Randi placed a hand on the mare's flank and leaned under her belly. Drops of milk clung to her nipples. Feeling her touch, the mare lowered her head and cranked her neck around to breathe warm puffs of air onto Randi's hair. She wrapped her arms around the horse's neck, twining her fingers through her mane.

Humans could speculate until eternity about the depths of animal emotions, but nobody could crawl into the brain of a horse to explore their feelings. Right now, unfortunately, Randi had more immediate dilemmas to tackle than whether or not the mare was grieving. Houston had entrusted Luke with the care of this valuable colt. Luke, in turn, had put his faith in her, and she'd failed.

She didn't have a clue as to how in the world she was going to break this news to him.

Three

THE BEST WAY TO forget about one problem was to tackle another. That theory had served Randi well over the past twenty-nine years and she didn't see a reason for today to be any different. The hurdle she chose to have a crack at after leaving the dead colt had been a thorn in her side for a long time.

Arms extended, she rubbed the sweat from her cheek onto her sleeve. Shooting wasn't brain surgery, for God's sake. Aim the thing and fire! She swallowed the stomach acid climbing her throat and, tightening her fingers around the semiautomatic pistol, visualized the punch of the kickback followed by the roar of the blast. Sweet satisfaction. Demon expunged.

The minutes ticked by. Nothing happened.

Maybe if she put Jaydee's face in the crosshairs. Surely she could pull the trigger if she tortured herself by reliving the events of that day back in September. She'd tootled down the driveway to Lucky Jack, humming a bouncy tune as she parked the shiny black F150 she'd bought for the move to California—after working her butt off waiting tables at Bennigan's—next to one of the barns. The first person she'd come across had been a striking strawberry blonde holding the lead to a dropdead gorgeous stallion with an unusual marking on his face.

"Can I help you?" The woman asked.

All smiles. "I'm here to see Jaydee." Belly flip-flopping.

"Is he expecting you?"

A warning flag went up. "He better be." She laughed and held out her hand. "I'm Randi. Randi Sterling."

She'd assumed Jaydee had boasted of her arrival to everyone he knew, beautiful women included.

"Hi, Randi." Strawberry-blonde took her hand. "I'm Stacey."

"Hi. Is... uh... is... Jaydee around?"

"I believe he's with a client. Is there something I can help you with?"

Bigger flags, waving harder. "Well... I don't know if he told you—I'm kind of surprised he didn't mention it..."

"Whatever you need to say to him, you can say to me. I'm his wife."

The gun slipped. The instructor at the Lakeside Shooting Club touched her shoulder. She lowered the pistol and slid her finger off the trigger. Handing Cole the weapon, she removed her ear protection. She'd been coming here every week for the past five months and wanted to be able to shoot for him almost as much as she wanted it for herself.

"Come back next week," Cole said over the crash of gunshots echoing through the indoor range. "Give it another go."

"It's such a simple thing. I don't understand. When I tell my brain to shoot, my body shuts down."

"Don't be so hard on yourself. Most people who've had an experience like yours won't even put a foot in the stirrup."

The paper torso hung untouched at the rear of the shooting lane. Even without a mouth and eyes, it managed to mock her. "Yeah, I get back in the saddle, then I get bucked right off. It's been nineteen years. I should be over my fear of guns by now." Randi collected her purse from a coat hook. "Can I tell you a secret? I always wanted to be Annie Oakley. We even share the same birthday."

"Really? You have something in common then. Channel her. It's all in the process." Cole was a bona fide rawhide and barbed-wire redneck and here he was, getting all metaphysical on her.

"I wasn't always like this. I won the skeet shooting competition at summer camp when I was nine."

"You told me," he said, though not like he minded hearing the story again. "Your dad mounted your trophy on the hood of his Chevy truck with baling twine. Stayed there till the twine rotted away."

Randi swallowed the lump in her throat. As far as crappy days went, this one ranked right up there with the best of them. First the colt and now this. She stared at her shoes, blinking fast. Cole would tell her cowgirls don't cry.

He reached out his hand and lifted Randi's chin. "Don't you dare give up, young lady. Is that clear?"

A rap on the glass jolted Randi awake, but it was too dark to see anything from her top bunk. She clutched the sheets to her chest and waited. Maybe Shane had bumped the wall while circling around on his dog bed.

She'd almost fallen asleep when the noise came again. Rap, tap, tap. Someone knocking. She bolted upright and when she saw what it was, she stifled a laugh, fluffed her pillow and lay back down. Branches, hitting a window. The wind in the trees. *Go back to sleep.*

In Colorado, when she was a kid, gusts had blown so hard on the plains she thought the roof would fly right off the house. Then there were nights when the wind woke her and through the wall she'd heard her parents arguing. Her mother called her dad a drunk; he retaliated with whore. Old enough to know those weren't terms of endearment, she'd put on her robe and sheepskin boots, then sneak out of her bedroom and cross the yard to join Georgie in the stable. Inside the barn, with her arms around her horse's neck, fingers laced through his mane, was the only place she felt safe.

But Georgie was gone and so was her sense of comfort. Her flannel sheets were wrapped too tight around her legs, her mouth felt dry as a cotton ball, and a nagging sense of something left undone refused to leave her in peace. She gave up and threw the comforter off her legs. No wonder. It wasn't the sheets making her feel constrained, it was yesterday's jeans. She put a hand to her chest. Yesterday's sweatshirt, too. *Weird.* When was the last time she'd slept in her clothes?

She clambered down the ladder. Her feet hit the wood floor with a slap as her eyes found the clock on the end table. The numbers glowed red: 11:55.

An icy shiver zipped down her spine. She'd forgotten to give Zany his second daily dose of eye meds. Hurrying to the table, she rummaged through her leather bag. One good thing about sleeping in your clothes—you were ready in a flash. She pulled out her keys. Shane lifted his head and cocked an ear.

"I know what you're thinking. That's what I get for taking my work to bed with me. Stupid, stupid, stupid."

The beers she'd downed while working on her *HorseWorld* article hadn't helped. Too much, too fast. Self-medicating to dull the pain of finding the dead colt. She, of all people, should know alcohol created more problems than it solved. "Come on, buddy, we're going for a ride."

A whoosh of air rattled the bungalow's windowpanes. Shane stayed put, tucking his nose under his tail. Most times he'd do anything just for a spin around the block, but tonight he lay curled in a ball, staring at her like she'd lost her mind.

"I don't like the wind either, husky-dog, but there's no way in hell I'm going to Lucky Jack in the middle of the night without you." She tugged her boots over her socks and opened the front door, holding it steady as the gusts tried to push it closed. "Don't forget who buys your dog chow, fur-face. Now get in the truck."

The wind shoved the F150, forcing Randi to overcorrect to stay between the lines. She drove too fast, on the verge of losing control, but at least the rumble of the engine gave her the sense she was doing *something* to remedy her mistake. Zany's treatments were crucial—she'd screwed up royally. Luke had been understanding about the colt. More so that she thought he'd be. He was upset, naturally, but he told her there was nothing that could be done, and that she wasn't at fault. *This* was a different story.

Shane's hindquarters trembled as he perched on the seat, glancing out the window each time the truck went sideways. He looked like a wolf, tough and scared of nothing, but he didn't like the way the wind whistled through the cracks or blew his fur the wrong direction. Go figure. Randi felt around the floorboards with her free hand until she found his toy, a well-chewed, worn-out stuffed monkey named Abu. She put it at his front paws, a peace offering which he flat-out refused.

Seven minutes later, the truck rumbled over the cattle guard at the mouth of Lucky Jack's driveway. The dirt road ended in a keyhole parking lot a quarter mile down. Once there, she maneuvered as close as possible to Zany's corral and shut off the motor. Fast-moving clouds blocked the moon. She'd been in such a hurry to get here, she'd forgotten to grab a penlight from the kitchen drawer on her way out.

Digging beneath the seat, she got her hand on some greasy goo from the bench rails, a ripped up map of the Denver metro area and her favorite baseball cap. She'd thought it was lost. Her fingers traced the words, *Cowgirl Up!* before she slapped it on her head. *Rise to the occasion no matter what, and when the going gets tough, tighten your belt buckle and get 'er done.*

The glove compartment also turned up nothing useful for checking Zany's eyes. Darn flashlights were like men. Always around when you didn't need one. Never around when you did.

She cracked the driver's door, and a blast of wind wrenched the handle from her grasp. The door swung wide and bounced on its hinges, rocking the truck. Shane kept his butt glued to the seat. She wrapped her fingers around his collar and tugged him out of the cab. He flattened his ears, tucked his tail and trotted five yards to the left to park himself at the base of a tree. She hoped this wasn't an omen. She never wanted to stumble upon something dead again.

At Zany's corral she rattled the chain and took the halter off the gate, talking constantly as she entered the enclosure. Zany couldn't see very well and she didn't want to startle him. She found him near the corner and put a hand on his shoulder. His ears flicked back and forth as he lowered his head and sniffed for mints. Her pockets were empty. Mumbling profuse apologies, she buckled the halter around his head.

If his eyes were badly swollen or, worse, had ulcerated, she'd never forgive herself. He shouldn't be outside with blowing dirt in the first place. He'd be living in the barn if his owner wasn't such a cheapskate, but that was another story.

Zany didn't seem distressed, which put her a hair more at ease, but she needed to get a good look under the barn lights to make sure his eyes weren't going into spasms. If they were, he'd need some atropine to relax and dilate his pupils. The meds were in the barn anyway. She called for Shane and the three of them left the corrals and climbed the wide, curving path leading to the main barn. Lightning flashed in the distance, illuminating the limbs of towering eucalyptus as they creaked and groaned beneath the punishing wind.

The sooner they were inside, the better, but the fixture above the door was dark. She groped for the edge of the massive slider and leaned into it. Something cold and wet splatted the nape of her neck and she stifled a scream.

Lightning lit the sky again, this time to the west over the ocean, and the tempo of raindrops crescendoed to a dirt-pum-meling torrent. She braced her shoulder on the metal frame and shoved the door wide. Zany bolted through the opening, drag-ging her along with him. Shane wasted no time bringing up the rear.

She flicked the wall switch up and down. Clack, click, clack. Usually the barn's interior glowed pale yellow from dusk to dawn as each stall contained an overhead light to keep the prize show horses from growing winter coats. Sleek horses were a must at the higher echelons of the Quarter Horse show circuit, but darkness triggered the hormone that made their coats grow full and fuzzy. Trotting into the ring like a wooly mammoth wasn't acceptable, so the competition horses slept with the lights on wearing heavy blankets.

Murky shadows made it possible to maneuver down the barn aisle. It was after midnight and her eyes hadn't adjusted and the wind howled something fierce, but there was nothing to be scared of. Really. *Nothing.* It was a barn filled with horses, not a dark alleyway downtown. If she stayed focused, she could get the job done, no matter what time it was, no matter how tired she felt, no matter how hard the wind blew.

Midway down the aisle she pulled Zany to a stop and fumbled for the crosstie ropes hanging from opposite walls. She secured the clasps to the gelding's halter and gave him a reassuring rub on the neck. Next task: find a flashlight and get a good look at his eyes.

Roberto lived in a groom's apartment adjacent to the breeding barn. He'd have some kind of light, for sure. Randi made a ninety-degree turn and felt her way through the "kitchen," a narrow pass-through room with a sink, rows of cabinets and drawers and a refrigerator containing horse meds, carrots and the occasional twelve-pack. If Zany needed the atropine, stashed high in one of the cabinets, she'd be hard-pressed to find the medication without a flashlight.

Shane panted, toenails clicking the heels of her boots. She closed the kitchen door and stepped into the breezeway, a wide path covered on top and open on the sides, that connected the main barn to the breeding room. The wind hit her hard, and slanting rain, so cold and painful it had to be hail, pelted her face.

Roberto lived at the end of the passage. Half a minute after her third knock, she knocked again. Still nothing. She felt bad about waking him; he worked long, hard hours and had recently suffered the wrath of Piper, but she had to have a flashlight for Zany's eyes. Pressing her mouth to the crack in the door, she called Roberto's name then quickly traded her lips for her ear. No answer. No sound. She tried the knob. Locked. Now what?

Maybe Houston kept a light in his office at the other end of the barn. She retraced her steps along the breezeway, back through the kitchen and down the aisle, running her fingers along the panels of the stalls so as not to crash into anything. Zany pawed the dirt from where he stood in the crossties.

"Back soon," she called over her shoulder. "Hang in there."

Houston's office was detached from the barn, so she told Shane to stay with Zany and left the sliding door open a few inches so he could see where she went. He grumbled audibly to let her know he wasn't happy about being left behind.

The rain poured in sheets. Randi scurried to the door, leaping over puddles, surprised to find the office unlocked, but didn't stop to ponder her good fortune. The light switch proved useless in here, too. Houston's desk—a massive piece of furniture—sat in the middle. File cabinets lined the walls on her left and bookcases filled the space to the right. She made her way with care, knowing spurs and doggy chew toys littered the floor, lying in wait for someone to step on them and twist an ankle.

She pulled opened the top desk drawer and a flashlight hit the front panel with a satisfying thunk. Pay dirt! It was one of those big old heavy metal things, but who cared? She'd be able to see Zany's eyes now, and that was all that mattered. Flashlight in hand, she followed the beam toward the door but forgot about what lay beneath her feet and stepped on one of the rawhide bones that only a few seconds ago she'd made a point to avoid.

The bone rolled under her foot. Legs tangled, she stumbled. She flung out her arms to regain her balance, but as she twisted, her shoulder slammed into something hard. A file cabinet rocked and *bam*! a dark shadow fell and glass shattered at her feet.

One hand on the wall, she swept the flashlight beam across the floor. Curled on the terra cotta tiles, surrounded by shards of glass from a jar, was a pickled horse fetus the size of a newborn kitten, like something you'd find in a high school science lab.

A perfect little body: miniature hooves, delicate ears and tiny oval nostrils. Fascinating in a grotesque sort of way, though an unusual bit of décor to have in one's office. She knelt, blinking away the stinging stench. A paper label clung to one of the larger pieces of glass. She picked it up and centered the light on the words: *Bay colt, by Whata Rebel Man.* She couldn't make out the rest, so she placed the formalin soaked slip on Houston's desk and wiped her hand on her jeans.

Whata Rebel Man? *Hesa* Rebel Man? Could Stacey's stallion somehow be kin to this thing on the floor? Good chance. They had two names in common, and the AQHA took lineage as seriously as Queen Elizabeth.

Stacey's bitter words from yesterday afternoon came flooding back: "He's my goddamn horse, not yours." What did it mean? Were Houston and Stacey battling over Rebel? If so, why? Wasn't keeping him in the family good enough? Who cared whose name was on the papers?

Thunder rolled, booming along the walls. She had to get back to Zany, but couldn't leave the fetus on the floor. Houston's wife had a pack of Jack Russell terriers, feisty little dogs with sharp teeth, that would make quick work of this thing. She grabbed an old jacket off a wall hook and set the flashlight down, pointing it so the beam illuminated the broken jar. She was in such a hurry to wrap the fetus inside the coat, she cut her finger in the process. Wincing, she rolled the unusual bundle tight and set it on the desk.

She shivered as she held her bleeding finger and hurried out the door. Zany had been waiting far too long.

Four

INSIDE THE BARN, RANDI held the flashlight steady in front of her as she made her way down the aisle. She put a hand on Zany's crosstie rope. A sharp *crack* startled him into a sideways stutter step, and in his panic he stepped on her boot with his hoof, but the ropes kept him in place.

"Roberto? Is that you? Shane?" Where was her dog? She traced the flashlight from one corner of the barn to the next. He *always* came when she called and, except for not letting him follow her into Houston's office, he'd been underfoot since they left the bungalow.

The cracking noise sounded like it had come from the kitchen. It took all of three seconds to find the culprit. A rope-like tail curled up from beneath a block of wood. Ha! After all these years hanging out in barns, she should've recognized the sound of a rattrap being sprung. At least it was dead and wouldn't be scampering across her feet.

The rat's tail whipped to the side. Randi jumped. Her hand flew open and the flashlight clattered to the floor, going dark as it hit and rolled beneath the cabinets. A stream of vile words gushed from her lips. She didn't have time for this! Damn it! What else could go wrong? She dropped to her hands and knees. Dirt and pebbles poked her palms, and she had to stop mid-crawl and brush them off. Shuffling around the floor wasn't the brightest idea since there were bound to be more traps set and ready to spring, and she didn't relish the idea of a finger snapped in half, but she needed that blasted light.

Her hand traversed grainy things, rolled over a pencil, touched a couple of nails, then crashed into a wooden handle with a large metal head. A hammer. Coated in something sticky. She used her pants as a towel again, adding the yucky stuff to the formalin already on her jeans, and continued her search.

The flashlight was cocooned in dust bunnies and nestled against the bottom of the refrigerator. She picked it up, clambered to her feet and flicked the switch, but the worthless thing didn't light up. She shook it. Unscrewed the top, jiggled the batteries, took them out, put them back in the wrong order, then the right. Had to be the bulb. Must have broken when she'd dropped it. Now what?

She turned in a circle. Where the hell was Shane? Worry spread through her veins. "Shane!" She used her *I mean it* voice, but instead of the obedient clatter of dog tags as he realized the error of his ways, a growl rose from the far end of the barn aisle.

In the barely-there glow of a skylight, Shane crouched, shoulders low to the ground, like he was stalking prey. Another rat? Randi put the broken light on the counter and took some twine from a drawer to fasten a makeshift leash. A horse kicked out as she passed by, hooves slamming into the wood. Reaching for her Pegasus charm, she forced her feet to keep going. She had an eerie feeling Shane was after something bigger than a rodent.

The next enclosure was empty; the one beyond that belonged to Rebel. Shane scratched the dirt and sniffed the bottom of the stallion's door. Randi wrapped her fingers around the bars lining the top portion of the stall and peered inside, half-expecting to see the horse on his side, thinking maybe he'd colicked—or worse. She was wrong. Rebel stood hooves down, always a good thing where horses were concerned, but he had a halter on with a lead rope dangling from his chin to the wood shavings below.

Roberto would never have left Rebel's halter and lead on. If the stallion stepped on the end of the rope, he could panic and end up hurting himself. It was an unwritten law the more a horse was worth, the greater the chance for bodily harm, usually of the stupid variety and resulting in hefty vet bills.

She slid the bolt and pushed the door along the track. Speaking low and soft, she stepped into the stall and reached for the clasp securing the rope to Rebel's halter, but it slipped from her hand. She was having a hell of a time holding onto things tonight. Keeping an eye on Rebel, she bent to pick up the lead. Near the back corner of the stall, a ray of moonlight streaming through a knothole caught the reflection of something shiny. Shiny things weren't the norm in stall bedding. She squinted and moved closer to check it out. Stacey's Rolex, with her wrist still attached.

Before Randi's brain had a chance to register everything that was wrong with what she'd seen, the door at the end of the barn rumbled wide, bringing a rush of wind, the beating rain and a yellow orb that bobbed up and down, growing bigger as it swept back and forth across the width of the aisle.

"Randi?"

"*Houston?*"

"What the hell are you doing in that stall?"

"I..." Blinded by Houston's flashlight, she shielded her eyes, at a loss for words. What was *he* doing here? He was supposed to be at the show in Burbank.

"Is something wrong with Rebel?"

She reached for one of the bars to steady herself. "No." She pointed. "Look."

Houston tilted the light, illuminating a pair of boots, jeans, a long-sleeve shirt and Stacey's eyes that stared at nothing. Blood covered her face, her arm rested on a pile of manure.

Houston stepped inside the stall. "Jesus H. Christ."

Rebel had backed himself into the opposite corner to avoid stepping on Stacey. Houston collected the lead rope from the shavings and attached it to Rebel's halter. "We've got to get him out of here."

"What about her?" Someone had a hold of her throat. At least that's how it felt. There was no immediate threat to Rebel. Houston should be more concerned with his daughter-in-law.

He squatted and picked up Stacey's wrist to check for a pulse. When he let go, her hand flopped back into the wood shavings. He stuffed the flashlight in his back pocket as he stood, grip end down so the light illuminated the rafters. "You go home. I'll handle this."

In the shadows, she couldn't read his face. "How did you know, Houston? I mean... what brought you out here so late? I thought you were at the show."

"Got rained out." He paused. "Guess I should be asking you the same thing."

"Zany. I forgot his treatment. He's in the crossties."

Houston didn't respond.

"You'll call the police, right?"

"I said I'd take care of it." Houston retrieved the flashlight from his pocket. "Are you okay?" He ran the beam from her feet to her neck and back again, slower the second time, stopping at mid-thigh and holding it there for a good five seconds. "What's that?" He took two steps closer. "Is that blood on your jeans?"

Randi wrapped her fingers around the steaming mug but couldn't get them warm. If she kept sitting at her kitchen table downing cup after cup of coffee on an empty stomach, she was going to puke, but she didn't know what else to do. It was too early in the morning for a drink, and she'd already woken Kira with a phone call, purging every detail of how she'd found Stacey's body, along with how she'd put her hands all over the hammer that was likely the murder weapon.

Kira had wanted to come over, but Randi was all talked out and needed time to think things through. Who wanted Stacey dead? She'd blatantly threatened Houston in the breeding barn, and Piper said she owed Houston her life. Houston had shown up in the barn last night. Why? The whole damn thing was a muddled, confusing mess.

When Jaydee had given his sales pitch to get her to move to California, he told her Rancho del Zorro was a nice town, a peaceful place to live. He'd lied.

Her plan: start packing. Twelve hundred miles and two freeways later, I-15 N to I-70 E, and she'd be home, leaving Jaydee and his dead wife far behind. The sooner she got out of here, the better. She kicked aside some boxes on the way to the closet, took out her suitcase and flipped it open.

She made a mental inventory of the furniture she'd bought since her arrival. One bunk bed, two lamps, five chairs, a kitchen table and her desk. All she really needed was her dog, a couple pairs of jeans, her boots, her laptop and a handful of sweatshirts. She'd leave the bungalow furnished as a gift to Luke. He'd given her a job and a place to live. She was about to run out on him. It was the least she could do.

Shane lay on his dog bed, fast asleep, ribcage rising and falling with a steady tempo, chin planted on Abu. Randi had a strategy, so back at the table she pushed the coffee mug away and using the crook of her elbow as a pillow, put her head down on the wood instead of her bed so she wouldn't sleep too long. A ten-minute catnap was all she needed.

Five

TIRES CRUNCHED THE GRAVEL outside, followed by two car doors slamming in quick succession. Randi raised her head, swiping away a line of drool connecting her sleeve to her mouth. She wobbled toward the door, dizzy from lack of sleep, braced her hands on the frame and stuck her eye up to the peephole. Two men came up the porch steps. A stocky one in front and a tall, thin guy bringing up the rear. Cops. Had to be. Shane stood on Randi's toes, hackles raised. She reached down to push him off and found herself staring at the brownish-red streaks striping her jeans. The doorbell rang.

Skittering to the bathroom, she kicked off her pants and shoved them in the dirty clothes bin. Next she grabbed a pair of sweats from the corner by the shower and tugged them on. A glance in the mirror showed she resembled something the cat had dragged in. She splashed cold water on her face and ran a brush through her hair. Useless.

Knock, knock, knock.

"Just a minute." She put Shane in the backyard, crossed the room and opened the front door, arm shaking as she pulled it wide. The stocky man wore a bolo tie. She hadn't seen one of those since she'd left Colorado.

"Good morning." He rocked on his heels. "I'm Detective Paul McWynn."

Everything about him was wrinkled, and he looked a bit cross-eyed. It wouldn't have surprised her if he said his name was Lieutenant Columbo.

"And this is Joe Reed."

Reed stood a head higher than McWynn, with black curly hair and skin the color of molasses. His clothing was pressed, with distinct creases in all the right places.

"Randi Sterling." The words stuck in her throat. She'd learned once, in a Native American studies class, that some tribes believed giving away your name put you in a stranger's power. Until now, that had been a foreign concept.

"May we come in?" McWynn asked.

She stepped back and allowed them to pass. "Coffee?" Her mother's Southern upbringing had instilled in her at an early age that being polite took precedence over personal apprehension and physical discomfort.

The detective fiddled with the silver longhorn skull buckling his tie, pressing his thumb into the point of the horns. "No. Thank you, though."

"Okay. Let me know if you change your mind." She adjusted the thermostat so the heat would kick on. The old dinosaur of a furnace did an adequate job of taking off the morning chill, though it made the place smell like the inside of a toaster. She needed a normal task to do; she couldn't show fear. Like horses, cops sensed anxiety.

McWynn and Reed sat at the table, leaving her to perch on the edge of the futon that also made up her bottom bunk. Despite McWynn's disheveled apparel, not a hair on his head was out of place. Too neat to be real, yet too real to be a rug. Her eyes traveled to his feet. Back home, guys in shiny boots with pointy toes were called "drugstore cowboys." They stood out front and looked good—all hat, no cattle. She'd been hanging around Kira too much and was starting to think in the clichés her friend was so fond of, but something about the way McWynn's eyes took in everything all at once had her thinking he was sharper than he dressed.

The detective cleared his throat. "Ms. Sterling, you left the scene of a crime last night." His tone might have been laid back, but his words carried heavy purpose.

"I didn't know I wasn't supposed to." After Houston showed up, she'd made sure Zany's eyes were okay, then put Shane in the truck and took off without looking back. Squaring her shoulders, she sat up straight. "I mean... I thought it was okay. Houston was there. He told me to go."

McWynn looked annoyed. "Mr. Hill informed us that when he arrived at the barn, you were already in the stall with the body."

"Well, yeah, I was." Her mouth went dry. "My dog started acting strange, and I thought something might be wrong with the horse. I was checking on him when I found Stacey."

The detective reached down and picked a lone spur off the floor. He spun the rowel with his finger. "Why were you on the property after midnight? Kind of late, don't you think?"

"I'm a veterinary assistant." Her heart beat faster. "There was a horse that needed medical attention."

Joe Reed gave a polite cough. "The horse in the stall with the body?"

"No. The Appaloosa tied in the barn aisle." From their puzzled expressions, these guys didn't know an Appaloosa from an Appalachian.

"Any idea what happened?" McWynn asked. "Did the horse in the stall with Mrs. Hill have something to do with her death?"

She shook her head. "I doubt it. Horses avoid trampling people if at all possible, and they rarely strike out unless they feel threatened. Besides, it didn't look like horse-inflicted damage." Which brought to mind the hammer and the fact she'd touched it.

"Are you aware of anyone who might have wanted to kill

her?"

"No." It didn't feel like the truth, but it didn't feel like a lie, either. "Are you sure she was murdered?"

"We found a weapon."

Her jeans were in the bathroom, crumpled in the hamper, stained with Stacey's blood. They couldn't search the place without a warrant, could they?

"Tell me why last night's visit couldn't have waited until morning."

"Zany has an eye disease."

"Go on."

"It's called moon blindness. Equine recurrent uveitis. ERU, for short. His eyes need twice-daily steroid treatments. If something goes wrong, he could end up losing his sight in one or both eyes."

Joe rubbed his chin. "What does that have to do with the moon?"

"Way back when, in the sixteen hundreds, people thought ERU coincided with lunar phases. It's supposed to be one of the first veterinary diseases ever documented."

"Interesting."

McWynn crossed his legs. "I still don't understand. Why so late?"

"I forgot his evening meds. I fell asleep. I didn't mean to. When I woke up, I got in my truck and drove straight to the ranch. It's key his treatments not be skipped."

"Is there anyone who can verify your story?"

"Not really. I live alone." The tips of Shane's ears were visible in the window portion of her back door. "Well, not completely alone. I have a dog."

McWynn pinched the bridge of his nose. "What about the horse's owner? Couldn't he or she have handled the situation?"

"He lives in L.A., and he's not the type I would call for help."

"Why not?" Joe asked.

"He's Tim Tyler."

McWynn looked impressed. "*The* Tim Tyler?"

She nodded. Once upon a time a mega box office draw, now relegated to reality shows and infomercials, Tim Tyler was a pompous man for whom image was everything. Included in his self-worth package was the value of his horse. Having a "sick" animal was a ball and chain as far as he was concerned.

The detective cocked his head. "Tell me, if this horse's medication is so important, how on Earth could you have forgotten?"

She scratched her nose then remembered reading it was a sign of lying. Something to do with the body producing extra histamines when you weren't being truthful. Obviously not the case here, but she put her hand down anyway. "Yesterday wasn't the greatest. We lost a foal. I had a lot on my mind."

"Do you often forget to take care of your patients?"

If she didn't already feel so guilty about her mistake, she would have taken offense. "I was up late working on a magazine article. And no, it's not a habit."

"You have a boss?"

She pointed out the window. "Luke Andersen. He lives in the big house you passed on your way in."

At the end of the driveway, the corner of Luke's place was visible through the sycamores, his silver F350 work truck parked in the porte-cochere. What would he think if he knew the police were questioning her? Did he even know Stacey was dead?

McWynn scooted his chair back, stood up and stretched, but instead of going to the window to verify what she'd said, he sauntered toward a row of photographs lining her desk. "Do you mind?" He picked up the first photo, one of her as a teen astride her horse Georgie, her hair wild and blown by the wind.

"Go ahead." As if she had a choice. How soon before they left? She needed to pack.

McWynn pointed to the next photo in line. "Who are these people?"

"My parents."

Craning his neck, he reached for something between her desk and the wall. He stuck his fingers down the narrow space and pulled out a framed photograph. "You and your boyfriend?"

Why hadn't she thrown that useless thing in the trash? "Ex."

"Where was this taken? Tahoe?"

"Steamboat Springs. We were in college."

"You look happy."

"We were." She shrugged. "I was."

From the moment of their first date, she'd been a done deal. Jaydee wore his shirts unbuttoned one hole too far, with a braided leather cord around his neck. They both loved horses and the mountains and skiing. They stayed up late watching movies, eating popcorn from a bag and drinking champagne from crystal flutes. Jaydee's family's money meant ski trips to Switzerland, gondola rides in Venice and sunbathing half-naked in the south of France. It was a lifestyle Randi never dreamed of and a miracle she didn't flunk out. Then graduation came, and Jaydee disappeared without saying goodbye. Number changed, address unknown. Seven years later, he called out of the blue to say he wanted her back, and, like a fool, she believed him.

McWynn flicked his fingernail against the glass. "What's his name?"

She considered lying, but that would be dumb. "Jaydee. Jaydee Hill."

The detective nodded at Joe, who scribbled something on his notepad.

"It's over." She stared hard at Joe's bent head. "Has been for a long time."

McWynn crossed the room and handed her the photograph.

She closed her hand around the picture. McWynn studied her fingers.

Goose bumps prickled her skin. She'd washed her hands after touching the hammer, hadn't she? My God, how could she have been so careless? She hadn't done anything wrong. She had to keep that first and foremost in her mind.

"Did something happen? It looks like you've got a cut."

"I broke a jar last night when I went for a flashlight."

"Where?"

"Houston's office." If she hadn't overslept at the kitchen table, she'd be in Barstow by now instead of being interrogated by this very persistent man. "Didn't you see the glass on the floor?"

McWynn shook his head. "No." He narrowed his eyes. "What's under your fingernails?"

She closed her fist, pressing her fingernails against her palm. Her middle finger on her right hand had a thin line of brownish-red under the nail. She couldn't get a breath. Her side ached. "Probably from one of my patients."

"Animal blood?"

Her mind raced. Zany? No. The bay mare with the hoof wall separation? Couldn't be. What about one of the Arabians? Both recuperating from bouts of colic—no bleeding with a bellyache. Wait, that little pinto pony had a cut on his coronet band above his left rear hoof. The topical ointment she'd applied was cold and stiff and hadn't spread the way it was supposed to. She had to press hard on the cut to get the medicine in the right place. Oh hell... she knew whose blood it was and soon McWynn would too.

"Ever heard of a precipitin test?"

"It tells the difference between animal and human blood." Shouldn't she have an attorney present or something? *No.* Attorneys were for guilty people.

"I'll need a sample. Okay?"

Afraid saying "no" would make her look guilty, she choked out an, "Okay."

Joe got up and left the bungalow, leaving the front door open. A minute later he came back with a small package and gave it to McWynn, who removed a sharp object and, after asking for her hand, ran it beneath her nail. *Ouch.* She jerked away, but he'd gotten what he needed.

Her prints were all over the crime scene. They'd find them, of course. She had to tell the detective everything, because if he discovered it for himself—God only knew what would happen to her. Bile climbed her throat. She swallowed it down. "I accidentally handled a hammer with blood on it." She blurted the words before she lost her nerve. "It was on the floor of the barn."

McWynn collected his sunglasses from the table, his face not registering her confession or her concern.

"We'll be sending this sample to the lab. It will tell us everything we need to know." He pulled a business card from his shirt pocket. "I appreciate your cooperation this morning." He handed her the card, eyes shifting to her open suitcase next to the closet. "However, I'm going to have to ask you not to leave town."

Six

BOUGAINVILLEA SPILLED OVER THE patio trellis; colored spotlights bathed the stucco walls of José's Hideaway in shades of yellow, green and red. Luke gripped the wrought iron handle and pulled the door wide, allowing warm air, boisterous voices and the smell of fried corn tortillas to rush from the restaurant.

Randi planted her feet, restraining herself from hightailing it back to his Range Rover waiting in the parking lot. "I don't know, Luke. Maybe this wasn't such a good idea. I should be home working on my article. If I blow my deadline, I'll never get another chance at *HorseWorld*."

"You have to eat, and this place is your favorite."

"I know, but I feel weird tonight."

"Weird how?"

"I don't know, anti-social and kind of lost."

"You're not lost." Propping the door with his boot, Luke extended his hand. "You're with me." His fingers closed around her wrist. "And you look nice." It was the same tone he used to calm frightened horses. "I like that skirt. Blue's your color."

"Thanks." She'd taken a hot bath, put on some mascara and lip gloss, and even spent more than the usual ninety seconds on her hair, figuring cleaning up a bit might make her feel better and less like a fugitive. It had, a little. "It's not easy to get me out of my jeans."

"I know." Luke closed the door behind them.

Strands of lights, toy plastic margarita glasses alternating with red chili peppers, hung from the perimeter of the bar. An enormous open firepit filled with gleaming quartz rocks divided the cantina from the dining room, and a pudgy jukebox bubbled neon colors to the beat of a thumping bass.

Luke stepped up to the hostess stand. "Do you have a quiet table?"

"Let me see what I can do for you, sir." She placed her fingertips on his arm and stood on her tiptoes to survey the place. "Be right back."

Women took to Luke like ducks to water. Young, old, plain, beautiful and everything in between. He was either oblivious to the attention or a good actor. He tucked his car keys into his pocket. "I don't want to rush you into talking about Stacey."

She nodded. Maybe after a beer. Or two. She longed to wash last night away but needed to keep her mind sharp. On the car ride over, she'd come clean about forgetting Zany's eye meds, her reason for heading to the ranch and finding Stacey dead. Luke hadn't been pleased. Though, considering the circumstances, he'd at least been kind.

Above the din of voices from the bar came the repeated thud of the walk-in cooler behind the counter, the rattle of ice being scooped into plastic tumblers and the hiss and splatter of sizzling meat. The hostess returned, motioning for Luke to follow. At a booth near the back, she placed oversized menus on the tablecloth and lit the candle. "Enjoy your dinner, sir." She left him with a wink. Randi might as well not have been there.

Luke picked up a menu. "I saw an unmarked car pull up to your place this morning."

The thought of McWynn made her nervous all over again.

He'd been out of her mind for at least two and a half minutes.

"Would you like a drink?"

"Sure." Way too eager. "Thanks."

Luke glanced over his shoulder. "I don't see our waiter. I'll go up to the bar."

As soon as he left, she could have sworn people at the nearby tables stopped their conversations and found an excuse to turn and look at her, but that was crazy. This wasn't the Wild West. There weren't WANTED signs posted on the beams with her picture on them. She studied her fingernails. She'd clipped and cleaned them after the detective had taken his baggie and left, something she should have done earlier if she'd been thinking straight—or thinking like a guilty person.

Luke returned with two beers, set them down, made another trip and came back with a shot glass in each hand. "I got Hornitos for you, with salt, a lime and a Negra Modelo chaser."

The man knew what she liked. She had to give him that much. Jaydee couldn't even remember her favorite donut. "Cheers, I guess." They toasted and she threw back the tequila, the warmth of it searing her throat. She sunk her teeth into the lime. Cool, tart relief. "Thanks for handling my rounds for me today. I'll make up the time."

"Don't worry about it, but Zany's got some orbital swelling. Make sure you give him some Bute in the morning."

"I will. You know how I love that horse."

Luke scrunched his face. "Remember what I told you."

"Yeah. 'Don't get too attached.' Easier said than done. Not only with Zany, but with all of them. I'll never forget how I felt when I realized we'd lost that colt and there was nothing I could do about it. I knew from school it would happen sooner or later, but it didn't prepare me for how helpless I'd feel."

"Animals die. Sometimes for no reason. It's just one of those things."

She refused to accept that. "Can foals die of SIDS?"

"Sure, it's called endotoxemia."

"Think that's what happened?"

"It's a possibility."

She touched the lime to her tongue. "I need to know for sure."

"I'm working on it, but you're going to have to be patient."

"I'm not good at being patient."

Luke managed a grin. "Tell me something I don't know."

A waiter appeared at their table, pen poised, a blank expression on his face. Luke ordered the carnitas, Randi a chile relleno. Luke drank his tequila and set the empty glass down. "I had a talk with Tim Tyler this afternoon."

"You didn't tell him I forgot Zany's ointment, did you?" If Zany's egomaniac of an owner found out, that would be the nail in her coffin.

"How could I? You just told me on the way over here."

"Oh... yeah." Definitely losing her marbles.

"Anyway, I would never rat you out. You're good at your job. Since you've been with me, I've seen nothing but excellent work. I don't worry about you not being responsible."

"It won't happen again." She wrapped her hands around the beer bottle.

"I know." He paused. "So anyway, after beating around the bush for a while, Tim finally got to the point of his call."

"Which was?"

Luke hesitated. "To ask if I thought Houston and Helen might consider selling the ranch."

"Sell? *Seriously*? Why ask you?"

"Tim hinted at a kickback if I helped him."

"Helped him how?"

"By convincing Houston the horse business is in a downturn and to get out before it's too late. He said the murder publicity would ruin the ranch and I should make that point clear to Houston."

"He thinks you'd do that for money?"

"I guess so."

She shook her head. "Unbelievable. What would Tim Tyler do with a horse-breeding farm, anyway? He's an actor."

"He has a real estate partner."

"Real estate?" She leaned back. "Uh-oh. I don't like the sound of that."

"It's not like he's had any box office hits lately, and I think rather than downsize his lifestyle, he's searching for other means of income."

"In other words, he wants to pave paradise and put up a row of timeshare condos."

"Looks that way."

"Why Lucky Jack? Isn't there some other land for him to wreck? Something actually on the market?"

"There's nothing as big as Lucky Jack with such close proximity to the ocean. If he develops the ridge where the Hills' house sits, he'll get ocean views."

"The ranch has been in Houston's family forever. He'd never sell it."

Luke didn't look convinced. "Let's hope not."

If she had any appetite at all, she'd lost it now. "What are you going to do? Are you going to tell Houston and Helen?"

"No way. Tyler's on his own with that baby."

"Good." Feeling vindicated, she took a slug of her beer. "Did you see Helen today?" She didn't give him time to answer. "How about Houston?" She really wanted to know if he'd seen Jaydee, but that wouldn't go over well with Luke.

"Helen and I spoke briefly. Houston wasn't there." Luke picked up a tortilla chip and crunched it. "The barn's all strung up with yellow tape and everyone's walking around like zombies."

"What about Roberto? He didn't answer my knock last night."

"Helen said he had to go to Tijuana. His mother's sick. They don't expect her to live."

"Oh. How awful. Poor guy."

"Why were you looking for him?"

"I needed a flashlight for Zany's eyes. No power in the barn. I'm not sure if it was the storm or if somebody cut it off." She picked at her napkin, shredding it into little pieces. "Speaking of things you see in the movies, there's something I want to tell you, something you should know."

He crossed his arms.

Might as well get it over with. Didn't want him hearing it from anyone else. "I found a hammer on the floor of the barn, covered in blood."

"Did you touch it?"

"Sad to say, yes."

He picked up his beer. "Where is it now?"

She twirled a small white vase with flowers so fake they were hardly worth the effort. "In a bag marked EVIDENCE. The cops will be running DNA on the stuff they found under my fingernails. They're going to find it was Stacey's blood and match my prints to the hammer."

Platters of steaming carnitas, tortillas in plastic warmers and bowls of condiments arrived. The waiter set the relleno plate on the table. "Careful, *muy caliente.*"

Luke stabbed a piece of carnitas and slapped it in the center of a tortilla. Sour cream, a blob of guacamole and a spoonful of salsa went on top of the pork. He showed no reaction to what she'd just told him.

Randi cut into her relleno but didn't make a move to eat it. "The detective asked me a bunch of questions about Zany's eye meds. I explained it to him over and over, but he didn't seem to get it."

"Would you like me to corroborate your story?"

"Yes. Please."

"What else did he ask you about?" Luke shifted on his seat. His eyes were curious and hard at the same time.

"McWynn?"

"Yes, McWynn."

"He found out I had a history with Jaydee."

"You told him?"

"I didn't have a choice. He pulled out an old picture of us. How he spotted it wedged behind my computer is beyond me."

Luke shook his head. "Have you talked to an attorney?"

"No. Why would I?"

"I have a friend. I'll give him a buzz just to be safe."

"Don't go to any trouble. I'll be fine."

"No trouble." Luke snorted. "Jaydee's the one the cops should be questioning. Although, according to Helen, he was in Vegas last night. How convenient."

"Think she's trying to protect him?"

"It wouldn't surprise me." He pointed at her plate. "You haven't touched your food. Aren't you going to eat?"

"I'm trying."

"Know what I do when I have a problem?"

"No." She pushed the relleno around her plate.

"I reason things out. You didn't kill Stacey. Let's try to figure out who did."

"You mean form theories then go around and question people? 'Where were you last night?' That sort of thing?"

"Exactly. Taking action works."

"Okay. Where do we start? With Houston? I can't even say his name in that context without feeling guilty. He may have his quirks, but he's never been anything but good to me."

Luke took a bite, chewed and swallowed. "Everybody has their idiosyncrasies. Thing is, does he have a motive?"

"He and Stacey argued Thursday afternoon at the collection. A lot of tension between them over Rebel."

"Houston also had means and opportunity. Unfortunately, he stays on the list. Next?"

"Piper? There's no love lost between her and Stacey. She's on Houston's team all the way. He helped her out in the past when she thought she was beyond hope."

"They both have ready access to the barn. Stacey wouldn't question their presence. Keep going. You're on a roll."

Maybe Luke had something after all. Talking it over with him made it easier to sit up straight and her food was starting to smell good enough to eat. "Tim Tyler. From what you just told me, a murder at the ranch might create a scenario where he could pick the place up dirt-cheap. If he wants to flip it, he'd be looking at a nice profit."

"Anybody else?" Luke had one eyebrow raised and was looking at her funny. No secret who he had in mind.

"Jaydee."

"Motive?"

She closed her eyes. "I have no idea." She was sick of thinking of Jaydee and why he did the things he did.

"Forget about him." A minute passed before Luke cleared his throat. "There's a party I've been invited to tonight. A client friend of mine from way back. Come with me."

"Thanks for the offer, but a party is *way* out of my league right now."

"It'll help get your mind off things. We'll have a good time, I promise. Besides, you said yourself it's not easy to get you out of your jeans, and you don't want that pretty outfit of yours to go to waste, do you?"

Seven

"**I** FEEL ABOUT AS social as a leper. If you'll give me the keys, I don't mind waiting in the Rover."

Luke took Randi's arm. "You'll be fine." He led her past a swimming pool lit on the perimeter by a row of tiki torches. The flames danced, reflecting off the surface of the water, and a soft glow fell in the grassy space between the house and pool. Laughter and jovial conversation floated from the rear of Rickert Donovan's sprawling ranch-style compound.

Having Luke by her side was a comfort, but she wasn't giving herself over to the party scene yet. "It doesn't feel right, chatting about the weather, making small talk and whatnot with Stacey dead and all the trouble hanging over Lucky Jack."

"We can't leave now," Luke said. "Rickert is one of our best clients. If it helps, consider this business."

"Luke!" A man broke from the throng, striding toward them in an all-black suit with a long-ish coat. If he'd held a guitar, Randi wouldn't have been surprised to hear him bust out "Ring of Fire."

"Hello, Rickert." Luke shook the man's meaty paw. "I'd like

you to meet Randi Sterling."

"My pleasure." Rickert's eyes gleamed with confidence as he gave her a quick once-over. "Any friend of the finest vet in San Diego County is a friend of mine. I don't trust anyone but Luke with my horses."

Luke smiled and, beneath his Native American complexion... was that a blush? "She's my new assistant."

"Is that so? You seem young. Do you have much experience?"

She smoothed her skirt. "I have a degree from Denver Tech, and Luke is doing a great job of showing me the ropes."

"I see. Is vet school in your future?"

"Well..."

"I'm working on it," Luke said. "Pushing her in that direction."

"Actually, I'm a journalist."

Rickert cocked his head. "I'm confused. I thought you were a tech?"

"I am, but I write for horse magazines too."

"Veterinary publications?"

"Uh... not at the moment. I'm doing a piece for *HorseWorld*: they're an all-breed magazine targeted toward people who show on the A-circuit."

Rickert's smile faded. "Piece of advice, young lady. Diversification isn't always a good thing. I made my fortune in junk bonds while everyone was telling me to put it in treasuries. You get spread too thin and before you know it, you're a jack of all trades, master of none."

"Randi is extremely capable. I have no doubt she can handle all the irons in her fire."

Luke's words were kind, but she couldn't help think of Zany. Her favorite horse, a simple task, and she'd botched it good.

"I've got her working at the Hills' ranch."

"Shame about the girl." Rickert clasped his hands behind his back. "I met her once. A real looker, that one. They catch the guy?"

"Not yet."

Rickert lowered his voice. "Question the husband first, isn't that what they always say?"

Luke's eyes met Randi's. "Probably a good idea."

"'Course, with him being such a player, it might have been some filly got her panties all in a bunch and decided to take out the wife."

If Rickert knew she'd been duped by Jaydee twice *and* that she'd put her hands on Stacey's murder weapon, he'd rank her intelligence right up there with the cactus they were standing next to. Probably encourage Luke to find himself another tech.

"Whoever it was, I hope they get the bastard."

"We all do."

Rickert put his congenial face back on. "Listen, you two, I'd love to chat, but duty calls." He spread his arms, gesturing at the expanse of his palm tree-lined property. "Make yourselves at home. Conchita will get you a margarita at the bar, and my guys are roasting *carne asada* behind the orange grove." A telltale stream of smoke floated above the branches.

Rickert left, and as soon as she and Luke were alone, he lifted his nose. "How 'bout it?"

"Seriously? We just ate. Well... you just ate."

"Who cares? It smells fantastic."

Men and their stomachs. "You go ahead."

"You sure?"

"I'll be fine." Long as Rickert didn't corner her again. Maybe she could find a spot to chill by herself until Luke returned.

The night air was warm, fragrant with orange blossoms and the promise of spring. Rickert's lounge chairs, ringing the pool, faux wicker upholstered in weatherproof fabric, were in the full recline position. She lifted one of the backs until it clicked into place and sat, stretching her legs in front of her. On the opposite side of the water, next to the bar, the partygoers carried on multiple conversations. Nobody looked her way, which suited her just fine. She knew she was being a huge party pooper, but hopefully after Luke wolfed down his food and shook the requisite number of hands, they could head on home.

The tinkle of ice cubes against glass, the croaking of frogs and the gentle lapping of water made her sink deeper into the chair, but it didn't cradle her body the way it looked like it should. She shifted her weight and twisted her hips. Nothing worked. Finally, she gave up on comfort and swung her legs to the side to perch along the edge.

The chatter of party talk rose and fell, punctuated by a woman with a high-pitched voice standing beside a stage where a band was setting up. "I told them I wanted a skier for my ice sculpture." The woman spoke loud enough to be heard over the chaos of the sound check and guitars being tuned. "I had all of Blake's important clients at the house, and those bozos sent me something looking like the Easter Bunny on a snowboard. I nearly died. I know people were laughing behind my back. I'll tell you what, I'll never use Perfect Party again."

A second woman chimed in: "I hope you didn't tip."

"I gave them a tip all right: Seabiscuit in the fourth."

A twitter of laughter followed.

Ugh. Enough. Randi had a hard time mustering up any pity for these people and their disastrous shindigs, and had just risen from the chair to go in search of Luke, when another exchange diverted her purpose.

"The U.S. Army slaughtered every Appaloosa they could find," a man said. "Did their damnedest to annihilate the breed. Almost succeeded, too."

"Whatever for?" A female.

"Revenge. See, occasionally, the Nez Percé beat the shit out of the Army and, because it couldn't *possibly* have been the result of military ineptitude, they blamed it on the horses the Indians rode."

Most people who pretended to know about horses at parties like this one spouted silly statements meant to impress, rarely based on fact, but everything this man said so far was close to the gospel truth. Who was he? Curious, she located the source of the conversation and made her way around the pool. The speaker, a tall man holding himself rather stiffly, stood across from a well-dressed man in a business suit chatting up a blonde and a brunette in clingy cocktail dresses. The blonde had her fingers wrapped around a martini glass and the brunette cradled a tea-cup Chihuahua.

"Didn't the guy we see on TV all the time ride an Appy?" The blonde took a dainty sip of her drink.

"His name," the brunette said, "is Tim Tyler."

Randi stiffened at the mention of Zany's owner.

The man in the suit retorted something about Tyler being a washed-up has-been. "Then again, you gotta pay the bills. Especially if you've gained fifty pounds and lost all your hair."

"Don't be so shallow." The brunette jumped in. "Looks aren't everything."

Randi lingered close to the group, positioning herself behind an outdoor propane heater.

"What you two don't know," the brunette shifted the Chihuahua to her hip, "is that Tim Tyler is an old friend of mine."

The blonde giggled. "Who isn't?"

"Timmy's horse is a beauty, and so is he. You're just jealous."

"I saw that guy at a horse show in LA once," the tall guy said, "but I wasn't impressed. He got on, rode his pattern, jumped off and tossed the reins to one of his minions. I'd hardly call him a horseman."

The brunette scowled. "Did you hear what I just said? Leave Tim Tyler alone."

The top of Randi's head warmed to the point of discomfort. She put her hand to her hair—hot! Yelping, she jumped away from the heater. The nearby group turned and stared.

"Excuse me. I don't mean to interrupt, but I couldn't help overhearing."

The women raked their eyes over her billowy skirt and cowboy boots. The material of their dresses hugged all the right places and their high heels were the type that drove men crazy.

"You can eavesdrop on me anytime, little lady." The owner of the Southern drawl sucked in his gut and stuck out his chest.

Randi narrowed her eyes. *Little lady?* The last time she'd

heard those two words side by side was when she'd gone to Furr's Cafeteria with her grandfather. She cringed every time he held up a finger and summoned the waitress.

"I'm Bob, by the way. Bob Knight of Fort Worth. Got myself a couple a car dealerships down there. Bob Knight'll do you right! Come see me if you're ever in Texas." His smile exposed teeth as straight and white as she'd ever seen. "Anyway, this here's Coco and Amber. I call them Camber. Know why?"

"I can't imagine." Where the heck was Luke?

"Because when they get to drinkin', they tilt to the side." Bob's belly shook as he roared with laughter. "Either that, or when *I* get to drinkin' they tilt to the side."

Amber, the blonde, giggled. "Oh, Bob! You're too much."

Randi forced a smile. The tall man stuck out his hand. "Conrad." Three pen tops protruded from his shirt pocket. "I'm Coco's cousin. From South Dakota."

"The Appaloosa expert."

"Comes with the territory." Conrad's expression was refreshingly relaxed and natural. Nobody here he needed to impress.

She smiled. "I heard you mention Tim Tyler." Information equaled power. She'd love to throw a wrench in the actor's alleged plan to raze the ranch. Just how badly did he want the property? Enough to kill for?

"Bob here," Coco said, "thinks Timmy's washed up, but I'm a personal friend and I'm telling you, the guy's still got it going on."

"You'd be the one to know." Amber crossed her arms, thrusting her boobs even higher.

"It's not like you think, and sexiness isn't always about ripped abs, *AMBER*."

Randi ignored the brewing catfight. "I heard Tim Tyler might buy a ranch somewhere around here." She put on her best starstruck face. "Wouldn't that be awesome? I mean, you walk into the grocery store, and guess who's right beside you checking out the cantaloupes?"

Coco drew back her dark red lips and exposed her pointed

canines. "Don't get too excited, honey." She stroked the Chihuahua's miniscule head. "I don't think your melons would be his type."

Randi had hardly given her chest size a second thought in Colorado. In this town it seemed boob judging was a favorite pastime.

"Speaking of nice tatas," Bob sloshed his drink on Randi's feet, temporarily making her forget Coco's uncalled for put-down. "Y'all hear what happened to Stacey Hill?"

Solemn nods. Randi wiped her boots on the grass. She wasn't going to get anywhere with this group. Waste of time. She stood on her tiptoes and peered over their heads. Luke was coming down the hill from the orange grove. Thank God. "I've enjoyed chatting with you all, but I see my date."

"Not so fast there, girlie. How 'bout a drink? I can fetch you one of those Cosmo things the girls are havin'."

"No, thank you." She took a step backward. "I have to be going."

Bob made a face like he wasn't used to hearing *no* for an answer. "Wait a minute. I didn't catch your name. Can I at least get that much?"

"Randi." She held out her hand. "Sterling."

Coco tilted her head and played with an earring. "You look familiar. Have we met?"

"I don't think so."

Coco's eyes grew wide. She threw her hands up and the Chihuahua fell to the ground. "I know who you are. My friend told me about you."

"What friend?"

Coco scooped up her trembling dog. Its eyes bugged out and the jeweled collar twinkled in the light from a tiki torch. "He said you two had a thing going on in college, but when he broke it off you never got over him."

"*Jaydee?*"

"He said you followed him out here."

"No." Randi shook her head. "Not exactly."

"He told me he felt kind of silly, being stalked by a woman."

Was she serious? "*He* asked *me* to come to San Diego." This was nuts. What else had Jaydee said? Why was he spreading rumors? "I didn't know he was married until I'd already moved here. By then it was too late."

Clearly, Coco didn't believe a word she said. She stared at her like she was Susan Smith after she'd been declared guilty of drowning her children.

"Funny," Coco tapped her toe, "that's not the way Jaydee told it."

Upon closer inspection, Coco wasn't nearly as polished as Amber. Her shoes were scuffed, the seams of her dress bulged in places where the threads were bare, and she'd been far too heavy-handed with her makeup.

Coco lifted her chin. "He said when you found out he was married to Stacey, you went off the deep end."

"I guess that depends on your definition of *deep end*. Personally, I think I handled it pretty well."

"That poor girl," Amber said. "Anybody know the details?"

Coco tucked the little dog back under her armpit. It seemed to warm him and make him feel more secure at the same time. "Ask *her*."

A palpable silence fell over the group. Even Bob, Randi's only ally, coughed and said something about heading to the bar to freshen up his drink. Randi turned to weave her way through the crowd and didn't need to look over her shoulder to know all of their eyeballs were boring a hole into her back.

Eight

SHANE WAGGED HIS TAIL, eyes fixed on his leash hanging from the hook. Randi pushed her chair away from her desk. "Okay, but just a short one. I have work to do."

Work, shmurk, he seemed to be thinking. Nothing was more important than investigating the sights and smells around the neighborhood.

A walk might do her good. Forty-five minutes at her desk this morning and Randi's progress on her *HorseWorld* article was snail-paced. A paragraph here, a quote there, but her mind wasn't in the game. At the very least, she'd have some time to ponder why Jaydee painted her a stalker, leading total strangers to jump to the assumption she'd killed Stacey.

Shane vaulted over a pile of clothes and loped for the door. She clipped his leash to his collar and stepped onto the porch just as a white Maserati sedan pulled up in front of Luke's house at the top of the driveway.

Well, well, well. Barbra Dubois. Barbra ran Ridgemark Saddlebreds, a successful operation where, according to the Rancho del Zorro rumor mill, she tied chains around her horses' ankles and set off fireworks in the arena to get the high-stepping action the five-gaited people coveted. Regardless of whether or not the rumors were true, Barbra and her horses cleaned up at the shows. People from all over the world came to her with their checkbooks in hand. Everybody in the saddlebred circle knew Barbra; if they didn't, they pretended they did.

Barbra stepped from the Maserati in red pumps and skin-tight pants, a cropped fur jacket and billowing black hair. She looked like she'd just come from an '80's Whitesnake video and sashayed up to Luke's door like a mare in heat. Randi had yet to decipher the nature of Barbra and Luke's relationship and was afraid to ask. She hated to think Luke had such superficial taste in women.

Luke's door opened then closed again, taking Barbra with it, and while Randi stood stewing on her porch, the phone inside the bungalow rang. Shane, no dummy, knew from experience the ringing meant a possible delay. He tugged on the leash to dissuade her from answering.

Randi debated. Only solicitors called her house line—and sometimes her dad. She dragged Shane back into the kitchen, took a chance, and picked up the phone.

"Miranda?"

"Hi, Dad." She pictured him at his desk, inside his red brick office at the University of Colorado, cigarette in hand, surrounded by mounds of papers and back issues of *The Economist*. It was Sunday, but he usually went in on the weekends. Said he liked it when the students weren't there to bother him.

"I thought I'd call and see how things are going in the land of the beautiful people." His words flowed fast and clear. A relief.

"I'm all right, but I have some bad news." She bit her lip, regretting her choice of words. Boozers and bad news weren't a good mix.

His voice grew tight. "What is it?"

"Remember Stacey Hill?"

"The one that son of a bitch dumped you for? They split up? I told you it wouldn't last."

Your Receipt

Customer ID: **********7353

Items that you checked out

Title: Rode to death : a Randi Sterling
      mystery
ID: 39085400720625
Due: March-12-20

Total items: 1
Feb-20-2020 19:16
Overdue: 0

Closed on Christmas and Boxing Day, and
New Year's Day. All locations will close at 5pm
on December 24 and 31.
www.reginalibrary.ca

"Stacey was murdered Friday night."

There was a pause. "He killed her?"

"I don't know about Jaydee's involvement. The problem is, the police think I might have had something to do with it."

Two beats of a black silence later he said, "*You*? That's ridiculous. Why the hell would they think that?"

She gave him a rundown of finding Stacey's body, adding an explanation of how her prints came to be on the hammer.

"I'm coming to California. Give me a couple hours to find a sub and I'll catch the next flight from Denver. United runs—"

"No." More trouble she didn't need. "Really, Dad, it's not necessary."

"You're in a jam, sweetie. It's the least I can do."

"I'll be fine."

"It's a father's job."

"How about this? Let's give it a day or two and if I feel I need you, I'll call."

"Promise?"

"Promise."

"Did you tell your mother?" He sucked in a breath, taking a drag off his cigarette.

"How could I? I have no way of finding her until she wants to be found."

"Still touring the country with that trust-fund baby?"

"I don't know."

More silence.

Randi prayed he was sifting through the pieces of what she'd just told him and not trying to remember where he'd left his flask.

Ninety minutes later, beachside at The Surf & Stirrup, Kira put her hands on her hips. "You look like shit."

A yellow sign hung from one of the back bar's cabinets: *No assholes, No hookers, No tweekers*. Under the words, to soften the blow for any closet-type patrons who might take offense, a universal smiley-face.

"Thanks." Randi settled onto a barstool. "With friends like you..."

Kira wore a fitted purple T-shirt that read *A Hangover is the Wrath of Grapes*. Kira hadn't had a hangover since she moved to San Diego from Austria fifteen years ago at the ripe old age of twenty. She wore it because bartenders in tight shirts, she claimed, sold more booze. Capping a bottle of Crown Royal, she put it back on the shelf.

Kira's saloon-style back bar was her pride and joy. She'd had it shipped to the restaurant in three separate pieces. The massive piece of furniture had ornate woodwork and graceful arches above the mirrored segments from the late 1800s Tombstone era. The bar spent Prohibition in Mexico to avoid destruction by Temperance fanatics before it made its way back to the States. Kira had wheedled it away from an antiques dealer for a steal, she'd said.

"You can't exist on caffeine and *Negra Modelo*, alone." Kira bent over to pick up a bottle cap off the floor. A tattooed outline of wavy hair and curvy breasts peeked over the waistband of her jeans.

"No offense, but it's hard to take motherly advice from someone who sports a tramp stamp."

Kira straightened and wagged her finger. "Bite your tongue. Freya is a warrior goddess. You could use a bit of her mojo. Your skin is pale, your hair's all stringy and your jeans are hanging off. That's just for starters."

"I'm sitting down. You can't see my jeans. Plus, I have plenty of meat on my bones."

"Did you eat dinner last night?"

She nodded. "Luke took me to the Hideaway."

"Nice of him, but it doesn't mean you ate."

To avoid the topic of her food intake, or lack thereof, she told Kira about Rickert's soiree and how Coco spread her poisonous accusations, leaving her feeling like she'd been branded with a scarlet *M* for murderer.

"I know that Coco chick. She bartends down the street at The Triton. Keep in mind this is Southern California, Ran. Land of the fruits, flakes and nuts, remember? No one's going to take her babbling seriously. Not to mention, I'm sure Jaydee's sipping a little hot Coco on cold nights."

"Sure looks that way."

Kira plunged her hands into a sink full of suds and glassware. "And as it turns out, Stacey wasn't exactly an angel."

"Other than the obvious, is there something you haven't told me?"

"Didn't I tell you about her and Matt?"

"Matt Watson? The horseshoer?"

"Yep."

"No."

"The two of them were in here last week, looking pretty damn cozy."

Randi propped her elbows on the bar. "Explain what you mean by *cozy*."

"He tickled her. She giggled. Back and forth for hours. They didn't bother to hide it, either. Houston, or Helen, or *Jaydee*, could have walked in on them at any time. Judging from the look of rapture on Stacey's face, I don't think she would have cared."

"Are you sure? Matt doesn't seem like Stacey's type. He's a laid-back surfer dude."

Kira rinsed the last glass and dried her hands. "He's hot. She liked 'em pretty. That's why she went for Jaydee, right?"

"I guess so, but rumor has it Matt's a born-again Christian. I don't think adultery is something he'd be likely to practice."

"Everybody likes sex, even the converted, and people let down their guard in here. *In vino veritas*, and Matt likes his grapes. Maybe Stacey finally realized Jaydee was nothing but a lead weight around her neck, so she sought solace in the understanding arms of her farrier. Jaydee found out and gave her what he thought she deserved."

Randi shook her head. "I can't see it. No matter how hard I

try, I can't picture Jaydee killing anyone."

Kira crossed her arms. "I don't mean to sound harsh, but you need to face the facts. The man you believed was the one for you—your soul mate and all that—didn't turn out to be who you thought he was, and you're having a hard time swallowing it. Bottom line: the more distance you can put between yourself and that creep, the better."

Out the window, palm fronds swayed in the breeze. Couples walked hand-in-hand along the shore, dogs chased the surf back and forth and children played in the sand. "Thanks for the coffee, but I should be going."

"No." Kira grabbed her arm. "Stay. I'm concerned about you, that's all."

"You haven't said anything that wasn't true." She gathered her purse but didn't get up. "Anyway, my stomach doesn't feel that great and my head's starting to hurt."

"I can fix that. Some scrambled eggs and a Surf's Up and you'll be good as new."

She hooked her purse over her knee. "What's a Surf's Up?"

"Jäger and a little bit of whipped orange juice."

"*Jägermeister*? That stuff is vile swill, especially at ten-thirty in the morning."

"When I was a kid, my mother gave me a tablespoon full whenever I got sick."

"Sure, and then you got sicker but you didn't know it because you were too buzzed to feel it. Besides, it kinda stinks. Jäger is probably the reason you gave up alcohol."

"Nonsense." Kira reached down and grabbed a square bottle from the freezer. She removed the cap and poured. Blackish-green liquid topped off with not nearly enough foamy orange juice. "Drink it." Kira had been in the States long enough to have adopted American lingo, but her stubborn traditions were rooted in Austria.

"Talk about peer pressure. Do you do this to all your customers?"

"It'll help. Promise."

"What's the thing on top?"

"Chocolate mint leaf. It's delicious."

Randi chewed it. Kira was right. Quite tasty. As for the rest of the concoction, she closed her eyes and gulped her poison.

Kira popped her gum. "Give it a minute."

Five seconds was more like it. A warm glow trickled through her limbs. Felt like her bottom was melting into to the barstool and the will to leave along with it. She hated to admit it, but Kira's theory might have some teeth.

Kira, looking pleased with herself, turned toward the coffee machine. "You mentioned Tim Tyler when you came in. What's the scoop?"

"He's trying to get his greedy paws on Lucky Jack by pressuring Houston and Helen to sell."

"What would he do with a horse ranch? Turn it into a Hollywood backlot?"

"Worse. High-density condos with ocean views."

Kira's happy face faded. "Forget about it, Ran—don't go sticking your nose into Tim Tyler's business."

"Do you realize what'll happen if he gets his way?"

"Do you realize what'll happen if you get *in* his way?" Kira narrowed her eyes. "Backyard pool. Floater. Ring any bells?"

"Floater?"

"A couple years ago. Don't you people read the news in Colorado? It was all over the place, remember? The blood on the porch? Tyler's affair with his trainer, Philip? Keep in mind the wife was an Olympic swimmer. No trace of alcohol in her blood and she drowns in her pool? Doubt it." Kira shifted her gaze toward the door and her smile reappeared. "Hey, look who's here."

Luke settled on the stool next to Randi, wearing a San Diego Chargers baseball cap and a Colorado State sweatshirt. "Morning, ladies."

Judging from his chipper mood, his visit with Barbra had been a success. A growl rumbled deep in Randi's chest, same way Shane's did when he spotted a coyote trotting—*trespassing*—across their yard.

Kira poured a glass of grapefruit juice and set it in front of Luke. "What about you, Luke? You ever hear about Tim Tyler's wife?"

"She drowned, right?"

"That's his story, but I'm not buying it. Please tell Randi not to poke around in a hornets' nest."

"I have." Luke gave her a patriarchal stare.

"Good. Two against one." Kira gave Luke's arm a squeeze. "Talk some sense into her while I go get her some food, will ya? She won't listen to me."

Randi took a deep breath. No need making herself crazy over Barbra. It was none of her business. She and Luke had no claims on each other. He was free to see whomever he wanted and so was she. "Thanks for pulling me from the lion's den last night. I know you wanted to stay at Rickert's longer than we did."

Luke shook his head. "Nah. It's okay."

He smelled good, like the soap he wore.

"Kira thinks Stacey had a thing going on with Matt Watson."

Luke drew his head back and blinked with surprise. "No way."

"What do you know about him?"

"He's a damn good farrier." Luke drained his juice. "We don't talk about anything other than horses."

"Kira said he and Stacey met here last week for drinks."

Luke twisted the silver cuff he wore around his wrist. "Maybe they were discussing Rebel's feet. He's low in the heels."

"Maybe."

Luke wasn't a gossip. He listened but rarely repeated. If he knew something, it would be like getting water from a rock.

She pushed her empty glass away. "Any news on the colt?"

"From the initial investigation, there were no signs of trauma or illness. Gordon, from the clinic, is doing the necropsy. We'll see if it shows anything conclusive."

Kira burst through the swinging kitchen doors and set a steaming plate of eggs on the bar. "Eat."

Randi picked up a fork. "You sure are bossy this morning."

"It's part of her charm," Luke said.

Kira flashed him her brightest smile. "Thank you, Luke. I'm glad somebody appreciates me." Her expression changed. "Hold it." She held out her hand like she was stopping traffic. "Someone's phone is ringing."

Luke checked his cell. "Not mine."

Randi dug inside her bag, but by the time she found the phone, she'd missed the call. She went to drop her cell back in her purse, but her fingers maintained their death grip. Speak of the devil and, lo and behold, Jaydee Hill came calling.

Nine

SCRAMBLED EGGS AND JÄGERMEISTER sat heavy in Randi's belly while Jaydee's call was a burden on her mind. Five more minutes on the road and she'd be at Lucky Jack. Hadn't had a face-to-face with the guy since he dumped her, but not for lack of trying. He'd simply made himself unavailable. Didn't take her calls and darted the opposite way at the barn when he saw her coming. Now, with Stacey dead, he popped up on her screen. *Why?*

Cresting the last hill before the ranch, she eased off the gas. If Jaydee thought she'd jump at the prospect of seeing him, he was in for a rude awakening. Whatever he was selling, she wasn't buying.

The descent into the valley that housed Lucky Jack was steep, but she downshifted instead of riding the brakes the way most San Diegans did. When she was fifteen, permit in hand, her dad had driven her up to Trail Ridge Road along the Continental Divide. She spent the day at 12,000 feet negotiating a winding two-lane road, much of it without a guardrail. Best driver's ed class ever. She missed her dad. Missed the way they used to be and wondered what the future held for their relationship. If she didn't find out who murdered Stacey and McWynn arrested her for the crime, her future might include nothing more than endless days spent staring at four walls and a toilet.

That would send her dad into a bottomless binge.

El Camino Real leveled out and her blood turned to ice. Zany's spotted rump flashed along the double yellow as he thundered up the other side of the ravine away from Lucky Jack. Danny, a teenager who worked at the ranch, sped after him on foot, a halter slung over his shoulder, the lead rope trailing in the dirt.

She cranked the wheel to the right. The F150's tires dug into the soft shoulder and the truck jerked to a stop. Chasing Zany by car was pointless. It would only make him run faster and there was no time to catch him before he hit the hairpin turn. She tossed the keys under the seat and jumped from the cab. Snatching a bucket from the bed of the truck, she threw a handful of peppermints inside, praying to Pegasus that Zany would hear the rattle of his treats and slow the hell down.

Danny yelled something over his shoulder, but his words were lost on the wind. Zany sped toward the blind corner at the top of the hill, panic evident in the tempo of his hooves on the slick pavement. Even in the best of circumstances, Zany had trouble with his eyesight. He had to be terrified.

Randi's heart raced as her feet slid out from under her. Her thighs burned with the effort of running in such thick, soft dirt, but she didn't seem to be making any headway. She jostled the bucket hard, but the noise wasn't enough. Zany showed no signs of slowing and Danny wasn't closing the gap between himself and the horse, either.

The rumble of an accelerating motor filled the valley. Randi's stomach lurched. Her favorite horse was going to die and all she could do was watch. A front grille appeared, a flash of blue hood, then the rest of a BMW sedan. Zany swerved, but so did the car. Horse and vehicle plowed into each other with a horrific screech of brakes, a shrieking cry and a sickening thud.

Zany went down and the car fishtailed out of control before it slammed into a shallow ditch.

A lethal silence followed, punctuated by the slow hiss of a radiator.

Randi staggered to the scene and snatched the halter out of Danny's hand. "Check the car!"

The idiot at the wheel of the Beemer had been driving way too fast, but he didn't deserve to die.

She sprinted to where Zany lay motionless and fell to her knees, the blacktop tearing through her jeans. She put a hand on his neck. She couldn't see his eyes through the mesh of the fly mask. Were they open or closed? He didn't move beneath her touch. Was he dead?

"Zany?" She gave his mane a tug. "Get up!"

His hind leg jerked, scraping a hoof against the road. Other than that, he wouldn't budge. Had to be shock. The next car to come zooming around the corner would finish him off, and her too. Looping the lead rope around Zany's neck, she pulled. He raised his head a few inches off the pavement, then quit trying.

Randi tugged the rope loose and flicked her wrist. The line hissed through the air and popped Zany on the haunches. "*Get up!*" Hating herself, she hit him again and again, harder each time until, finally, with a stupendous heave, Zany righted his body and rolled his legs under his belly. He still had to get to his feet. The sound of another car coming up the hill behind them fired Randi into action. She screamed, waving her arms and jumping up and down.

It worked. Zany struggled to his feet. Knees locked, sides puffing, nostrils flared, he shook, jiggling the flesh below his shoulder that had split open, exposing equal halves of raw meat. Blood dripped onto the pavement.

Randi's hands trembled as she approached the horse. Every muscle in her body screamed for her to hurry, but she had to get the halter over his head without scaring him into another mad dash. "Easy, boy." Two steps closer. He trusted her, even after she'd whipped him, but as soon as she lifted her hand to secure the rope around his neck, the car she'd heard coming topped the hill. The driver laid on the horn and Zany started. She grabbed for the fly mask hoping to hold onto his head, but it tore away beneath the Velcro straps, leaving her with the mask, but no horse.

Zany stumbled and lost his balance then scrambled with a desperate clatter of hoofbeats to the other side of the road where he tripped over a low rock wall and plunged over the side of the canyon.

The second car pulled behind the first and shut off its engine. The driver of the blue X5 that hit Zany, a round man in a muscle shirt and running shorts, stood in front of his crumpled hood, arms flailing. "Keep your goddamn horse behind a fence! Who's going to pay for this?"

Danny ignored him, focusing on his task of helping the woman climb out of the passenger side of the BMW.

Randi kept her eyes glued to the spot where Zany had disappeared over the edge and called to Danny. "Everyone all right?"

"Seem to be. Physically, at least."

"Good." She poked a portion of the fly mask down her waistband to free her hands. "Follow me."

On the other side of the wall the brush was dense, five, six feet high in some spots, a tangle of branches. This wasn't going to be easy. She slid down the bank, clawing her way through the thicket, stopping every five yards or so, to listen for the sound of Zany busting his way through the bushes and to pull the thorns from her hair. "You with me, Danny?"

"Right behind."

She trudged along the trail. No-see-ums swarmed her face, but Zany's eyes were what mattered now, not hers. Prickly pears pierced her jeans and the dense scrub oak fought her every step of the way. The road rash blistering her knees hurt with each movement, but she didn't care.

A flock of crows shrieked and dove at something on the ground. A new rush of dread rippled through her, amplified by the drumming in her ears. If she came upon a clearing and found her brave and beautiful Appaloosa crumpled in a bloodied heap with the black scavengers diving at him, she'd lose her mind. Forearms held high to shield her face, she plunged through the chaparral.

She lost track of time until Danny called, "Hold up. I think I heard something. Bear left."

She changed course, but it was slow going—agonizing, minuscule progress. Another thirty yards and the chamise thicket closed in completely. It rose at least six feet high with branches interlaced like chain mail. Randi's arms stung from the brambles and something warm trickled down her cheek.

"Hey!" Danny stood beside an ancient, gnarled manzanita, its lowest branch barely high enough for a horse's back to clear. "Over here!" He held up his hand to show his position and waved her over. "Check this out."

Blood. A long smear of it on the trunk. "We're on the right track. Come on, hurry."

A thin path opened up enough so they were able to make a tiny bit of headway. Randi picked up the pace and, not watching where she put her feet, stumbled into a gopher hole.

Danny was there in a flash, breathing down her neck. "You okay?" He held out his hand.

"Yeah." She'd reinjured the ankle she twisted falling in Houston's office the night Stacey was killed. Panting, she accepted Danny's help up, brushed off the dirt and limped on. She had to swerve to avoid a colony of cacti and, rounding the next corner, stopped short before running into an enormous oak. The widespread tree sat smack in the middle of the trail with no way around it. She'd never seen brush so thick. If they couldn't get through, there was no way Zany managed it. *Where is he?*

Danny's shoulders fell. "We're screwed."

"Maybe not." She studied the trunk. The wood wasn't thick, but it was strong. "You're taller than I am. Climb up there and see if you can see anything. He has to be to be either to the right or the left. We know he's not behind us."

"If you say so." Danny scrabbled, spider-like, up the trunk

of the oak. The branches bent beneath his weight but held firm. Three-quarters of the way to the top he shielded his eyes and surveyed the horizon.

"See anything?"

He swiveled in all directions, holding a hand to shield his eyes. "Not a thing."

Randi's heart sank.

"What now?"

"We're not going to get anywhere by standing around. Climb down and we'll double back and look for another way."

The leaves rustled as Danny shifted. "Wait! Three o'clock. Something's moving."

"Is it Zany?"

"I think so... wait a second... Yes!" Danny's high-pitched voice buried all traces of his maturing teen self. "I see spots. Has to be him."

With Danny giving directions from high atop his perch, Randi worked her way toward the Appaloosa. When she reached the target area, once again, a side canyon was choked with brush. Bees buzzed around her head and the sun beat down on her shoulders. All different shapes and sizes of cacti huddled in great clumps, more scrub oak obstructed the path, and juniper twigs scratched her face. None of it mattered. The canyon was boxed in. Zany stood at the head of it, trapped by a wall of rock.

His head drooped and his sides heaved with exhaustion. Randi brushed the flies away from his red, weeping eyes, dug the mesh mask from her pants and put it on. Next she fastened the halter around his head. He seemed eager to put his destiny in her hands.

Danny sacrificed his beloved George Straight T-shirt to staunch Zany's bleeding, holding it against the horse's shoulder wound as they walked. Randi led the way, weaving in and out of the thick tangle of vegetation, back to the road and home to Lucky Jack. Despite the trauma of the experience, Zany had gotten off light. The damage could have been much worse.

"Danny, how in the world did he get out of his corral and end up on the road?"

"I don't know. He was already running like hell when I got here."

When they reached El Camino Real, Randi coaxed Zany into crossing the street. Eager to get it over with, he pranced across the pavement like it was a bed of hot coals and his hooves were on fire. Danny jogged to keep up with him and hold his shirt in place on the wound.

At the barn, Randi tucked the Appaloosa into a clean stall with a bucket of alfamo and just enough of the tranquilizer Acepromazine to take the edge off him. She cleaned the wound as best she could before Luke arrived, then went in search of Houston. She spotted him in the distance leaning against a sycamore trunk on the outskirts of the broodmare pasture. The boards of the old wooden bridge creaked as she crossed. The ranch felt deserted. At least she hadn't seen Jaydee. She still didn't know what he wanted and she was happy to keep it that way.

Houston turned at her approach and gave her a nod. The clouds had blown in and it was sprinkling lightly, just enough to dirty windshields and make the air smell like rain. She joined Houston at the fence and together they watched the herd of pregnant mares, bellies swaying as they walked. She propped a boot on the bottom rail and thought about bringing up the jar she'd broken in his office, but something about the curve of Houston's back, like he wanted to retreat into a shell, told her he wasn't having a good day. It could wait. There was plenty of bad news to go around already. "Did you hear about Zany?"

Houston plucked a weed sprouting near a fencepost and stuck it in his mouth. "He wasn't the only one that got loose."

"Who else?"

"Clients' horses. Two of them were found grazing by the road, and one wandered back into his corral of his own accord."

"What are the chances four horses escape at the same time from different pens?"

"You think somebody did it on purpose?"

She ran a hand through her hair and pulled out a twig, leaves still attached. "You see Tim Tyler around today?"

Houston eyeballed her as if trying to decide how much she knew about Tyler trying to get his hands on Lucky Jack. "Don't you go thinking he had something to do with it. Why would he? His horse was one of them that got out."

"He doesn't care about Zany. For all we know, he's taken out a fat insurance policy on him."

Houston scowled. "I'm sure Tim Tyler didn't open a bunch of corrals and shoo the horses onto the road."

Randi wasn't convinced; if clients' horses got out with a major road close by, they might be tempted to take them away from Lucky Jack, strengthening Tyler's position that Houston should quit before the ranch went down the tubes, but she kept quiet.

Houston shifted the weed to the other side of his mouth. "Regardless, I don't like it. We don't need any more bad publicity. Twelve more boarders left today. *Twelve.* And all those horses were in training. That's a lot of money. *Gone.*"

"Did they give you a reason?"

"Oh, sure. You name it. Found a cheaper place, no time to ride anymore, blah, blah, blah. The truth is, they're worried about their kids after finding out about Stacey being killed on the property. They don't come right out and say it, but I know what's on their minds. Now they're going to worry about their horses, too. All of a sudden they're willing to move fifteen, twenty miles east to the heat and dust just to get away from here. Last week that would have been unthinkable."

Randi shoved her hands in her back pockets. One could hardly blame them—a murdered woman, a dead colt and a bunch of horses getting loose. "What about the thirty-day notice? It's in the boarding contract, right?"

"People don't give a damn about a piece of paper."

"Can't you do something? It's a legally binding agreement."

Houston shook his head. "I can take them to court, but even if I had the time to go downtown, and I won a few bucks here and a few bucks there, it ain't gonna pay the mortgage."

"Mortgage? It's none of my business, but this ranch has been in your family forever. Don't you own it free and clear?"

Houston looked away. "Had to pull damn near most of my equity out."

Southern manners forgotten, the question flew out of her mouth before she could stop it. "*Why*?"

Houston gave her a long, hard stare. He looked older than she remembered—and sad. "Like you said, Randi, it's none of your business."

Later, Randi stood in front of Zany's stall, watching him breathe, when Luke came up from behind and touched her shoulder. "How's he doing?"

"My mind is playing tricks on me. I can't tell if he's relaxed or fading away."

"Don't worry. He's not dying."

She exhaled.

Luke stepped to Zany's side, taking the gelding's pulse at his jawline with one hand, palpating his shoulder wound with the other.

"I would have stitched it if I could."

"Just as well. We don't want him looking like Frankenstein's monster."

"Very funny."

"You know I'm kidding. You did an excellent job getting it cleaned and dressed." Luke reached into his bag and removed his suture needle.

Randi studied the ten-inch gash running the length of Zany's shoulder. "That's a heavy hunk of flesh. Do we have to use wire?" The idea of running metal through the horse's skin made her shudder. She'd watched it being done in school, but on Zany it was a whole different ballgame.

"I'm going to try to get by with catgut. I think it'll hold. If he were out in the pasture moving around a lot, I might go for wire, but I know you'll be here every day exercising due diligence—and then some. Did you get a look at his corral?"

She nodded. "No breaks in the rails and no gaps. Nothing broken. No way he could have gotten out on his own."

"Maybe one of the guys forgot to latch his gate."

"I tracked all of them down while I was waiting for you. The last one to clean the corral swore up and down he put the chain on."

"Who was it?"

"José."

"Probably the truth then. He's got enough seniority not to be fired for an accident, especially a first-time offense." Luke's fingers, accurate and nimble, brought the edges of the wound together so there'd be no puckering or folding of the skin. "Hold this, will you?" He motioned with his head to where he'd pulled the flesh together.

She put her hand where he indicated and, as Luke stitched, she was aware of each time his hand brushed up against hers. "You're good at that."

He stopped what he was doing, raised his eyebrows and looked at her with an expression that could have been construed as flirtatious—or maybe it was amusement again—or maybe it was just her imagination.

"We'll give him some antibiotics in an IV drip. We can go to pills tomorrow. He'll also need some light massage on a regular basis. We don't want fluid building up."

"Got it. We practiced massage a lot in training. The patients loved it."

"No doubt." Finished with his task, his eyes roamed her face. "What's on your cheek?"

She touched the spot where his gaze landed. Dry and crusty. "Blood, I guess." She waited for him to make a big deal out of it. He could be a regular fusspot sometimes.

Luke brushed the mark his thumb. "You'll live."

Ten

RANDI RETURNED THE SUPPLIES she'd used on Zany to the medicine cabinet. Under the high ceilings of the main barn, the horses in box stalls dozed, watching her go about her business under heavy-lidded eyes. There were no stable hands grooming horses, no owners tacking up for a midday ride, no mounts steaming in the washrack after a turnout. Unusual for a Sunday. Weekends at the ranch were always busy.

She realized Houston had never answered her question about whether he'd seen Tim Tyler on the property, but unless Tyler was the type to hide out like an arsonist and watch his destruction come to fruition, he probably wasn't here. What would she do if they came face to face? Perhaps if she showed him Zany's wound she'd get a reaction that would tell her whether or not he was guilty of trying to get his horse killed. Then again, he *was* an actor.

A breeze blew down the aisle, carrying the smell of sun-baked hay. Finches chirped and, from a distance, a radio played a bouncy country tune. Despite the sunny day cheer, Randi's skin prickled as she passed Rebel's stall, cordoned off with police tape. Like the scene of a horrific traffic accident, once the victims had been removed but mangled steel remained, she couldn't help but stop and stare, wondering what led Stacey to such a violent and sudden end.

Stacey was killed late Friday night. It was Sunday afternoon. What was that statistic? After forty-eight hours the trail went cold? Didn't leave much time. She checked her watch.

Before the disastrous chain of events, Piper had agreed to be interviewed for the *HorseWorld* piece. Randi needed the breeding manager's expertise on artificial insemination, otherwise the article would lack authority and kill her chances of seeing her name in *HorseWorld's* table of contents. Not only that, but she was curious. Did Piper hate Stacey enough to kill her? Piper had the means and the opportunity, but was devotion to the man who saved her life enough of a motive for murder?

Piper was in the lab. Randi poked her head in. "Have you got a minute? I need to cover some basics for my article and I've got some questions."

"Yeah, sure. I told you I'd help." Piper motioned with her hand. "Come on in."

The lab, located in the breeding barn, was the size of a singlewide trailer with counters on both sides and a closet at the back. Fluorescent bulbs flooded the space and the smell of antiseptic made Randi cover her nose. "Do you have a recorder I can borrow? I left mine in my truck when I went after Zany, and I haven't had a chance to go back. It's still parked on El Camino Real."

"Sure." Piper took a thumb-sized device from the drawer and pushed it along the counter. "How's he doing?"

"Okay." No need to retell the story. Reports of accidents spread through the ranch like wildfire. "Luke stitched his shoulder. It kills me to think of how scared he must have been with that car coming straight at him."

"Did you find out how he got loose?"

"Not yet, but I will." She flicked the ON switch into position. "Go ahead and introduce yourself when you're ready."

Piper shut the door to the lab and put on the self-conscious face people tended to wear when being recorded. "My name is Piper Powell. I'm the manager of Lucky Jack Performance Horses here in Rancho del Zorro, California. We breed world-class Quarter Horses and are currently standing at stud Hesa Rebel Man, winner of the National Cutting Horse Association Championship Futurity. Our ranch has a state-of-the-art facility for collection and shipment of cooled semen on-site, which means we're able to service mares all over the country." Piper removed a sturdy blue container, about the size of a coffeemaker, from one of the cabinets. "This is an Equitainer, made specifically to ship cooled semen. After I check the motility and package the sperm from the collection, I send the product off to the buyer inside this baby. I'm responsible for seeing that it reaches its destination in a timely manner and I work closely with the clients and answer any questions or concerns the mare's owner might have."

"Houston asked you about motility after the collection. Tell me about it."

"Movement. Live sperm. That's the goal." Piper nodded toward the microscope. "We're fortunate. Rebel's swimmers are extremely active. I've got a batch right here. Want to see?" She prepared a slide and slid it under the viewer. From the dark gray backdrop, countless miniscule forms flurried. "Eager little devils, aren't they?"

"I'll say." Impressed, Randi lifted her head from the scope. "What do you call the thing that looks like a rifle case?" Funny that's what she'd likened it to, given her phobia. "The one Houston held to collect from Rebel."

"You mean the AV?"

"AV?"

"Artificial vagina. We use the Missouri model. It's the lightest system, so if Houston's not available, I can handle it without him."

"There's more than one model?"

"Yep. The Colorado is the most common, but the casing is

metal and it's heavy."

"Oh. Right. Isn't it uncomfortable? It must be rough on his—"

"Nope." Piper shook her head. "The bladder on the inside is filled with warm water. Makes it cozy for him."

"Cozy?"

"Yeah. The stallion ejaculates based on the temperature and the pressure exerted by the water bladder. With the Missouri, we adjust the pressure by pumping air inside it. As far as we know, he can't tell the difference between the real thing and the AV."

"Say I have a mare I want to impregnate with donor—uh—sperm." She could *write* about reproduction all day long, but spitting out the words—different story. "How much will it cost me?"

"Depends on the stallion. You might as well ask how much a car is. Take the price of my Corolla, for example, and compare it to Stacey's new Mercedes SL." Piper cocked her head. "Or maybe it's Jaydee's now."

She didn't want to talk about Jaydee. "How much for Rebel's, uh... product?"

"Rebel's an SL, for sure. At the moment his stud fee is five grand a pop, not including collection and shipping fees, and with lifetime earnings running at six figures, his sperm is in high demand. If his offspring prove to be winners, like we all think they will be, his fee will go through the roof."

"Then you all get rich?" Houston needed the money, she was sure of that now.

Piper couldn't hide her smile. "That's what we're hoping. Although, keep in mind, it's a curve. When Rebel has some proven colts in the ring, the market could force his fee to drop again."

"How?"

"If his sons also have successful careers, as we believe they will, people can choose to breed to them instead." Piper leaned against the counter, holding her hands to illustrate tipping scales. "Save money. Get the same bloodlines. It's tricky. We have to cream it while we can, so to speak. In breeding, as in life, timing is everything."

"What's going to happen now? With Rebel, I mean."

"Beats me." Piper shrugged. "Hopefully nothing. It's business as usual as far as I'm concerned."

"Why did Stacey feel the need to point out Rebel was her horse? And why do it out there with a breeding room full of people?"

Piper chewed her thumbnail for a good five seconds. "I don't know if Houston would want me to talk about it."

"Off the record, then."

Piper rolled her neck. "When Stacey bought Rebel, she and Houston struck a deal. Houston already had several mares in foal to Rebel. All good chances for champions to give him a head start on everybody else in this game. The first colt was the one you found dead." Piper's eyes flashed, and for half a second Randi could have sworn they shifted blame her way. "This year Stacey opened up the breeding. That's one of the reasons she was mad at Houston for not waiting for her. My guess is she wanted those people in her back pocket, not Houston's."

"I don't get it. You said they had an agreement."

Piper tucked a pencil behind her ear. "They did, but Stacey was about to renege."

"How?"

"In return for helping Stacey negotiate Rebel's, shall we say, somewhat complicated purchase, Houston was to receive thirty-five percent of Rebel's stud fees. If the horse keeps producing like he is, we can collect up to ten doses from him every other day. After you do the math, and multiply it by thirty-five percent, you come up with close to five hundred grand per breeding season. Rebel is the only stallion we have who gives us those kinds of numbers. And this is between you, me and the wall, but Houston and Helen have pulled all the equity out of this place just to keep it running. They're in hock up to their eyeballs. I overheard Stacey on the phone last week. She told whoever was on the other end she was going to change the terms. Cut Houston out."

Randi didn't like what she was hearing, not one bit, but she wasn't going to mention she already knew about Houston's monetary woes. "Well, Houston doesn't have to worry about not getting his share now."

"Maybe," Piper said. "We'll see what comes out of the will."

"You think Stacey had one? She was pretty young for that."

"I'm sure she did. She guarded Rebel's welfare like the horse was her flesh-and-blood child."

"Could she unilaterally change the terms of her and Houston's deal?"

Piper gave a bitter laugh. "If it had been done right, no, but Houston thinks a handshake is good enough to seal an agreement. A man's word and all that. I warned him. I told him he needed to kiss her ass, and if she wanted to be at every collection to make sure Houston wasn't skimming or double-crossing her somehow, he damn well better wait for her. Manicure or no manicure."

"You didn't like her, did you?"

Piper cupped her chin. "Still off the record?"

"Still off the record."

"There's far more involved in standing a world champion at stud than Stacey could wrap her head around. Houston had experience. She didn't. It's not 4-H. This is the big leagues." Piper rubbed her arms like she felt a sudden chill. "I don't mean to sound catty."

"No biggie. I understand."

"Yeah, I guess if anyone could, it would be you. I don't know how I would have handled being treated that way by Jaydee. Overall, you've been far more gracious than I would have been."

"I wouldn't call it gracious. There are things you don't know."

"Really?" Piper seemed intrigued. "Like what?"

"It's embarrasing to admit, but the day Stacey broke the news she and Jaydee were married, I drove straight to my bungalow, grabbed the bottle of Dom I'd been saving to drink with Jaydee, popped the cork and consumed the entire thing in the bathtub. I didn't even bother with a glass. My skin was like a prune, the water was cold and it was almost dark when I finally got out."

"That's mild. You didn't do anything to *him* personally. I would have stuck a knife in his ribs."

Matt Watson's horseshoeing truck sat beside the crossties. He glanced up from his anvil and stood straight when he saw Randi. His hair, curled in loose ringlets and bleached by the sun and saltwater, hung almost to his shoulders, framing a wide face with large, hazel eyes and a straight, narrow nose. "Hey." His smile was anemic. "How ya doin'?"

"Hanging in there. You?"

"Same old stuff. Working. Trying to keep busy. I got in a morning surf sesh at Swami's at least."

"Swami's?"

Matt's smile widened. "It's a reef break below the Self-Realization Fellowship. Started out as a nickname. It stuck."

Matt smelled like the bubble gum and coconut-scented goo surfers smeared on their boards. Whenever Randi got a whiff, she was instantly transported to a white sandy beach, eating chunks of pineapple and listening to ukulele music. "Can we talk?"

He reached into his back pocket, took a pinch from his Copenhagen tin and tucked it into his lower lip. Brushing some grime from his farrier's apron, he settled himself on the tailgate. "What's up?"

She was itching to ask about Stacey, see if the rumors of them getting cozy were true. Best to ease into the topic with small talk. "I was thinking about Jezebel. The mare with the hoof wall separation? Think you can cut away more of the dead part of her hoof? I'd hate to see it abscess. You know the saying, 'No hoof, no horse.'"

Matt almost smiled. "Yep, heard that one a few times." He clacked the heels of his boots together. Dirt clods fell to the ground. "As soon as I finish here, I'll give her a look."

"Great. Thanks. Did you know Zany and three others got out today? Zany got hit by a car."

Matt nodded. "Damn shame. Nice horse. Hope it doesn't leave a scar."

She nodded. "Me too. Physical *or* emotional." She let her eyes roam while she considered the best way to broach the subject of adultery, but nothing clever or creative popped into her head. "Mind if I ask you about Stacey?"

Matt shoved himself off the tailgate; the metal groaned. "I'll say the same thing to you I've said to everyone else." His amiable tone hardened. "I told that cop anyone could have taken the hammer off my truck and I wouldn't have missed it." He spat greenish liquid onto the dirt.

"The hammer was *yours*?"

He nodded.

"How do you know?"

"My initials. They're branded on the side."

Randi liked Matt, but this wasn't a popularity contest. Once McWynn got the DNA results, he'd be back on her porch, this time with a warrant in his hand. "There's a rumor going around that you and Stacey were more than friends."

Red crept across Matt's cheeks. He placed a horseshoe over the anvil and, gripping the hammer, moved the curved piece of metal across the iron block, closing the angle of the steel—bang, bang, bang—to get the fit just right. Five strikes later he held the shoe up to the sky and studied its shape. "It wasn't like that with me and her and I'll tell you why."

He put the horseshoe to the grinding wheel. A stream of sparks shot from the metal sphere. Finished, he walked the shoe over to a sorrel gelding with a broad white blaze waiting patiently. He picked up the horse's leg, clutching its hind foot between his thighs. "I don't believe I chose to shoe horses. I believe I was chosen. I could have done something else with my life, but this is what I was put on Earth to do." He stuck a nail between his lips and worked the rasp across the bottom of the horse's hoof. "This ranch is my biggest client. Why would I jeopardize that?"

He had a point.

"Your prints weren't the only ones on that hammer."

Matt removed the nail and cranked his head around to make eye contact. "Who else?"

"Me. My prints."

"How'd that happen?"

"By accident, but I don't think the detective is convinced."

Matt grunted and lined the shoe up with the horse's hoof.

She couldn't tell if he believed her or not. "Did Stacey ever say why she and Jaydee hooked up in the first place?"

"You don't know?"

She shrugged, felt like an idiot. "Nobody ever told me."

Matt held the nail steady as he tapped. "They met at a yearling sale in Bakersfield. Stacey said Jaydee came onto her like a Mack truck. I don't think she minded too much at first, then things changed and he started moving too fast. He asked her to marry him and she said no. He didn't give up, though. Took him three days to talk her into it." Shoe in place, Matt put the horse's hoof down. "It wasn't Stacey's fault, what happened with you. She didn't know you existed until you showed up here looking for Jaydee."

"I figured."

"I'm surprised either one of you would take on a guy with those kind of issues."

"Issues?"

"Yeah. Gambling."

Randi was confused. "He had some late nights when we were together in college, and he might have visited an Indian casino or two, but I'd hardly call him a gambler."

Matt scoffed. "You have no idea. He's got it bad. Stacey's father was one of the original dot-commers. Made a killing. When he died a few years ago, Stacey and her sister inherited his entire fortune. Jaydee's doing his best to piss it away." Matt waved his hand. "Vegas, satellite wagering, horse races, football pools—you name it, he'll blow it."

Jaydee dumped her to marry money? What a materialistic,

superficial jerk. "You think his supposed gambling had anything to do with Stacey's death?"

"It had everything to do with it. She wanted him to stop. First he burned through their joint savings which, of course, was mostly Stacey's money, and if Houston and Helen didn't own Jaydee's half of the duplex, I'm sure the bank would be fixin' to foreclose."

Is that why Houston pulled out his equity? To cover Jaydee's debts? People with gambling problems were always in the red, weren't they? Owing money to sharp dressers with a fondness for linguine? "How much was Stacey worth?"

Matt looked uncomfortable. "She never mentioned specific numbers, but I have the feeling that if you put the richest person in Rancho del Zorro up against Stacey's estate, he, or she, would feel like a homeless bum." He spat again. "Not enough for Jaydee, though. Never enough. He always wanted more. He even tried to put *his* name on Rebel's papers. Stacey refused. She was afraid Jaydee'd whisk him away in the dead of night and she'd never see him again. The horse, that is. I don't think she cared if she ever saw her husband."

"What do you think will happen to Rebel with Stacey gone?"

Matt shrugged. "Time will tell. If Stacey didn't specify someone else in her will, Jaydee's got himself a valuable chunk of horseflesh, and I guess, with nobody to stop him, he'll do what he wants with him." He shook his head as if the movement pained him. "I'm telling you, you watch your back, Randi. When a guy has a serious problem like he does, it has a hold on him... he ain't gonna quit for nothing or nobody."

"What does that have to do with me? He's not coming after me for my bank account."

"Maybe not money, but you've got something Jaydee wants. I've seen it in his eyes when he talks about you. He's got you in his crosshairs. Not a good place to be."

Eleven

DANNY APPEARED OUT OF nowhere, tripping over his coltish legs in his haste to block Randi's path. "I need your help." He bent over, out of breath, and braced his hands on his knees. "It's Sydney."

"Don't tell me—he got out too?"

"No. He's in his stall but he won't stand up." Danny swiped the back of his hand across his lips.

Sydney was the type of horse who would stand stock-still while small children frolicked under his belly. He was also prone to colic. If he rolled, a twisted gut could kill him. Randi hung a left, taking a shortcut toward the barn. "With Roberto in Mexico, I don't know who Piper has feeding. Is his sign still on his stall door?"

"It's there." Danny jogged to catch up to her. "You'd have to be blind to miss it."

The kid was right. At the gelding's stall, a large wooden plaque, attached to the bars with baling wire, read: NO ALFAL-FA. SEVERE ALLERGIES. PASTO SOLAMENTE.

The big gray horse lay on his side. Randi surveyed the bedding. "There's a lot of poop in here."

Danny made a face.

"It's not a potty joke." *Teenagers.* "It's important if he might be colicking. The manure is actually a good sign."

"What do we do now?"

"Grab a halter. We'll try to get him on his feet."

Sydney had other ideas. Danny tugged on the rope but the horse wouldn't move. Randi crouched and put an ear to his belly. His hide was sweatier than it should have been, but his stomach gurgled. Things were moving through the pipes the way they should be, so why wouldn't he get up?

A bucket filled with pellets hung from the bars. Randi unhooked it and shook the feed. Sydney showed zero interest. His hay-net was also full. At this time of day it should have been empty. "He didn't eat his breakfast. At least we can see he got grass hay and not alfalfa. That's the good news."

She ran her fingers through the pellets. Something didn't feel right. "Did you add anything to these?"

"No."

"There's something strange mixed in. Looks like leaves." She pulled one out. Dark green, long and slender. She snapped it in half and gave it a sniff. The leaf was bitter, the smell distinct. "Danny, get Luke on the phone. Fast."

The poor kid. It was hard enough for adults to come to grips with the evil side of human nature, but as a teen you still held out hope that passing a magical age threshold vaulted you to a higher plane of morality. Not the case for whoever had mixed poisonous oleander leaves in with Sydney's feed.

Danny stroked his horse's neck while Luke injected a mixture of oil and charcoal.

"I spoke to the groom who fed lunch today," Luke said. "I mentioned the leaves. He had no idea what I was talking about."

Danny's mouth turned downward. "Do you believe him?"

"No reason not to."

Randi collected the empty syringe from Luke. "The leaves could have been added after the fact."

"Absolutely." Luke gave Sydney a pat and got to his feet. "I don't think he ingested very much, and being such a big horse is working in his favor. His heart rate is a little elevated but still within range. He'll need to be monitored tonight."

Danny stood up next to Luke and was almost as tall. "I'll stay."

"Are you sure?" Randi had her cell in hand. "I can ask Piper. She spends most nights here during foaling season."

"It's fine."

"What about your parents?"

"Randi's got a point," Luke added. "They might not be wild about the idea."

The kid set his face in stone. "I'm staying."

The three of them stood in a semicircle, all eyes on the bottoms of Sydney's platter-sized feet. He was a good horse who'd never wronged anyone. Worth his weight in gold.

First Rebel's colt, then Stacey. Horses set loose and poisoned leaves delivered. What was going on? What kind of sicko were they dealing with? "Danny, you're here at the ranch every day, right?"

"Yeah, 'cept on Sunday mornings when my mom drags me to church. Afterward she always drops me off at the end of the driveway and makes me walk, that's how come I saw Zany running down the road today."

"Next time I see your mom, remind me to thank her for 'dragging you to church.'"

Danny gave a half-hearted smile.

She knew he'd say nothing of the sort, but it was okay. "Did you work on Friday?"

Danny thought about it. "Yep. About two o'clock I was fixing the south fence line. It had some broken boards."

"Did you notice anything strange? Something strike you as different from the way it usually is?"

Danny shook his head as he stepped from the stall to pick up a handful of hay from the barn aisle. "I liked Stacey. She was nice to me. But, no, Friday seemed quiet. Other than Jaydee, there was nobody strange hanging around, if that's what you mean."

The sun hung low in the sky when Randi returned to the barn for Zany's last treatment before she called it a day. A cold beer and a hot bath sounded like heaven.

She stepped into Zany's stall and let out a shriek. A man stood half hidden in the shadows before he moved into the light. Tim Tyler was shorter than in the movies, with more wrinkles and less hair, like an older version of himself, a brother or cousin, and the way he lurched toward her made her wish for something to defend herself with.

"Who are you?"

"My name's Randi. I work for Luke."

"Are you the one responsible?"

Was he joking? "Of course not. Danny and I were the ones who saved him."

"I don't know what you're talking about." Tyler pulled an envelope from his pocket and waved it like a flag. "What I'm talking about is this bill. Where do you people get off? And what's he doing in a box stall instead of his corral? It took me fifteen minutes to find my damn horse. I've been wandering around like a fool with nothing better to do." Tyler sent the envelope spinning to the ground. "I didn't ask for him to be moved and I'm not paying the extra board."

A bill? Extra board? What about Zany's brush with death? She curtailed the urge to retrieve the paper he'd flung on the ground. Tim Tyler might be a celebrity with an ego the size of California, but he sat on the toilet just like everybody else. She wasn't going to let him intimidate her, nor would she pick up his trash. At least not while he was watching.

"I'm losing year-end points as we speak." Tyler's face grew darker as his volume increased. "Some fat bitch on a piece of shit nag kicked ass in Burbank this weekend because my horse is laid up. No way that would have happened if I'd been in the ring."

"Mr. Tyler, you don't understand." He'd have to be blind not to see the stitches in the horse's shoulder. Maybe, having been the cause, he was purposely ignoring the wound. "Zany's eye condition is–"

"No. You listen to me. That horse," Tyler stabbed the air, "was ApPHA western pleasure champion two years in a row. If I can finish out the season on him and win the title *one* more time, I keep the Surf and Sun Perpetual Cup. Otherwise, I have to hand it over to the fat one and I'll be sittin' empty-handed."

"It's just a piece of wood and metal." Then again, her skeet shooting prize she'd told Cole about at the range might as well have been the Stanley Cup.

"Are you kidding me? I *need* that thing in my trophy case, and since you're charging me an arm and a left testicle to fix my horse, I believe it's your responsibility to make it happen."

Oh God. Where was Luke when she needed him? He'd know how to handle this mental case.

Tyler crossed his arms. "Tell me exactly what you're doing to this animal's eyes so he can make his way around the arena without running into the goddamn judge."

Must remain calm. "Well, for starters, he gets twice-daily steroid treatments." Somebody had left a grooming brush in the stall. She picked it up and rubbed her hand across the bristles for something to do. "And atropine if his eyes start to spasm—"

"*Atropine?*" Tyler craned his head and scratched at his neck, looking down at the ground like he'd dropped something. Seconds later he lurched to attention. "I used that stuff to kill a guy in *Darkness Before the Dawn.*"

"What?"

Tyler threw his hands in the air. "You're charging me to poison my horse!"

Zany jerked his head up and pinned his ears.

She didn't want to delve into how, or at what levels, atropine became harmful. Tyler wasn't listening to a word she said anyway. "Mr. Tyler, Zany is my favorite patient and I take excellent care of him. I've got his situation stabilized and—"

"Get the wax out of your ears, girl." Tyler rolled his eyes. "I don't want my animal stabilized. I want him winning. Philip says I can make up the points if I get a few blues, but I'm short on time."

Philip? The same Philip he supposedly had an affair with before he allegedly killed his wife? "We're making strides." Her heart drummed. "The progression has leveled off. It's the best we can hope for at this point."

Tyler shook his head. "Not good enough. I need someone competent to take over his treatment."

"I'd be happy to give you some literature on—"

"I don't want your goddamn literature."

She squeezed the brush, the bristles digging into her palm. What was his problem? How could anyone be so stuck on himself? Why wasn't he asking about Zany's shoulder?

"Look here," Tyler seemed to be making a supreme effort to calm down. "The bottom line is if this horse isn't healthy enough to be in the money, then he's pointless to me."

"Pointless? He's an innocent animal."

"If he can't bring home the trophy, I don't need him anymore. He's dead weight, and I assume I don't have to tell you what happens to useless horses."

"You can't be serious."

"Hey, anything that eats while I'm sleeping better provide me with some kind of return. I don't do charity."

"Meaning?"

"Meaning, things that suck energy and don't return it are called *baggage*."

"You can't just sell him, Mr. Tyler." She'd copped a pleading tone. "Zany's not marketable in his condition."

"They'll take anything at auction. Long as it's still standing."

"*Auction*? Don't you know what happens to most of those

horses?"

"Of course I do. Alpo. Or steaks for the French. Those people will eat anything. I think the going rate is—"

Blood roared in her ears, followed by a high-pitched whine. One moment the brush sat heavy in her hand, the next it flew through the air and slammed into Tyler's head.

Tyler put his hand to his temple. Fury twisted his features. "Why, you little *bitch!*" He dropped his shoulder and charged. Before she could duck, she was airborne. Her back slammed up against the wall and a board cracked beneath her ribs. She landed crumpled in the corner. Couldn't breathe. Her mouth was open but the air was stuck. He'd killed her somehow. She just wasn't dead yet. She kicked her legs, waved her arms and willed herself to scream. One last sound before it was over. With a sudden, violent rush, oxygen filled her lungs. She wheezed, gasping and coughing, her arms wrapped around her ribcage.

Tyler raised his fists, eyes black with hate, ready to finish the job. She threw her hands over her head and yanked her legs to her belly, waiting for the blows to rain down upon her.

The door to the stall slid open and Matt Watson stepped inside. He took one look at Randi and slugged Tim Tyler in the jaw. Tyler stumbled, tripped over his heels and went down. Blood trickled from his lip. He moaned, cradling his face.

Randi struggled to a sitting position. She opened her mouth to thank Matt for stopping Tyler before he did serious damage, but the way Matt's knuckles stretched white around his farrier hammer rendered her speechless.

Twelve

TIM TYLER'S WHITE ESCALADE sped down the driveway, leaving a rooster tail of dust in its wake. So much for heading home to a cold beer and a hot bath. Houston and Helen needed to know what the creep had done. She climbed the path leading to the Hills' house as fast as her scraped and bruised back allowed. Her ribs were sore but probably not broken. She'd snapped her wrist ice skating backwards once trying to show off for some guy. This pain wasn't pleasant, but nowhere close to that.

The home of Houston, Helen, Jaydee and Stacey sat high on the ridge. Each side of the duplex comprised about five thousand square feet. A modest size by Rancho del Zorro standards, yet it lorded over its domain.

Years ago, when she and Jaydee had come "home" to visit on breaks from Colorado State, Houston and Helen talked about how someday Jaydee and his future bride would take up residence in the east half and eventually take over the breeding and training business. Randi'd sat in their living room feeling shy and smug, quietly daydreaming herself into that role.

The cry of a hawk, flying perilously close, made her turn her head. At the bottom of the ice plant-covered slope, a few small birds picked at the sand, a dog meandered beside a hedge and a ghost-like silence hung over the arena. She stared through unfocused eyes at the ring while an image from the past floated into her brain.

The first time she saw Jaydee ride, he was putting a reining horse through its paces and she'd parked herself next to the entrance gate to watch. The horse had thundered down the rail, wheeled to the right, then executed a picture-perfect flying lead change. A few strides later, Jaydee, in a fitted white button-down so crisp it crackled, cued the horse to half-halt before he swung him into a spin. The sorrel's legs were a blur as he twirled, mane unfurling like a flag. Jaydee dropped the rein on the horse's neck, and he planted all four feet in nothing flat.

Jaydee tipped his hat and, from a dead standstill, with a blinding burst of speed, horse and rider flew all the way across the arena, barreling toward the rail. Just when it appeared they'd run out of room and there was no place left to go but over, or *through*, the fence, Jaydee leaned back in the saddle and the horse tucked his hindquarters to pull off a flawless sliding stop.

The dust settled and someone along the rail let out a low whistle. She'd been so proud. That guy was *hers*.

Facing Houston and Helen's front door, worlds away from her twenty-two-year-old schoolgirl self, a weariness settled on her shoulders. She lifted the heavy brass knocker, fashioned in the shape of a spur rowel and let it fall on the door three times. After a brief pause, it swung open. Helen seemed surprised to see her. "Jaydee didn't do it." Her scowl could've scared crows off garbage.

Randi shifted her feet. "I didn't come to talk about Jaydee." At least not yet.

Helen's expression softened. "Okay. In that case, come on in."

Randi stepped over the threshold. In the corner by the window sat the same leather couch she remembered from seven years ago. Cushy chairs were scattered around the living room, and a potbellied stove took up the far corner. One thing, however, *was* different: A framed eight-by-ten of Jaydee and Stacey in front of the Luxor Hotel hung from the wall. She took a step closer. Jaydee wore a suit and Stacey a black cocktail dress with spaghetti straps and a plunging neckline. She held a martini and smiled with white teeth and full lips. She looked happy, radiant even.

Randi followed Helen to the floor-to-ceiling window, where all of Lucky Jack was visible below. To the west, above a thin line of water, the sun prepared to dunk itself into the ocean. On the eastern ridge, row upon row of enormous tract homes with backyards hardly big enough for a lawn chair, let alone a lawn—and with an optimum view of your neighbor's bathroom—had metastasized over land once covered with manzanita, sage and California golden poppies.

Luke was right. It didn't take a real estate whiz to know the Lucky Jack property, with its considerable acreage and proximity to the ocean, would be worth a fortune stacked with high-density condos. If Tim Tyler had his way, views of frolicking foals would be replaced with the scenery of Bob's butt crack.

A beam of late afternoon sun streamed across Helen's face. The skin around her lips showed shades of blue and purple sloppily coated with makeup.

"What happened to your mouth?"

"A dog jumped up and got me. It's a whole lotta nothing." She waved it off. "Houston told me you saved the Appaloosa after he got hit by a car."

"Danny and I did. I couldn't have done it without him."

"He's a good hand, but he's too young and inexperienced to handle a touch-and-go situation like that by himself."

"He was a trooper."

"Teenagers are tricky." Helen grabbed a tissue and blew her nose. "Sometimes you get the adult, sometimes you get the child. There seems to be no rhyme or reason as to who is going to show up when."

Helen wasn't giving Danny the credit he deserved, but Randi hadn't come here to discuss the level of the kid's maturity. She relayed the information about finding the oleander leaves in Sydney's feed, then told her about Tyler's tantrum over his vet bills and how he'd threatened to sell Zany at auction unless he got enough points to keep his stupid trophy. She added how he shoved her into the side of the stall and threatened to beat her, but left out the part about winging the brush at him. She told her how Matt had intervened but kept the part about the hammer to herself. Helen was sharp. Matt had saved her butt and she owed him for that. If he hadn't come along, she'd have been pulverized in a corner, clutching Tyler's crumpled vet bill.

Helen glowered. "I've had it with Tim Tyler. Next time I see him, I'm going for Houston's gun. As for the oleander, I'm sure it was an accident so don't go spreading rumors. It's bad for business."

"How could poisonous leaves accidently find their way into a batch of pellets?"

"Well, if I knew, I'd tell you."

Helen was obviously in some sort of denial. "When did Houston get a gun?"

A ruckus at the back door diverted Helen's attention. Her Jack Russell terriers must have realized they'd been left out of the conversation because they barked and scratched, whining and raising all sorts of hell to come inside. Helen complied, and a moment later they were lined up in the kitchen, wagging their stumpy tails as they begged for biscuits. The dogs were pleasant enough as individuals, but in a pack they were a nightmare. Helen loved them, but it was no mystery why they were called the Manson Family behind her back. She doled out treats, then began hefting jugs of drinking water onto a pantry shelf, the subject of the gun and the oleander apparently closed. "Coffee's still on."

Randi straddled a barstool, the setting sun warm on her back.

Helen held up the carafe. "Want some?"

It smelled burnt, but turning Helen down was never a wise move. "Sure. I'll take a cup. Thanks."

"How 'bout a little somethin' to go with it?" She banged open the liquor cabinet. "It's been a rough couple of days."

"Agreed." Five o'clock somewhere.

"You see my class yesterday? Pathetic. Parents are yanking their children out of my program so fast it's like this place has a revolving door. We just about had a horse trailer traffic jam in the driveway. I even had one guy tell me, 'I can't have my daughter riding at a ranch where there's a killer on the loose.'" Helen took two mugs and poured a generous shot of Black Label into each one. She slid Randi's across the counter.

"Houston's worried too." Randi took a sip. It was un-cowgirl-like to make a face when you drank whiskey, but she couldn't help it. "Have you seen Jaydee?"

"Not today." Helen put away the doggy jar, but not the booze. "You said this visit wasn't about him."

She shrugged like it was no big deal. "His number came up on my phone. I'm not sure what he wanted."

Helen set her mug on the tile countertop. "Look, Randi. I know how bad Jaydee made you feel. Everyone does. Things change and people move on."

"I have moved on." It didn't ring as true as she meant it.

"He was in Las Vegas when Stacey was killed, you know."

Southwest ran flights from San Diego every couple of hours, and Kira told her it was only a five-hour drive to Vegas if you hauled ass. Plenty of time for Jaydee to arrive by cocktail hour. "I heard he makes frequent trips there these days."

"No more than the average Joe." Helen mashed her lips together.

Who to believe? The guy who might have been having an affair with Jaydee's wife? Or his overprotective mother? She waited for Helen's glower to subside. "What about you? Who do you think killed Stacey?"

"Truth be told, it could have been anyone."

"Anyone?"

"Sure." Helen set both hands on the countertop. "Couple of years ago we had a guy down by the border. Cut off hookers' heads and stacked them in a wheelbarrow. Left 'em on the side of the road."

"You think it was a serial killer?"

"I like to think everyone is a good soul, though it's probably not the case." Helen touched her fingers to the side of her mouth. "We get a ton of people running through this ranch every day. I can't keep track of each and every one of them."

Randi took a gulp of her whiskey coffee. It didn't sting quite as bad this time, and she appreciated the way it warmed her belly. "I'm sure glad Houston came into the barn when he did. I was in shock when I found Stacey. But he never told me why he was there."

"I sent him over. I heard strange noises."

"Like what?"

"Voices."

"From this far away?"

"Sound carries. I sleep with a window open."

"In February?"

"I like a cold bedroom. And fresh air." Helen glanced at the clock. "What difference does it make?"

"Any idea what Stacey was doing in the barn so late that night?"

"How would I know?" A flash of irritation crossed Helen's face. She checked the clock again. "I've got a roast that has to go in the oven."

"How did Jaydee and Stacey get along?" Didn't take much booze to make her brave enough to ask questions of Helen she normally wouldn't have.

"They got along okay."

"They never argued? I can remember a few heated moments with your son, myself, no offense."

"Of course they fought. Why ask such a silly question? Nobody ever really knows what goes on inside somebody else's marriage."

Felicia, who'd been the Hills' housekeeper ever since Randi could remember, came through the kitchen clutching a handful of dirty sponges.

When she left, Randi asked, "Did Felicia work for Jaydee and Stacey too?"

"Sure. She doesn't speak English, though. So if you're looking for dirt, try Matt Watson. If anyone's keeping Stacey's secrets, it's him."

She raised her eyebrows like this was the first she'd heard of it. "Matt? Why Matt?"

"Stacey had been spending a lot of time with him." Helen went to the fridge, retrieved the roast and put the meat on the counter.

"Did you see the two of them together?"

"Plenty." Helen opened the cabinet under the sink and removed a flyswatter. She gestured toward the window, swatter flapping. "I don't miss a thing from up here."

Hadn't she just said she couldn't keep track of everybody?

"Matt's truck would come rumbling up the driveway, then I'd hear the door slam." Helen jerked her thumb in the direction of Jaydee and Stacey's house. "Next thing I know, she's hightailing it down there, chatting him up while he's trying to work."

"Hardly incriminating evidence. Matt's a personable guy."

"Thursday, when Stacey was *supposed* to be in the breeding barn with Rebel, I was washing dishes and heard a car. I looked out the window. There they were in her convertible, flying down the drive and kicking up a big cloud of dust. Matt was at the wheel and I couldn't see where Stacey's head was."

"Oh."

"Oh, is right. She's *married* to my son." Not bothering to correct her tenses, Helen swung the flyswatter against the counter with a smack that left a small blackish-red blob smeared on the tile. She wiped up the remains with a paper towel and tossed it in the trash. "None of it matters now, anyway. I'm too old to do anything else. I've done everything I can, so if all else fails, wrap me in a tarp and bury me out at Coffin Bone Canyon, that's what I told Houston."

"I don't get it."

"I'm trying to save the world's last wooly mammoth. Those goddamn developers would do anything to get their hands on this property. Training horses, teaching kids to ride, putting them all in the trailer and hitting the road, it's all I know. Think they care? Think again."

"What're you going to do?"

"Tough times call for tough people." Helen brightened a bit. "We still have Rebel. If anything can save us, it'll be that stallion."

Randi carried her mug to the sink, surprised at how fast she'd drained it. "I don't want to make you more worried than you already are, but if you're right and Stacey and Matt were having an affair..." She let the idea dangle for a few seconds. "Say Jaydee's marriage was in trouble–and if Stacey had a will, then it's possible she cut him out of it before she died."

Helen stared out the window. Her hand shook as she lifted the empty mug to her lips.

Thirteen

MONDAY MORNING, SHANE LAY curled under Randi's desk, paws twitching, ears flicking back and forth. Randi rubbed her toes across his ribcage. At last she was getting down to business. Should she be so fortunate as not to be interrupted, she might finish her article by the afternoon. Her editor expected something emailed to the office ASAP, yet not before it was ready. Always a unique dilemma.

She pushed the PLAY button on the recorder and Piper's voice filled the room: "*Each time we collect, we hold back a control sample in case the buyer claims the semen's not viable. The control will prove when it left here, it was.*"

"*How long does sperm live?*" She winced inside at the sound of her recorded voice; it didn't match what she heard in her head.

"*Usability with cooled semen starts to decrease after about twenty-four hours, so we pack and ship as fast as we can. Then it's out of our hands.*"

"*Twenty-four hours? I thought sperm died quicker than that.*" As the interview had progressed, she'd settled into using the terms "sperm" and "semen." Perhaps in time they'd feel as comfortable rolling off her tongue as words like "sweater" or "to-mato."

"There are coolant packs in the Equitainer and I add an ex-tender fluid. Kind of like a meal for sperm. Helps it last longer."

"What do sperm eat?"

"Powdered milk, egg whites, sugar and antibiotics. The kind we buy is pre-mixed and comes from France."

"I'm impressed. You really know your stuff."

"I love my job. I see it as a sort of sexual arts and crafts."

Randi's fingers flew over the keyboard. She was on a roll, in the zone, but when she paused to look out the window and or-ganize her thoughts, a white four-door sedan filled her view. It came to a stop in front of the bungalow like someone throwing a bucket of cold water on her progress.

Shane leapt up and headed for the door, hackles raised. She caught up with him, hooked a hand under his collar, made a U-turn and steered him into the backyard.

The detective stood on the porch. "Hello, Ms. Sterling."

Beside him, Joe removed his sunglasses.

"Hello." Were they here to arrest her? She needed to sit down.

"May we come in?" McWynn asked.

It wasn't against the law to refuse them, was it? "I'm kinda busy right now. Can it wait?"

"Shouldn't take long. A few minutes, max."

The expression on his face said he wasn't leaving so she held the door open. The sun made a rectangle of light through which the two men passed. "Would you like coffee?"

Joe shook his head. "I'll pass. Thanks. Already had my quota this morning."

"I'll take a cup." McWynn pulled out a chair and set his hol-stered pistol on the kitchen table along with his keys. "Black."

Did he have to go and do that with his gun? "Are you sure? No milk or sugar? I make it strong."

"I'm sure."

She reached into the cupboard, fingers closing around the

mug from Kenny's Pest Control. Fitting. She poured the brew inside and handed it to McWynn.

His eyes flickered over the cockroach logo. "Tell me again about your relationship with Stacey Hill."

"There's not much to tell." From the backyard, Shane shoved his nose against the screen door, causing it to rattle in the casing.

"Were the two of you friends?"

"Stacey and me? We knew each other, but we didn't hang out or go to lunch if that's what you mean." Why was he beating around the bush? Just get it over with. Not knowing what he had up his sleeve was torture.

The detective plucked a dog hair from his elbow. "How did she feel about you being involved with her husband?"

They'd already covered this. Was he trying to trip her up? "It was before Stacey came along."

"What happened with you and Jaydee? I don't think I've heard the whole story."

She took a deep breath. Apparently this was going to take more than a few minutes. "After we graduated from college, Jaydee disappeared."

"Disappeared?"

"He moved out of the apartment in the middle of the night. Didn't tell me where he was going, or why."

"Did you try to contact him?"

"At first I did. I wrote. I called. I did everything short of getting on a plane and heading to Lucky Jack in person."

"What stopped you?"

"My mother always told me not to chase guys. She said it was a turnoff. I figured if I waited it out, he'd realize what he was missing."

"The old 'if you love something set it free' theory?"

She shrugged. "I guess. Took him seven years of 'freedom' to come back, though."

"And then what?"

"He begged me to give him another chance."

"So you jumped at it?"

"Not exactly." She leaned against the counter and crossed her ankles. It was designed to be a casual move, like his questions weren't getting to her, but he probably wasn't fooled. "I gave it a lot of thought, and when I finally decided to come to San Diego, it wasn't only for Jaydee."

"What else?" Joe asked.

"My home situation wasn't the greatest. I was enabling my father by living with him and being his alcohol watchdog. I thought if I left he'd be better off without me as a crutch." Why was she telling him this? It was none of his business and nothing he needed to know.

"Is he?"

"Is he what?"

"Better off."

She recalled their latest conversation. "I think so."

McWynn gave a dry cough. "When did you last speak to Jaydee?"

"I don't remember." God's honest truth. "Are you sure he was in Vegas the night Stacey was killed? His mother would say anything to keep him out of trouble."

Joe nodded. "A desk girl at the Bellagio vouched for him."

"Yeah, well, Jaydee could charm paint off a wall. Desk girls are sitting ducks."

"We're following up." McWynn put on his glasses. "Is that what happened to you? He won you over with his charm?"

She thought about it. "He convinced me I could have it all. A job I loved, life on a ranch, a horse of my own, maybe even kids someday. I was foolish enough to believe him."

"It happens." McWynn stood, slapping the wrinkles from his pants. "May I use your restroom?"

"Sure." He'd only had a couple sips of coffee. Couldn't possibly be time to recycle it. Maybe he planned on pocketing her toothbrush for more DNA evidence.

"You okay?" Joe asked when the bathroom door closed.

"I'm all right." She smiled to prove she wasn't that uptight or anxious... or hiding anything.

He pointed to her guitar in its stand. "Nice Gibson."

"Thanks. It was a high school graduation present from my dad."

"Good stress reliever."

"Yes, it is." She rubbed the fingertips of her fretboard hand. Her calluses were fading. "I need to play more."

Joe lowered his voice. "I noticed your reaction to his gun."

"Why did he do that? Is he trying to intimidate me?"

"He usually has to take it off when he sits down. Needs to watch his Jumbo Jack intake, if you ask me."

"I have a hard time with them. Guns, that is. Jumbo Jacks are easy."

Joe smiled. "I used to have the same problem."

"No way." She pulled out a chair and took the seat next to him. She was being played with the ol' good cop/bad cop routine, but it was working: she liked Joe. "You're a cop. What'd you do? How did you get over your fear?"

"Just kept at it. Sink or swim. No choice. " Joe scratched his chin. "What's your story? Something happened?"

"I was a kid."

"Tell me about it." His voice soothed, like a kindly family doctor or an elderly church pastor.

"I remember how the front door banged open. Snow and cold air swirled into the house."

"Snow?"

"Colorado." She slipped her hair into a ponytail with an elastic band from her wrist. "We'd just finished dinner. One of my father's students rushed in and started screaming. The guy was incensed at something my dad had said, or done, during a lecture. To this day I'm not sure why. I don't think my dad knew, either."

Joe nodded. "Sometimes people get rubbed the wrong way over things that seem small to us but huge to them. Not much you can do about it."

"Yeah, well, this guy was *very* rubbed. He pulled out a gun and pointed it at my dad. I have no recollection of what happened next, but according to my mom, I jumped up and grabbed the shooter's arm before he could pull the trigger."

"Brave," Joe said.

"Or reckless, depending on how you look at it."

"Then what?"

"He turned the gun on me." She'd never forget his hands. Thick fingers with half-moons of dirt beneath his nails. "Said he was going to kill me. Then my dad. My mom last."

"Where was your mother at this point?"

"Standing in the doorway. She'd been washing dishes in the kitchen. When he fired, I thought my head exploded."

"How'd he miss?"

"My dad blindsided him at the last second and the bullet ended up in a painting of Pike's Peak instead of between my eyes."

"Wow, you were lucky."

"My dad kept the painting. Hangs in his kitchen to this day."

Joe's face was empathetic. "Don't give up. It'll come."

"That's what my guy at the range keeps telling me." She glanced at the bathroom door. McWynn was still in there. "Did you know Annie Oakley could hit a dime tossed in the air at ninety feet?"

"Little Sure Shot."

"I gotta hand it to you, Joe. You're good. You're so good I know what you're up to and don't even care."

McWynn emerged from the bathroom before Joe could respond. The detective settled himself in a chair and picked off more dog hairs, this time from his thigh. "Are your parents still in Colorado?"

Of course he'd been listening. "Just my dad."

Shane started to howl from the backyard. Randi let him in. He went straight for Joe and sat at his feet, waiting for a pat.

"What is he?" Joe asked. "German Shepherd and what else?"

"Part husky and I think Shiloh Shepherd because of his long hair."

"Never heard of a Shiloh."

"They're rare, bigger and less angular than the Germans."

Joe scratched Shane's neck, jingling his dog tags. "Where'd you get him?"

"Adopted him from the shelter when I did my volunteer work there. His owner had to give him up because he was going into the military and—"

McWynn interrupted with an exaggerated sigh. Unlike Joe, he apparently wasn't a dog lover. "What about your mother? Where is she?"

Randi sat back. "I'm not sure. She travels a lot with her boyfriend. Last I heard they were passing through Jerome."

"Arizona?"

She nodded. "My mother has a thing for funky ghost towns."

"Divorced your father then?" McWynn's lower eyelid twitched.

"Yes."

McWynn stared at her. Her eyes sought Joe's. Joe glanced at McWynn. Was the detective out of questions or just reloading? She didn't see any handcuffs. Maybe they were in the car.

Shane shuffled to his water dish and started lapping, the noise absurdly loud. Randi allowed her gaze to travel, doing her damnedest to focus on something other than wondering what incriminating notions were running through McWynn's head.

In the corner by her bed, her bookcase held everything from Jack London to *Jack in the Beanstalk*, including an abundance of murder mysteries. Strange to think she used to read about death for the fun of it.

McWynn scooted his chair back. "Did you ever confront the two of them? After Jaydee dumped you?"

"You mean did I slash his tires? Or key Stacey's car?"

"Something like that."

"The worst thing I did was rip up every old picture I had of the two of us, except for the one you found the other day." *That* should have been the first to go. "Then I stuffed the pieces into the soundhole of Jaydee's Martin."

Joe winced.

"I was careful, didn't hurt the guitar, and I'd be willing to bet he hasn't found them yet."

McWynn got up and walked to the window, looking beyond the jacaranda and the morning glory-covered fence line, toward the mountains to the east. "Rancho del Zorro's a pricey place to live." He crossed his arms and turned to face her. "Must be tough for a single gal to make ends meet."

"I eat a lot of Top Ramen." Did he think she was after Stacey's money? That after she got rid of Stacey, she and Jaydee would ride off into the sunset together, saddlebags brimming with cash? "I don't understand what my financial situation has to do with the murder."

The detective stretched his arms, laced his fingers together and cracked his knuckles. "Maybe nothing. My gut says this killing was a crime of passion."

She didn't like the way he looked at her.

"I think you and Stacey argued on Saturday night. I think she started to rub things in your face, or maybe she was gloating over how Jaydee chose her over you."

She shook her head. "It wasn't like that. Not even close."

"You picked up the hammer, not initially meaning her harm, but things got heated, then they turned ugly and Stacey ended up dead." McWynn held out his hands like he'd just happened upon the world's simplest explanation for the fate of Mrs. Jaydee Hill.

"You're wrong." Felt like ants were scurrying inside her stomach. "I wasn't in the barn when she was killed."

McWynn's voice softened. "Voluntary manslaughter is a possibility if you come clean now."

"Detective." She made sure he was paying attention. "I didn't kill Stacey."

"Then again, a good prosecutor might convince the jury you lured her out to Lucky Jack late at night with the intent to kill. Now we're talking murder."

If her jaw hadn't been attached, it would have fallen on the floor. "This is crazy."

"Of course, murder for financial gain carries its own set of special circumstances."

"You have no proof of that." She balled her fist and pressed it into her belly to squash the ants.

He picked up the keys to the sedan. "Your prints are on the murder weapon, and there was blood under your nails."

Fourteen

RANDI PULLED INTO A parking space facing a strip mall a block from the beach and killed the engine. The moon, half hidden by the clouds, topped a trio of eucalyptus. A rustler's moon. Sufficient for running horses across the Rio Grande like Gus and Captain Call, but not bright enough for someone to draw a bead on you and shoot your horse-thievin' ass.

The Triton was a racetrack bar, and impossibly packed during the summer race meet. Kira said the place, her biggest competitor, catered more to the grooms and lesser-known jockeys during the season than it did the owners and trainers. This time of year, parking wasn't a problem.

Randi chewed a hangnail. On the drive over she kept telling herself that coming here was a bad idea. This afternoon, presumably as she'd walked Shane around the golf course in a futile attempt to wipe McWynn's beady stare from her mind, Jaydee had stabbed a note through the nail on her front door instructing to her to meet him here at nine thirty. Twice in two days he'd tried to get a hold of her. Why? What did he want?

If curiosity killed the cat, where did that leave her?

On the other hand, he couldn't do anything diabolical to her in public, and she might learn something to help her case. Jaydee liked to talk. He might let something slip. She dropped the keys into her purse. No sign of his white Dodge Ram, which wasn't a big shock. Punctuality had never been high on his list. Ten minutes. Then she'd be out of here.

A waft of stale booze and cigarette smoke blasted her as she flashed her I.D. at the bouncer and made her way to the long bar. In the center of the room were three pool tables. Two of them were taken. The sound of balls hitting each other echoed off the walls, and the generic country music had turned familiar: Brooks and Dunn, "Boot Scootin' Boogie."

Most of the guys in the place had on faded jeans, scuffed boots, T-shirts and baseball caps. Their female companions wore as little as possible, showing flesh that would look better covered. From the prices marked on a chalkboard, the drinks were cheap, and, from the looks of it, so were the women. Taking a seat at the bar, Randi was surprised, and at the same time not, to see Coco, Jaydee's *friend*. The woman who came to the defense of Tim Tyler at Rickert's party and accused her of being a stalker. "I didn't know you worked here." Had Kira mentioned it? She couldn't remember.

Coco bristled. "I didn't know you came here." As cold as ever.

She ordered a Coors Light, craving something stronger, but she needed her wits about her to deal with Jaydee. Jilters held the upper hand for all of eternity. "So... how do you know Tim Tyler?"

Coco slid the beer along the well-worn counter. "What is this? Twenty questions?"

"Just one. I was hoping to meet him someday. I thought maybe—"

"Cut the starstruck crap. He comes in here when he's in town. That's how we met. Anything else?"

"What about Jaydee?"

"This bar. Same way."

"I have to let you know, you've been misinformed. It's over

between Jaydee and me, and I've never *stalked* him, or anybody else, for that matter."

Coco shrugged and turned to face the TV above the bar where a college basketball game played, volume off.

Figuring Coco had just given her the brush-off, which was fine, Randi closed her fingers around the beer bottle, taking in the photos lining the walls. In addition to an oil painting of the establishment's namesake, there was a gallery of racing superstars, equine and human alike: Cigar, the Shoe, Seabiscuit, Barbaro, Chris McCarron, Mike Smith, and the Queen Zenyatta, herself.

"Buy you a drink?" A rush of moist breath flowing into her ear almost startled her off her seat as Jaydee slid onto the adjoining barstool. His dark blond hair had been cut short, military-style since she'd last seen him, and his pale green eyes, the same color as hers, glittered like he was high on something.

"Got one." She tilted the bottle.

Jaydee put an elbow on the bar. "Hey, Coco. Gimme the usual."

Coco poured him a shot of Bushmills and cracked open a Pacifico. "Sure thing, darlin'." She reached over to squeeze his arm before moving down to the next customer. The way she touched Jaydee made it clear that if the two of them were just friends, as Coco claimed, benefits were included in the package.

Randi felt Jaydee's eyes on the side of her face.

"Am I making you nervous?"

She pretended she hadn't heard. "Hey, listen... I'm sorry about Stacey."

"So much for small talk."

"We're past the chitchat stage, don't you think?"

Jaydee hung his head, but not for long. "You look good." He ran his eyes from the top of her head all the way to her feet.

She'd dressed for comfort, not to impress, in her faded purple AQHA sweatshirt, ballet flats and a pair of Cruel Girl jeans. Marks were carved into the bar. She traced a five-point star, a swastika and a heart. "Any ideas?"

"About what?"

"About who killed her."

Jaydee chugged his whiskey. "If I knew that, we'd have two murders on our hands."

"Why was she was in the barn that late on Friday night?"

"Stacey was a night owl, and she couldn't get enough of that damn horse. She'd stand there and stare at him all night if I'd'a let 'er."

"So... no idea who did it?" She peeled the label from her bottle of Coors Light. The mountains had turned from cold blue to warm white beneath her sweaty palms.

"No idea."

"Helen said you were in Vegas."

Jaydee's lips thinned to a sneer. No mistaking that in the neon glare.

"Where'd you stay?"

"What's it to you?"

Always trying to one-up her. Why had it taken her this long to figure out he was constantly playing a role, never showing his true self? "You said you'd take me to the Bellagio someday."

"You still haven't been?" His face relaxed. Was that a flicker of regret?

"Still haven't been."

"That's unfortunate."

Her pulse throbbed at the base of her throat. "What'd you tell McWynn about me?"

Jaydee drew his head back. "You? Nothing."

"Your friend Coco is spreading rumors. Someone told the cops I wanted Stacey out of the picture. I doubt the detective made it up, and he's breathing down my neck because of it."

"Really? Well, hell, Ran. I have to say, I'm kind of flattered you're still carrying a torch."

Unbelievable. His conceit was off the charts. She'd been a fool to come here. She slung her purse strap over her shoulder and pushed herself off the stool.

He grabbed her arm. "Hold it. I'm not finished with you."

"I'm suspected of killing your wife and you're flattered? Let go of me."

He relaxed his grip but didn't do as she asked. "Sit down." He smiled. "Let's start over. No more smart-ass comments. I promise."

From the other side of the bar, Coco gave her a look like she was a wicked witch tormenting the poor grieving widower.

"Come on." He patted the stool. "Put your booty in the chair. Hey, Coco Butter, what's your best bottle of champagne?"

"Let's see..." Coco bent over to check the cooler under the bar. Jaydee leaned forward to get a better view. She fumbled around, clanking bottles, then pulled out a magnum and set it on the counter with a flourish. "J. Roget." She pronounced the "T" at the end. "The good stuff."

Randi crumpled the beer label she'd been holding between her fingers and let it fall to the floor.

Jaydee nodded his approval. "Do it."

Coco sent the cork flying. It bounced off a San Diego Padres pennant in the far corner of the room and a trail of dust rained down upon one of the pool tables. She poured the champagne into wineglasses, foam spilling over the sides and onto the bar. She didn't bother to wipe it up.

Randi excused herself to go to the bathroom and when she finished thought about slipping out the back door, but the industrial-sized bolt was thrown and it was probably hooked to an alarm.

She slid back onto the stool. This was the last place she wanted to spend her evening, but if Jaydee kept on drinking he might let his guard down about his gambling debts. Maybe he needed Stacey dead to get at her money.

Jaydee hoisted one of the glasses. "To the future." He downed the contents in one swift gulp.

Whose future? Surely he didn't think she'd be so reckless as to fall for him a *third* time.

Coco crossed her arms, lifting her cleavage in the manner she'd perfected. "Aren't you going to drink it?"

She stared at the glass. Large bubbles clung to the side. The result of carbonation with carbon dioxide, as opposed to a healthy stream of pinpoint bubbles that rose to the surface when it was fermented in the bottle. This was bulk method champagne. "Headache material," Kira called it. The cheap stuff. Just like Coco. "No thanks. I'm full from my beer."

"Oh, brother." Coco rolled her eyes. "What are you? Some kinda lightweight?" She and Jaydee shared a look. "Or are you just a snob?"

Jaydee snickered. "She's both, and most Colorado girls can hold their liquor. Randi's the exception."

She found their conspiracy infuriating. Jaydee always made her play the fool and was forever getting the best of her, making her the subject of people's gossip and pity. Against her better judgment and feeling a pointless need to prove them wrong, she tossed back the champagne and pushed the empty glass across the bar. It didn't taste as bad as she thought it would. "Hit me again."

Fifteen

NAKED. CANDLELIGHT. DRUNK. THAT'S what she was. Well, drunk for sure, and naked too, but you couldn't be candlelight. How silly. She slid her arms up and down the satin sheets like a kid making snow angels. *Heaven.* She cracked her eyelids and giggled. Hardly. Not unless Heaven had ceiling fans.

The blades spun in a blur. The warm glow surrounding her faded, and the more she watched, the worse she felt. The fan picked up speed and the bed began to twirl. She slammed her eyes shut and kept them closed until everything slowed. When the bed finally stopped spinning, she rolled to her side and dared a peek. The moonlight reflected off an outdoor pool, a rippling ball of light dancing on the water. She floated above the surface. Water. Moon. Luna. Sea.

Blazing, blinding light streamed through a window. Randi's head, her throat, her stomach—everything—hurt. And her hair was wet. How come? She flung the pillow over her face, engulfed in the smell of strong perfume that wasn't hers. Hurling the pillow to the floor, she struggled to her elbows and forced her eyes across the king-sized bed. On the other side of the mattress lay her worst nightmare. A satin-covered lump with a head of close-cropped blond hair protruding from the comforter.

Matt had said Jaydee had her in his crosshairs. Was this what he meant? Sexual conquest? Was she so desperate, so tormented, so lonely this is what she stooped to?

Naked, she padded to the bathroom and sank to her knees in front of the toilet. Her stomach bucked with dry heaves, but all that came up was some bubbly, vile-tasting yuck. She slumped against the wall. From the looks of things—bra slung over a towel rack, panties crumpled by the trash can, jeans tossed in the bathtub and her sweatshirt where it had somehow fallen behind the toilet—she'd been the life of the party last night. Too bad she couldn't remember any of it. Or maybe that was a good thing.

She reached for a glass on the white marble countertop. A smudge of lipstick marked the rim. She wiped it with her thumb and filled and drank water from the glass three times. Finished, she set it beside a toothbrush. Next to the toothbrush was an old pink teddy bear clutching a red fuzzy heart, a bottle that presumably held the sickly sweet perfume, a jewelry chest, a row of candles and a colorful variety of fingernail polish. In the rack beside the toilet, a copy of *HorseWorld* was folded in half, keeping Stacey's place.

She wiped her mouth with a fistful of toilet paper and stared at her reflection in the mirror. Puffy face, dark circles. The drawer held a hairbrush along with some elastic bands. She couldn't bring herself to use Stacey's brush, but she did borrow one of the bands. She pulled her damp hair into a ponytail. How strange. Had she taken a shower? Gone swimming? Skinny-dipped? Houston and Helen could see Jaydee's pool from their window. Oh, *God*. What else had she done?

She closed the lid on the toilet and, cradling her throbbing head, sat on the seat. A beer and some champagne and she'd blacked out? It didn't make sense. The last thing she remembered was Coco pouring her a second glass after she'd slammed the first. She knew better than to chug champagne, but how come the rest of the night was a complete blank? How was that possible?

She collected her randomly strewn clothing, helped herself to four Advil and swished some Listerine, though it was doubtful she'd ever get the taste of last night out of her mouth.

Dressed, and as presentable as she was going to get, she tiptoed past Jaydee, snoring away like he hadn't a care in the world. She didn't dare look at him, fearing the pressure of her gaze might pull him awake. Something round and white, about the size of a quail egg, lay on the floor next to the bed where he'd dropped his pants. She reached for it with her toes and rolled it around. Looked like a foosball. Felt like a foosball. Funny. She hadn't played that game since college. She kicked it under the dust ruffle and it hit the far wall with a *clunk*.

Jaydee twitched and mumbled something she couldn't understand. His eyelids fluttered.

She held her breath and froze in place until his snoring cranked up again.

Her leather bag was on the tiled entryway next to the flats she'd worn to The Triton. She slipped on her shoes and slid out the door without looking back. The fog was rolling in and she welcomed its cooling cover. At the bottom of the steep ice plant-covered slope, the hay truck chugged slow and steady, ranch hands tossing feed from the flatbed trailer. Except for the hungover, bewildered woman standing outside Jaydee's house, everything seemed to be a typical morning at Lucky Jack Performance Horses.

A handful of cars already filled the parking lot. She imagined McWynn down there, leaning out the window of his sedan, holding down the shutter to his camera and snapping off shots of her in rapid-fire succession.

Okay... deep breaths. No use letting paranoia run rampant. Caution. Not all-out panic. All she had to do was get to her truck. Ooh. Good question. Where was her truck?

A flicker of movement behind Houston and Helen's living room window gave her a start. She had no excuse at the ready in case one of them caught her. If she could just make it past their place and around back to the garage without having to stop and dry heave in the bushes, she could jump in the F150 and be gone.

She rounded the corner. *Snip. Snip, snip.* Danny trimmed an overgrown bougainvillea. His back was to her and he bopped his head to a beat. He seemed oblivious to everything but the music in his earbuds and the clippers in his hands. She scurried past him and finally had a clear shot of the garage. Good news: she hadn't driven drunk. Bad news: her truck was nowhere in sight.

A door slammed. "Danny?" Helen's voice.

Randi ran, flats slapping the ground so hard her feet hurt through the thin soles. Where the steep drive to the Hills' homes joined up with the road leading to the ranch, she ducked behind a hedge and pulled out her phone. The screen was black. Dead. Now what? She squared her shoulders and left the safety of the bushes. Long as no one asked why she was wearing flimsy flats instead of boots, or why she had her purse slung over her shoulder or why she hadn't brushed her hair and smelled like some ho from a dive bar, she was in the clear.

Her fortune took a turn for the better. José was cleaning a pen along the riverbed corrals. Most of the ranch hands had cell phones. She leaned over the bars. "*Hola, José.*"

"*Hola, señorita. Buenos días.*"

"Yes. *Sí.* Thank you. Uh... *por favor*, a *teléphono*?" Why hadn't she paid more attention in high school Spanish? She pantomimed dialing a number with her hand then held it to her ear.

"Ah. *Sí.*" José patted his shirt pocket and handed her a phone.

"*Gracias, José. Muchas gracias.*" It came out sounding like mooch-ass, grassy-ass, but it got the point across.

She dialed the number for The Surf & Stirrup. Kira answered after half a ring, as if she'd been expecting the call. She wasn't pleased, but she agreed to go feed Shane and let him outside. Luke was closer but *no way* was Randi calling him. She could never explain this to him. Ever.

Shane had been alone in the house all night and, if he hadn't wet the floor, he'd be upset about missing his breakfast. She felt awful. That she'd let her guard down around Jaydee was bad enough—not being there for her dog was a sin she'd never forgive herself for. "When you're done, can you pick me up at Lucky Jack? Across the riverbed behind the abandoned outbuilding?"

José eyed her sideways. Just because he didn't speak English didn't mean he didn't understand it.

"No way. I'm not taking my car down that road. It's all washed out and full of potholes."

"Kira, please. Don't make me beg. I promise I'll make it up to you."

Randi parked herself on a tree stump beside the unused barn where nobody could see her. Twenty minutes later, she sat in the passenger seat of Kira's yellow and black Mustang GT. Kira tapped her fingers on the steering wheel. Sounded like a galloping horse. "You owe me a carwash *and* an alignment."

"Whatever you want, you've got it. No problem. I'm forever in your debt."

"I'll let you off easy. Don't worry about the car. It's due for service anyway."

"Okay. What then? Please let me do something for you."

"Ride Oro. She really needs the exercise. As usual, I can't get away from the restaurant."

"When?"

"Today. The sooner, the better."

Randi groaned, pressing her throbbing forehead against the ice-cold window. For the first time in her life, she didn't feel a rush of excitement at the thought of sitting on a horse's back.

Kira didn't show the least bit of sympathy for her ailments. The Mustang rolled and rocked down the pit-filled road. Kira complained about her trashing her suspension and Randi lowered the window and stuck her head outside. The wind on her face felt cleansing in a bizarre, canine sort of way.

At El Camino Real, Kira put on her blinker and turned north. "Tell me about last night."

"What do you want to know?"

"Everything. Start from the beginning."

"Jaydee asked me to meet him at The Triton."

Kira took her eyes off the road. "You agreed?"

"I wasn't going to, but curiosity got the best of me. That, and I thought I might learn something about him and Stacey. I was hoping he'd get drunk and confess to the murder so I could turn him in and get on with my life."

"And somehow this meeting led to you not sleeping in your own bed? That's the part where I get lost."

"I don't know what happened, Kira. I blacked out. It's the weirdest thing. Everything about last night is gone, like it never happened, and you know I'm not a lightweight, despite what Coco says. She and Jaydee laughed at me."

"What's that A-hole doing now? Any morning-after conversation? I take it he didn't leap up and fix you breakfast."

"He's asleep."

"Does he know you left?"

"I don't think he's going to wake up for a while."

Kira adjusted her side mirror. "Was he ever alone with your drink?"

"Yes, when I went to the bathroom. After that I can't remember."

"Think, Randi. Think, think, think."

"It hurts to think."

"Okay. Try this. How about letting your mind flow gently over any recollections that might occur."

She shook her head. "Nothing there."

"Any sensations, moods, impressions stand out?"

"You sound like a shrink."

"Bartender. Same thing."

She contemplated until it hurt, which didn't take long. "I have a foggy memory of feeling heavy sitting at the bar. Like my limbs were sandbags. That's the best way I can describe it. After that, nothing until there was a ceiling fan and a pool. I woke up with wet hair, too. Not to mention I have a headache the size of China."

"Randi—don't you get it? Jaydee *drugged* you."

"What? He wouldn't do that."

Kira lifted her sunglasses and gave her a hard stare. "Seriously? If the man's committed murder, date rape is child's play." She looked straight ahead just in time to brake for a red light.

"I'm not entirely sure anything happened."

"You've lost your marbles. Of course it did."

"I don't feel any different. Physically, I mean. It's been so long I'm pretty sure I'd be able to tell if *it* happened." She didn't want to say the word. Saying *it* would give it life and power it didn't deserve.

"Randi, drunk plus naked equals fornication. It's basic math. Been that way since high school." The light turned green and Kira stomped on the gas pedal. They shot up the freeway on-ramp and, merging with traffic, the V-8 roared past a 350 Z. It was about a ten minute drive to The Triton, half that with Kira at the wheel.

"Did anybody see you leave this morning? Sex or no sex, you don't want the detective finding out where you spent the night."

"Danny was trimming the bougainvillea in front of Houston and Helen's place, but I don't think he noticed me."

"Anyone else?"

"José. I borrowed his phone, but I doubt he's interested in my activities."

"Don't be so sure. I dated a cop for a while, you know."

"Okay... I'll bite." Randi gripped the door handle. "But please slow down before I puke."

Kira ignored the request to reduce her speed. "I was young and foolish and impressed by the uniform, but I learned that if a cop asks you a loaded question, chances are he's already figured out the answer. What I'm getting at is if McWynn happens to inquire as to your whereabouts last night, you'll need to start looking for someone to take care of Shane on a permanent basis."

Kira did a double take in her rearview mirror. "Why is that truck on my tail? There's plenty of room to pass. If I stop all of a sudden, we'll be a hood ornament."

Randi glanced over her shoulder. "Oh. Not good."

Sixteen

RANDI TWISTED IN HER seat to get a better look. "He's catching up." A curled-horned ram from the Dodge's front grille filled the Mustang's rear window. "I never thought I'd say this to you, but step on it!"

Kira jerked the wheel and crossed two lanes of traffic to veer the Mustang down an off-ramp. Jaydee was ready for the move and stuck to them like glue. At the bottom of the ramp, the stoplight turned red. Kira banged the heel of her hand on the dash. "We're screwed."

"Guess he didn't sleep as long as I thought he would."

"What's he want?"

"Beats me."

Kira had her foot on the brake but the Mustang jolted forward as the Dodge made contact. A controlled bump, done with purpose to intimidate.

Kira's jaw dropped. "Dirtbag just hit me." She yanked on the emergency brake, flung the door open and had one foot on the pavement.

Randi grabbed her arm. "Wait!"

"Let me go." When Kira got mad, traces of the accent she'd worked so hard to shed returned, making her sound like a female Arnold Schwarzenegger. "I'm going to kick his ass."

"Not so fast. He's getting out."

Jaydee climbed over the touching bumpers and came around to the Mustang's passenger window.

Kira flung herself across Randi's lap. She hit the lever and the glass went down with a silky whirr. "Get away from my car!"

Jaydee stuck his head inside, his nose inches from Randi's. He was in a world of trouble if the light turned green. "Where is it?"

His breath could've raised the dead. Randi flattened herself against the back of the seat. "Where is *what*?"

"You know what. Give it back."

"I don't have anything of yours. Never did. Never will." A far too subtle dig for him to understand.

"I don't have time for this bullshit. Hand it over."

Kira put the Mustang in gear. "If you did anything to my car, you're getting the bill."

Jaydee pushed himself farther inside. "You have until the count of three." He opened his fist. "One... two..."

The word *three* hung on his lips when the stoplight changed. Kira hit the gas. Jaydee ducked and tried to back out in time but his head clunked the frame as he spun away from the car. Kira made a left and the Mustang shot down Loma Verde, heading west toward the ocean. She grinned. "He's gonna have a nice lump to add to his not-too-bright head."

"He's crazy."

"About time you realized that." Kira squinted through the windshield. Ahead, cars were everywhere, forcing her to reduce her speed. Unfortunately, the road behind them was clear. "Think he'll follow us?"

"You know he will."

"Can you call somebody? The cops maybe?"

"My phone's dead. Where's yours?"

"At the restaurant, where I left it."

"Terrific."

Kira gave the rearview mirror a glance. "What crawled up Jaydee's butt?"

"No clue."

"Whatever he's looking for, he wants it bad." Her eyes flicked back and forth between the road and the mirror. "We're stuck. I can't go *over* these cars and here comes the Dodge."

Seconds later, the vibrating growl of Jaydee's truck clawed its way up Randi's spine. "Watch it, Kira. Brace yourself."

A taillight shattered on the rear of the Mustang. Kira fought to keep the wheel steady. "*Bastard.*"

"If that intersection's clear, flip a u-ey."

"The light's red. I can't afford another ticket."

"You have to risk it. I've never seen Jaydee like this. I don't think he cares if he kills us."

"Maybe that's his plan." The Mustang's nose was halfway into the intersection with cars bearing down on them from both directions when Kira cranked a sharp left at the same time she rode the brakes. The front of the car dipped as the back lifted and swung out behind them. The Mustang whined and squealed and tilted and, for a horrible second, it seemed as if they'd roll end over end, but somehow they stayed upright. The GT fish-tailed back and forth but sped off leaving Jaydee stuck at the light, his path blocked by a pair of big rigs.

Kira's face was white. "Shit. I'm shaking. What was he going on about back there? Are you sure you don't have something of his?"

"I took one of Stacey's hairbands. A generic piece of elastic. That's it."

"Did you do anything before you left that pissed him off?"

"I got dressed in the bathroom, drank some water, moved a bottle of perfume and looked at a copy of *HorseWorld*. Oh yeah, I helped myself to some Advil. If he wants it back, it'd be easier to buy more at the store."

Heading east, the cars were stacked up like roadblocks. Kira did her best to avoid them, though they seemed to be on Jaydee's team as they puttered along, changing lanes at the last second to cut the Mustang off. Kira swore up, down and sideways at each one until, at last, the road cleared and opened up again. "Think he quit?"

"Nope."

"Me neither. At some point you're going to have to find out what he wants."

"I'd prefer to wait until he calms down."

"Then we'll keep on running." The road pitched and the curves tightened. "Catch me if you can, California boy. I grew up driving in the Alps." Kira downshifted and the car settled onto the road. Three minutes later they crested the hill that would drop them into Rancho del Zorro if they stayed the course.

The sun broke through the clouds. Kira waved at the glove box. "Grab my sunglasses, will ya? And my lipstick."

"Lipstick? Seriously?"

"It helps me think. See your maniac ex yet?"

Randi kept one eye on the mirror as she passed Kira the items she'd asked for. "Not yet."

"It's only a matter of time. If that Neanderthal's got one thing going for his sorry ass, it's determination."

The trees whizzed by in a blur. One-handed, Kira applied the lipstick. If something ventured into their path, it would be dead meat, catapulted into oblivion. "Don't kill anything." Randi gripped the door handle again, tighter this time. When they crashed, the EMTs would have to pry away her cold, dead fingers. "I have no desire to end up like Thelma and Louise."

"Not a bad way to go." Kira smiled. "Hold my hand."

"Funny. Get yourself another Louise."

"Just trying to lighten the mood. Okay, listen up. About a mile, maybe two, down this road, if I remember right, there's a tiny street hidden by the world's biggest hedge. If we can get there without Jaydee seeing us, he'll never know we made the turn and he'll keep heading straight into town. By the time he figures it out, it'll be too late."

A light flashed in the mirror. The Dodge truck appeared.

Randi grit her teeth. "We've got company. He must have taken a shortcut. Advantage: California boy."

Kira stomped on the accelerator. The engine responded with a roar. "What did you ever see in him?"

"I swear he wasn't like this in college. He was sweet. And thoughtful. And funny and intelligent."

"Hard to believe."

"Something's changed him. Matt Watson says he's got a gambling problem."

"You need to be more discriminating about who you go out with."

Randi kept quiet and watched the side of the road. Coming up on the right side a hedge towered. "Is that it? Is that the street?"

"Good eye." Kira turned and hit the accelerator. The Mustang swayed, hunkered down and hugged the road. "Is he still behind us?"

"Clear so far."

"Uh-oh."

"What?"

"I'm thinking I might have been wrong."

"Wrong how?"

"This road might end in a cul-de-sac."

"Great. We'll have to ditch the car and make a run for it."

"I'm not leaving my Mustang. No way in hell."

"Got any other ideas?"

"We'll cross that bridge when we get there."

A thick orange grove blocked the view around the next bend, but as soon as they'd made the turn, the cul-de-sac Kira feared was there appeared. She slowed the Mustang. "Look, there's a house."

"The gate's open. Take it. Somebody's gotta have a phone we can use to call the cops on him."

"Are you sure? We don't know who lives there. You know how trigger-happy you Americans are. We could get shot."

"In broad daylight?" Randi rolled down the window and listened. "His truck's coming. I hear it. Either we take our chances or deal with Jaydee. He wants whatever he thinks we have real bad. Stacey's dead. We could be next."

The iron partitions jolted and began to move inward. "Hurry! It's closing!"

"Oh, *hell*." Kira stomped on the gas.

They weren't going to make it; there wasn't enough time. Randi closed her eyes and tucked her head, anticipating the shriek of metal tearing against the side of the Mustang. The car bounced over the gutter and Randi's eyes flew open.

Kira blasted through the narrowing gap, clearing the gates by a margin too close to calculate. Behind them, the two sides met and locked in place with a reverberating clang. Kira eased off the gas and lifted her palm for a high-five slap.

Randi complied. "I bit my tongue and my mouth is bleeding, but your driving was brilliant. Don't slow down, though. Jaydee might be the one with a gun."

"Okay. Let's hope our hosts are the hospitable type."

They rumbled up a cobblestone driveway that emptied out in front of a Spanish-style house. Adjacent to a rolling lawn was a pool with a waterslide made out of rocks where music and raucous cackling came from a waterfall hiding a grotto-like room. Beside the pool a tall man wearing a Speedo stood holding a glass with a celery stalk protruding from the top. He smiled as he came toward the Mustang, lifting his glass in a salute. So much for the concern over trespassing.

Half a dozen topless women bounced and jiggled in the water. Kira shut off the engine. "I think we've stumbled upon Rancho del Zorro's very own Playboy mansion."

"Little early for a party, don't you think?"

Kira laughed. "Maybe it never stopped." She rubbed the end of her nose. "I can't believe that guy's wearing a Speedo. A white one. *Gross*."

"I thought you Europeans were into those things."

"That's one tradition I was happy to leave behind."

Speedo-man opened Kira's door and held out a hand.

"Ladies, welcome to my humble abode. To what do I owe the pleasure?"

"My ex is chasing us. We slipped in your gate to get away from him. Hope you don't mind."

"Can we hang out for a few? We'd like to use a phone, too," Kira said, "Mister... ?"

"Stefan. Call me Stefan." He stirred his drink with the celery stalk, his equipment clearly visible. "Stay as long as you want. Pretty girls don't need an invitation to my party. Sorry about the gate. I thought you were selling something, or that the Jehovah's Witnesses had taken to driving muscle cars."

Brakes screeched near the end of the drive. Stefan lifted his chin. "Is that your friend?"

Jaydee stuck his head out the window, yelling words that were drowned out each time he laid on the horn. He jumped from the cab. "Open the goddamn gate!"

"He's a charmer." Stefan flipped him off with one hand, cupped his hand to his mouth with the other. "Go to hell!"

Jaydee got in the truck, jerked the door closed and rolled the Dodge backward. To some it might have appeared he was in retreat mode, but Randi knew better.

There was a chirp of rubber as he rushed the gate. A sharp pop was followed by the sound of glass tinkling onto the pavement, but the gate held firm.

Stefan disappeared inside the pool house and came back holding a rifle that he pointed at the Dodge. Kira gave Randi a look.

"Okay with you if I shoot out his tires?"

Randi held up her hand and took two giant steps away from the rifle. "Don't. Then we'll never get rid of him."

"Good point. I'll scare the piss out of him instead." Stefan took aim and fired. The women in the pool screamed, throwing their arms around their breasts, as if suddenly noticing they were topless.

Jaydee gunned the Dodge and roared away.

"Nice work," Kira said.

Stefan took a bow.

Randi slumped against the side of the Mustang. Jaydee wasn't finished with her. With the exception of their relationship, he'd never quit on anything before.

Kira took off her sunglasses. "You look awful. Think it's safe to go? Or is the monster waiting for us around the corner?"

Stefan stirred his cocktail with the celery stalk. "I have an idea. Why don't you two stay and relax? Make use of the pool, or I can offer you one of my signature Bloody Marys. You won't regret it."

Kira put a hand on Randi's arm. "You up for a little hair of the dog?"

She shook her head. "The only dog I want right now is waiting for me at home."

Seventeen

FROM THE RUNNING BOARD of the F150, Randi scanned the ranch. Jaydee was here somewhere. She'd seen his Dodge parked behind the garage high up on the hill. Hopefully he was sleeping off his fit of rage. She didn't want him near her.

If he saw her, would he take up the chase again? She had something he wanted, but what? Give it back, he'd said. Did "it" implicate him in Stacey's death? Evidence he'd killed her? Since the cops already had the murder weapon, it might be something subtle, tying him to the crime in an indirect manner. Problem was, she'd taken nothing from his place but her pounding head, the band for her hair and the clothes she came with.

Jaydee had flipped, that was a given, and he didn't seem that broken up about Stacey. Not when he'd flirted with Coco and checked Randi out like a piece of meat in the bar, then apparently drugged her with something and she'd ended up in his bed.

Whatever Jaydee's deal was, she'd promised Kira she'd ride Oro and she still had her patients to attend to. She refused to let Jaydee run her off.

Piper was at the foaling pen beside a chestnut mare with a bulging belly lying on her side. Randi's heart skipped a beat, the memory of the dead colt far too fresh in her mind.

Piper looked up. "You ever see a foal being born?"

Relieved, Randi ducked through the bars. "Not in person. I've come close but always been a hair too late."

"You're in for a treat. Foaling usually happens at three in the morning, not three in the afternoon."

The mare thrust her neck sideways as her slick sides contracted and she let out an elephant-sized groan. Wood shavings peppered her fire-red mane. Using a gloved hand, Piper moved her tail to the side. One more push and a tiny pair of hooves protruded from inside the mare. Randi hadn't witnessed a live birth, but she'd seen enough videos to know the foal should come into the world like a high-diver, head tucked between its two front legs. "Who's the daddy?"

"Rebel. The mare is Houston's."

Without warning, the chestnut jerked her shoulders upright and rocked her hindquarters, heaving herself to her feet. She shook her head as if to say she'd had enough of this nonsense and could she just get back to her hay?

"Now what?"

"Not to worry," Piper said. "Give her a minute and she'll likely reposition herself to start pushing again."

It seemed as if the mare understood. She swung around and, with another moan, collapsed to the shavings. She grunted and pushed again. This time the foal's forelegs appeared, covered with a thick, milky-colored membrane. The legs seemed to go on forever until at last a muzzle followed. Next came the head and neck. After the shoulders, the hard part was over. Two more pushes and the rest of the baby horse, with a rush of fluid and encased in the clouded shiny sac, slid into the world.

Much less traumatic than some of the human labor stories Randi had heard about, but maybe it was because horses couldn't scream.

Piper pulled the membrane away from the foal's nostrils

then peeled the rest of the stuff away from its body. "It's a boy. A colt." Piper grinned as she plucked a couple of clean towels from a paper sack. Together they began rubbing the long legs of the dazed, blinking foal. The mare nickered at her newborn while she made swaying motions in preparation to stand and break the cord binding her to her colt. She rolled back and forth, struggled to her feet, shook her head and blew out her nostrils, showering them with a fine spray of horse snot.

"Yuck." Piper passed her a clean towel. "Here, this one's for you."

"Are you kidding? This is the best thing to happen to me all day."

"Must be a bad one."

"I've had better."

"Is Jaydee hassling you?"

How much did Piper know? What if Danny *had* seen her sneaking out this morning and blabbed it to everyone? "Why do you ask?"

"He roared in here a while ago, mumbling a whole bunch of crap. Your name came out of his mouth and not in a nice way."

"Did you talk to him?"

"Hell no. I steer clear of him when he's in one of his moods. He saddled up Jasper and I don't know what he did to him, but he brought the poor horse back dripping with lather like he'd just ridden the hundred miles of Tevis. Then he left him in the crossties and stormed off. Didn't even un-tack. I cooled the horse down, gave him a bath and put him away. Took me an hour—like I don't have better things to do. Think he'll thank me?" Piper propped her hands on her hips. "I'm telling you, if he wasn't Houston's son, I'd let him have it, both barrels."

The colt derailed the conversation by trying to follow his mother's lead and stand. He jerked and pulled and pushed himself to his knees, then, after a couple of unsuccessful attempts, teetered on stilt-like legs.

"Hey, Piper, look." A white marking stood out against the slick darkness of the newborn colt's face—the symbol of the Flying V guitar. "Check it out. Just like his daddy."

The foal met Randi's gaze and didn't blink or look away, struggling to control the four uncooperative sticks that kept wobbling beneath him. He opened his mouth and stuck his tongue out in a wide yawn.

Randi laughed. "He's quite the clown, isn't he?"

"Who cares about that? Look at those hindquarters. Check out that perfectly sloped shoulder. This baby's going to be something special. You watch."

The colt staggered sideways like a drunk at closing time, gained enough momentum to bolt forward, then tripped and fell to the ground. His tiny tail twitched as he flopped on his side, stretched his legs, flicked his tail one last time and closed his eyes.

Something Special. She'd make damn sure nothing bad happened to this little guy.

Day had almost surrendered to night by the time Randi led Oro from her stall. In the name of saving what little light remained, she did minimal grooming before tacking up and swinging into the saddle.

Steinbeck said a man on a horse was spiritually, as well as physically, bigger than he was on foot. Same went for women— maybe even more so. Ever since she'd been old enough to sit on one, Randi had known she belonged on horseback. She steered Oro along the eastern border of the ranch's property line, where the trail thinned before it ran along a stand of eucalyptus and plunged into the valley. Oro lowered her head and placed her feet carefully amongst the rocks. Shane played scout, nose down, tail up. The trail leveled near the bottom and lofty oaks cast long shadows across the path. With each step taking them farther from the ranch, Randi relaxed.

The narrow path widened once they left the hollow and she gave Oro a loose rein and let her trot. Coyotes yipped in the distance. Oro's gait was bright and eager. The chill of the evening had everybody feeling good. Shane ran up the trail and back again, diving into the bushes, probably hoping to flush out some kind of critter, tail wagging and mouth open in a happy grin. Next to car rides, walks and kibble, this was the best thing in his doggie kingdom, and this ride helped assuage her guilt over leaving him alone, trapped inside the bungalow last night. She'd wracked her brain all day, doing her damnedest to recall what happened at The Triton, and it was still a blank.

Another horse and rider came around a blind corner. Oro dropped her shoulder and scooted sideways with lightning speed. If Randi had been less experienced, she would have been dumped head first into the thorny brush.

Houston, on his stocky black gelding Caviar, rode toward them, reining his horse to stop once they pulled even with each other. He tipped his hat. "Didn't mean to spook your horse."

Caviar was unflappable. Oro, not so much. Shying was an art form for her, one she chose to sharpen her skills at every chance she could.

"It's okay." She gave Oro a pat.

Houston braced himself on his saddle horn and jerked his head toward the back of the property. "You see the outcasts?"

The outcasts were a group of about fifteen horses in a pasture at the far end of the ranch. The "cheap seats" of Lucky Jack's boarding. "No. Why? Is something wrong?"

"Their tails have been cut."

"Cut?"

"Below the docks. All of them."

"*What*? Really? Who would do that?"

"Don't know. Too bad whoever it was didn't get a swift kick to the head." Houston pulled a cigarette from his shirt pocket and struck a match that lit up his face. "'Course, they'll catch worse than that when I find 'em."

Oro tossed her head, eager to get a move on. Randi ordered her to settle down. "It's not like there's a black market for violin bows or show tail extensions."

"Don't be too sure. A pound of hair three feet long can go for seventy-five to about three hundred, depending on the color."

"Still, a lot of trouble to get it."

"It's got me baffled. One more damn thing to worry about around here." He took a long drag off his cigarette. "I've got a call into a security company. Gonna get one of those gates with a code and a bunch of cameras to put up around the barn. I don't believe in living like a paranoid pansy, but I don't have much choice. Helen's all over my back."

Houston's cell phone jangled from his belt clip. Flipping it open, he held it to his ear. He listened for a few seconds then his jaw went slack and the cigarette tumbled to the ground.

Randi kicked her feet out of the stirrups and leapt from the saddle to stomp on the glowing ember before it set fire to the foxtails surrounding Caviar's legs. She was about to scold Houston for being so careless when he snapped the phone closed.

"Son of a bitch."

The only other time she'd heard Houston swear was when he'd seen Stacey's body.

"That was Helen. There's been another colt."

Icy fingers circled Randi's throat. "Dead?"

"That makes two now. I wish I knew what the blasted hell is going on."

The air smelled of burning tobacco. She buried her fingers in Oro's mane. "Houston, call her back."

"What?"

"Call her back. Please. I need to know if there was a marking on his head." Not her Something Special. *No. Please, no.* She'd made a vow no harm would come to him. She'd promised.

"What kind of marking?"

"A V-shape. Like Rebel's."

Houston did as she asked. After an eternity, he hung up and shook his head. She sagged with relief and let out a breath.

Houston picked his reins. "I'd better go deal with it. Helen's always complaining she gets stuck with all the dirty work around here."

"Need help?" She asked just to be polite. If he said yes, she'd be sorry.

He shook his head. "You go on with your ride."

Four days. One dead human. Two dead horses. The outcasts' tails, Sydney's attempted poisoning, Zany set loose. Not to mention the overnight fiasco with Jaydee and the ensuing car chase. She couldn't shake the feeling they were related.

She rode, fast and hard, until she lost track of time and Oro finally slowed to a walk, her flanks and chest damp with sweat. Shane's tongue lolled from his mouth and his paws dragged the dirt. Only a handful of stars winked in the sky, and the moon had yet to show itself. The wind picked up, rattling the leaves in the trees. Oro pranced as the light faded and the temperature dropped. Long past feeding time, all she wanted was to have her nose in the hay bin.

Coming around the U of the loop, they headed for home. Randi sang to take the edge off the antsy mare: "Red River Valley," "Home on the Range," and the "Cowboy's Lament." The old western songs seemed to calm Oro. Maybe they struck a chord deep in her Quarter Horse DNA, or gave her something to think about besides ridding herself of her rider and hightailing it back to the barn.

Whatever the reason, it worked. Oro seemed happy enough now, swinging her hips with an easy cadence until they left the open space and crossed onto Lucky Jack property, where a broken backhoe and several rusted-out wheelbarrows—mere outlines in the overgrown weeds—seemed to shift shapes in the shadows.

Oro jumped and shied, leaping sideways at anything and everything. Phantom horse killers lurked everywhere. Leaves, branches, lizards, a sudden breeze, an owl—even Shane. Randi kept her seat deep in the saddle and her legs relaxed but ready, eyes alert as she scanned the horizon. Rounding the final bend in the trail, she spotted the outcasts. Far away from the barns, these horses had mainly absentee owners. Teens who'd traded horses for the opposite sex, people who'd lost their jobs or gone through a divorce, and her personal favorite, the ones who bought a horse to impress their friends then had no idea what to do with it. The outcasts were a skittish group with shaggy coats, unkempt manes and wild looks in their eyes.

She moved Oro closer to the fence. Houston had told the truth. The tails of each and every one of them were hacked off below the dock. They weren't in pain. No muscle, skin or bone had been cut, and there was no blood, but not being able to use their tails to swat flies and mosquitoes was a huge handicap. Come summer, this wouldn't be a happy group.

What a strange thing to do... a blatant act of vandalism. A message. A warning. Of what? And why? She wheeled Oro away from the fence and dug her heels into the mare's sides. Oro responded by covering the ground with powerful strides, moving quickly into a gallop, hooves flinging riverbed sand over their tracks.

Soon the sand turned hard and the trail narrowed. Oro's ears went up and she put on the brakes. Tractor headlights reared into the sky, shining bright off a fog bank rolling in to spread ghostly images over the branches of the nearby eucalyptus. Coffin Bone Canyon. Oro tossed her head, jigging sideways. Randi gave Shane a warning glance while she positioned the three of them behind a tangle of trees to check things out. The canyon extended farther than Randi could see, ending in a semicircle of scraggly mesquite at the base of a towering wall of rock. The lights dipped and rose and the tractor engine whined as a scoop shoved its way into the ground. Jaydee sat at the controls. To the right of the tractor, fresh earth was piled high to the side. A foal-sized lump, covered by a green tarp, lay beside it.

Jaydee jumped from the tractor, took off his baseball cap, punched it with his fist and studied the hole in the ground for a good minute or two before climbing back up to the seat. Randi understood the immediacy of moving the colt Helen had found. It wasn't good for business for clients to see a dead horse. But why no necropsy on this one?

It was key Jaydee not see her watching him. There were no witnesses to what he might do to her out here, at least not ones who could testify in court.

Randi picked up the reins and shifted her weight. Well-trained beast that she was, Oro took the required amount of backward steps until she faced the right direction on the trail and they were able to make a quiet, and hopefully undetected, exit.

They'd gone about six feet down the path when Jaydee starting hollering, "*Hey*! What are you doing? Get back here!"

She twisted in the saddle, glancing over Oro's rump. Was Jaydee gunning for her? As insane as he was behind the wheel of his truck this morning, he might be crazy enough to come after her in the tractor. Oro could outrun it, but being chased by a noisy machine would scare the living daylights out of her.

A rock the size of a baseball slammed into Oro's flank. The mare squealed and kicked out, bolting forward at the same time she tripped over an exposed root. She caught herself just before she fell to her knees and came out of her stumble at a full gallop. Randi grabbed a hunk of mane, but lost one of the reins. It dragged on the ground for half a second then snapped after catching beneath Oro's thundering hooves.

Trees hurtled by at blinding speed. Randi ducked low and, clutching the remaining rein, clung like a monkey on the mare's neck until she leapt a ditch and landed too close to a tree. A branch slammed into Randi's ribs. The force of it twisted her to the far side of the saddle, bouncing Oro off stride and she began to buck, a godsend because the up-and-down motion slowed her mad dash enough that Randi was able to reach her fingers halfway down the strip of leather and grab hold. Bracing her free hand on the mare's neck, she pulled, bringing the lone rein all the way to her hip in an emergency stop, forcing Oro's head and neck around and swinging her back legs into a spin. Round and round they went, and just when she was sure Oro would collapse on top of her, the mare slowed her panicked steps and came to a stop, all four legs braced, ribcage heaving, nose low to the ground.

Randi reached down and stroked the mare's steaming neck. "Not your fault, Oro-girl."

The barn was visible in the shadows. Three times in one day she'd escaped Jaydee. Her luck wouldn't last forever.

Eighteen

"**J**AYDEE JOINING YOU AGAIN?" Coco pushed a coaster along the length of the bar.

Randi dragged herself onto the barstool, clutching her ribcage where the tree branch had hit. "Oh man, I hope not." Come to think of it, Jaydee might be thirsty after all that grave digging. She better make this fast.

"Can I get you something?"

Randi twirled the coaster. *New Belgium Brewing. Fort Collins, Colorado.* If she had ruby slippers, she'd close her eyes and click her heels together three times. "I seem to have lost parts of last night. I'm hoping you can help me find them."

"Happens to the best of us." Coco smiled without showing her teeth. "Nothing to drink?"

"Water, please."

"Um... well, yeah... the boss doesn't like it when people take up a stool and only order water."

"There's nobody here."

Below the bar, near Coco's feet, a *yip, yip, yip* pierced the blaring house music. Coco bent down and scooped up the mini

Chihuahua she'd brought to Rickert's party. It quivered, staring at Randi with weepy marble-sized eyes. How could something so small make so much noise? How did Coco manage not to step on him?

"Fortunate dog, getting to come to work with you." It had to be a violation of some kind of health code.

"The boss won't be here tonight. Don't you dare rat me out."

"If he's not coming in, why do I have to order a drink?"

Coco raised her eyebrows and waited.

"Fine. How 'bout a 7UP?"

"I thought you wanted answers."

"Okay, make it a Seven and Seven."

That seemed to satisfy Coco. For all the sass she was dishing out, she better have loose lips.

"Does Jaydee come here often?"

"You asked me that last night." Coco scooped ice into a glass. "Why do you want to know?"

"Just wondering."

Coco poured then set the drink in front of her. "Every now and then. I wouldn't call him a regular."

"You two seem to have a nice rapport." Nice enough to need Stacey out of the picture? Maybe that was why Coco deliberately pointed the finger in her direction at Rickert's party, to deflect it from herself.

"We have some laughs."

"Laughs? You like him, huh?"

Coco snickered. "Not as much as you do. You were the one hanging all over him."

The conversation was rapidly deteriorating to a third-grade level. "Extenuating circumstances."

"If you say so."

Randi dug through her purse and put her last twenty on the counter. "Look, Coco, something strange happened in here last night. A beer and some champagne and I can't remember a thing? Highly unusual."

"Some champagne?" Coco slapped her palm on the bar.

"Honey, you damn near guzzled the entire big ol' bottle. Near the end of it, you didn't even bother with a glass."

Ouch. How many times had her dad sat at the kitchen table with a baffled expression while her mother listed all the asinine things he'd said and done the night before? "What about Jaydee? He just watched?"

"You weren't exactly in a sharing mood."

"I'm having a hard time swallowing this, no pun intended."

"You had no such problem last night."

"Is it possible Jaydee messed with my drink when I went to the bathroom?"

Coco propped a hand on her hip. With the other, she snatched up the twenty. "You think he slipped you a roofie?"

She considered what Kira had said. "It would explain a lot."

"Is that it for you?" Coco slung a towel over her shoulder and put the money in the drawer, not bothering to ask if she wanted change. "I'm kinda busy here."

"Almost." She hadn't gotten her twenty bucks' worth. "Did we stay very long?"

"You polished off the magnum, you guys shot a game of pool, then you left."

"One game? Used to be, when Jaydee got going on a table, it was impossible to drag him away."

Coco looked down her nose. "You kept ramming customers with the butt end of your stick. You were dancing with it too. I took it away before somebody broke a cue over your head."

"No way. You're making that up."

"Ask Clarence at the door. He saw the whole thing. I'm surprised he let Jaydee out of here with the empty. Said he wanted it for a souvenir. Seemed strange, but whatever. People have done far weirder things with a magnum."

"What about foosball? Did we play that too?"

Coco nodded toward the back of the bar. "Doubtful. I don't think the handles even turn anymore. It'd take an entire can of WD-40 to get it to work."

Randi slid from the stool and sidestepped between the tables, making her way to the darkened rear of the room where the foosball table sat. Coco was right. The handles turned, but not without making a horrible screech, and the rails were so rusty the little plastic players couldn't move the ball any more than an inch or two.

From the far corner of the room, someone started hacking. A deep mucus-filled sound coming from a man slumped over a table. There was something familiar about him. She moved closer.

His jacket was filthy, and his hair, entwined with twigs and bits of dried leaves, made him look like he'd slept the day away in a park. Led Zeppelin blared from the speaker grille less than six inches from his ear. His clothes were torn and covered in a layer of grit, and he was in serious need of a shower.

She touched his shoulder. "Hey," she said, loud enough to be heard over the music, "Are you all right?"

He raised his head a few inches. His mouth hung open, and his eyes were red and unfocused, but it was him, she was sure of it. Rebel's groom, Roberto, missing since the night of Stacey's murder.

"What happened to you? Are you okay?"

He put his head on the table and burped. It stunk so bad she pushed herself away and tried not to inhale. Roberto? It didn't make sense. The Roberto she knew had far too much pride to ever let himself be seen in public wearing filthy clothes and reeking of booze and B.O. If his mother died and he'd returned from Mexico already, why not go straight to the ranch, to his job where he was needed?

She patted her back pocket, but she'd left her phone in the truck. She put a hand on top of his. His skin was hot. "I'm going to call Houston and Helen and tell them you're all right." She added an unwarranted "Wait here."

On her way out, she stopped at the bar. "How long has that guy been here?"

"He came in about an hour ago. Ordered a double Cuervo, gulped it down and hasn't moved since. The double wasn't the first thing he'd had to drink today, I'll tell you that much." Coco wiped the bar with a rag. The smell of mildew wafted through the air.

"He works for the Hill family, you know."

Coco froze mid-wipe. "If he needs a ride home, I can call Jaydee to come get him."

"Good idea. Save me a trip to my truck."

Coco picked up the phone and dialed the number from memory, unable to hide her shy smile.

She had no idea what she was getting into. Jaydee would spit her out like a nasty taste when he'd had his fill.

"Whoops." Coco disconnected. "Too late."

"What do you mean?"

"See for yourself." She pointed toward the back of the room.

The back door hung open. The glow from an alleyway streetlamp made a yellow stripe across Roberto's empty chair.

Nineteen

EARLY WEDNESDAY MORNING, LUKE emerged from the mist as she was picking oranges in the yard. He crossed his arms and for a horrible second she thought he was going to say something about her being with Jaydee.

"This must be a treat for you. Oranges don't grow in Colorado."

"True." She relaxed her shoulders. He didn't know. At least not yet.

Luke checked his watch. "I've got to go treat a fracture in Escondido. Would you mind running to Lucky Jack to check on one of Helen's yearlings this morning?"

"What happened?" *Not the yearlings, too.*

"He got into some barbed wire around dawn. Wrapped it around his leg. Helen got him untangled and the cuts are superficial, but I'd like you to see for yourself. The way things are going, I don't want to take any chances with the youngsters. Ranch vets aren't supposed to let their clients' horses die."

He'd told her sometimes it happened. Horses died. Nothing anybody could do about it. Obviously these weren't normal circumstances.

"I'll throw on some clothes, then I'm out of here." She dropped the last orange into the bag hanging from her arm.

"Thanks." Luke started to walk away then stopped and turned around. "Oh, by the way, the initial report on the first foal came back inconclusive."

"Nothing?"

"Not a damn thing."

"How can that be?"

He shrugged. "Now we wait for further tissue diagnostics. It could take weeks."

"Damn." Something tickled her throat and she started to cough. Her ribs hurt even worse this morning than they had last night. She'd tell Luke about seeing Jaydee at Coffin Bone and Roberto at The Triton later, when he didn't already have deep worry lines etched in his face.

"I gotta run." He slapped his hat on his head. "Make sure you get some breakfast. Coffee won't cut it."

"You sound like Kira. Next I suppose you're going to ply me with Jägermeister?"

That brought a smile.

Lucky Jack's yearlings lived in a pasture below the Hills' house so Helen could keep an eye on her "projects." Randi parked along the fence, scanning the vicinity to make sure Jaydee wasn't waiting to accost her. It was only a matter of time before they met up. Not a moment she was looking forward to.

She grabbed her vet bag and went through the gate, surveying the group of twenty or so adolescent equines. Most hung around the food trough, foraging for leftover breakfast crumbs. The injured colt stood at the far side of the herd. He lifted his head, wisps of hay protruding from the sides of his mouth. He was eating, at least. An encouraging sign.

As she approached, angry red stripes below his left knee became apparent. He was a handsome guy. Dark bay in color with large, intelligent eyes, straight legs and athletic haunches. You didn't get to be the fastest breed in the world for a quarter mile without having a serious booty. More thought and planning went into the breeding of these horses than into many human pairings.

Years ago, Helen had explained the Hill family training system: After Houston and Jaydee got each of the yearlings used to being saddled, bridled and having a human on their back, Helen took over to polish and refine their training. The three of them worked well together and knew the others' strengths and weaknesses. Lucky Jack Performance Horses churned out show ring champions. Animals so well-trained that all you did was think of a direction, a speed or the best line of attack for an obstacle or pattern, and the horse would execute it as if it had a direct link to your mind. Riding such wonderful beasts had been one of the best parts of Randi's college trips "home" with Jaydee.

Now Rebel was the ranch's foundation stallion, the kingpin. Houston had put all his eggs into one DNA basket by basing his entire breeding program on a horse whose owner had been murdered and who had two offspring dead for no apparent reason.

She spied Danny digging a posthole near the north fence line. "Hey, kid, want a break? I could use a hand over here."

He put down his shovel and came toward her—slow enough to be cool, not so fast as to be disrespectful, but he didn't make eye contact, even when he took the lead rope from her.

"Everything okay?"

He shuffled his feet. "Yeah."

"Sydney's fine, right?"

"Yep."

"You haven't seen Roberto, have you?" She took hold of her Pegasus charm, hoping the groom had made his way back to the ranch of his own accord.

Danny shook his head. "No."

Was he out on the street? Living in the canyon with the coyotes and rattlesnakes? Where had he gone? Why did he take off when she told him she was calling the ranch? Was he guilty of something?

Randi plucked the remaining hay from the yearling's mouth and put her finger on the artery inside his jaw. Fifteen seconds later she multiplied the beats she'd counted by four. "Thirty-six. Normal. If his temp's good, we'll get the cut cleaned and wrapped and that'll be that."

Danny still wouldn't look at her. If she didn't feel so guilty about slinking out of Jaydee's house at the crack of dawn, she'd be seriously irritated with his behavior. She removed a thermometer with a long string tied to it from her canvas bag. "You got his head?"

Danny nodded once, watching her from the corner of his eye.

She slathered the end of the thermometer with Vaseline and, attaching the clip to some tail hairs, inserted it with care into the colt's rear end. He shifted his weight and flicked his ears but didn't make a big deal out of it. Situations like this, Randi was glad she worked with horses instead of people.

When time was up, she moved the colt's tail aside and tugged on the string. "Hundred and one. It's fine. No need to worry unless it goes above one-oh-two. I'll need to check it tomorrow, and I'd like to have you help me again if you'll be around."

He turned away.

"Danny, what's on your mind?"

"Nothing." His eyes followed a truck and a loaded trailer moving down the driveway, away from the barns, heading toward El Camino Real. Another customer—leaving.

"How was your night in the barn with Sydney?"

"Fine."

"Well, you look like you've seen a ghost." She hesitated, inspecting him up close. "Or maybe it's just me."

Danny shoved his toe into a patch of grass. "You're nice, like Stacey was. And Jaydee—well, he doesn't seem like your type."

Perceptive kid. "It's not what you think, believe me." She crossed her arms. "Did you say anything to anyone?"

"No."

Whew. "Can I ask you a question?"

"I guess."

"Do you think Jaydee and Stacey got along okay?"

"I don't know. He used to yell at her. I'd hear him when I worked in the yard and they were inside the house. I think something even broke once."

"How long ago?"

He shrugged. "I don't know... a week, maybe."

By the way he chewed his lip, there was more. "What else?"

Danny stared at the ground, heaved a sigh and spoke so softly she had to strain to hear. "I don't want to get anyone in trouble, especially me, but he told Stacey she wouldn't leave Lucky Jack alive, and neither would Rebel."

After a trip to In-N-Out, Randi took the coast route home. The sunlight reflecting off the water and the pelicans soaring in formation against a canvas of blue lifted her spirits. Easy to forget your troubles with such a beautiful backdrop.

When she'd left her beloved mountains behind—the pinecones, blue jays and snow-covered peaks of the Rockies—deep down she never believed the move would be permanent, even if things *had* worked out with Jaydee. She'd had moments of a changed heart since then. There was something freeing about living where your entire left-hand side was an expanse of water as far as the eye could see. The ocean was a huge hunk of nature houses couldn't populate. For a girl who could never get enough of wide-open spaces, it was hard to beat. She'd miss it.

Cruising down the road, feeling better than she had a right to, considering she had a loco ex-boyfriend after her for something she didn't have, and a cop after her for something she didn't do, she rolled down the window and let the breeze caress her skin. The remains of her fries sat beside her thigh and she still had some Neapolitan shake left. She sucked on the straw.

Why did people have a constant need to upgrade their houses, cars, diamonds and even the purses they carried, when the real joy to be found in life was in the smell of fresh-cut French fries carried on a salt-air breeze? Shane agreed, dripping drool on the seat to prove it.

Would feeding him fast food make her a bad doggy-mom? One fry wouldn't hurt. She selected the longest one left in the box and he took it gently from her fingers with the tips of his teeth.

Her phone rang. Kira returning her call. She pulled to the side of the road, wheels rolling across the sand. "I'm sorry about your broken rein, Kira. I'll get you another."

"Don't worry about it. I'm just glad my horse was fast enough to get you away from that monster and that neither of you were hurt."

"Oro has serious speed. She saved my butt."

"You can thank me later, but that's not why I called. I wanted to tell you about a guy who just left the bar. Reddest hair I've ever seen. Built like a lumberjack."

"Is this some Irish drinking joke?"

"No joke. Listen, it's important."

"Okay. You have my full attention."

"Like I said, he's this big dude. Calls himself Fitz. Freckles all over his face. Anyway, he starts bragging about this real estate deal he's about to close, telling me how it's going to make him a fortune."

She wiggled the phone closer to her ear. "Go on."

"When I ask him what he's talking about, he clams up. Gets all antsy and says he doesn't like to drink because booze gives him a big mouth. Keep in mind he's already had a handful of beers and it's not even noon. So I tell him my Mustang Mai-Tais are half-priced, and he drinks three of them. Of course he starts blabbing and won't shut up."

"What'd he say?"

"He told me a tragic situation—a murder, of all things—is going to make him rich. He feels bad about the moral issue, but not bad enough to pull the plug. The deal is moving forward, he says. Full speed."

Twenty

WEDNESDAY EVENING, ASSISTED BY a pot of coffee usually reserved for morning intake only, Randi corralled her scattered brain cells long enough to pick up where she'd left off on Piper's interview before McWynn's second visit had brought her progress to a grinding halt.

"How does the buyer know the sperm delivered to them is really from Rebel, that you're not running some sort of bait and switch scam?"

"Good question. This should answer it." Piper had read from a legal-size form: *"I do hereby certify cooled semen was shipped for the above-named stallion and certify the semen was not at any time frozen. Houston or I can sign it."*

"What's wrong with freezing it?"

"Nothing. Frozen has to be packaged differently from cooled. Overseas shipments have to go that way, because the cooled semen won't last. Transport takes too long. Frozen keeps indefinitely and is stored in specific tanks. We don't ship that far anyway. If someone wants Rebel's product, they're getting it cooled."

Two hours later Randi finished transposing her notes and organized the material in such a way it could legitimately be called a rough draft. Focusing on her article had been good for her, a pleasant change of pace from the constant worry that had taken up residence deep inside her bones. In the morning she'd polish what she'd done tonight before sending the piece to *HorseWorld*.

It was too early for bed, so she changed the strings on her Gibson, then spent the better part of an hour running through her favorite tunes. Old and new. Country and rock. Her voice wasn't great, and her chops were rusty, for sure, but Shane didn't howl the way he sometimes did, didn't even give her funny looks, and once she got warmed up, she fell into a groove and played until her fingers begged for mercy. At eleven she still wasn't tired, not surprising given her intake of caffeine, so she settled on the futon couch with Shane at her feet and flipped on the TV. How long had it been since she watched the boob tube?

Local late night news was promised after the commercial. Not caring about the talking insurance lizard, she muted the volume and tossed the remote on the futon before she went to the kitchen to make herself a snack. She poured some Cheerios into a bowl, added milk and a handful of dried cherries, took three steps, looked up at the TV and almost dropped the cereal on the floor. *Her* face filled the screen. A photo, an old one. It'd been cropped and enlarged, making the background indistinguishable.

She put the bowl on the table, milk sloshing over the sides, and sprang for the remote on the futon. It wasn't there. Must have fallen. Damn it! She plunged her arm down the crack between the cushion and the wall, felt the plastic with her fingertips but couldn't grab hold.

Sprawled across the couch, she cranked her head around and there was her name, MIRANDA STERLING, below her picture, now in the top corner of the screen for God and everyone to see. The attractive female news anchor said something with a serious face, then came a flash of Stacey standing next to her stallion followed by an aerial of Lucky Jack slowly pulling back to all of Rancho del Zorro. Randi's mouth went dry. Forget the damn remote. Scrambling off the futon, she stumbled over a boot on her way to the television. She stabbed the volume button on the front panel as her face faded to black and the woman said, "Back to you, Ted."

Shane ambled toward the table. The milk dripped over the edge and he licked it up before it fell to the floor.

Randi hurried to the window. A few of Luke's house lights were on but his truck was gone. If he saw her face on TV as all of San Diego learned she was being questioned for murder, would he fire her? Even worse, would he start to question her story and think there was a possibility she was guilty?

Her bungalow took on a sudden chill. She pulled on her sheepskin boots, put on a sweatshirt and, desperate for a familiar voice, called her dad. He didn't answer, so she hung up. It was midnight in Colorado and her father was the sort who kept the phone by his bed and the ringer on high in case of emergency. Besides, sober people were usually asleep by midnight. *Damn.* If he was out this late, chances were he'd be drinking.

The phone rang. She snatched it without bothering to check the caller ID. "Dad?"

"No. It's me, Kira. I've got the TV on at the bar. You're famous. Actually, more like infamous."

"What did they say? I couldn't hear it."

"Just that the police are looking at you as a person of interest. So far, you're their only lead."

Next morning, when it was six in Colorado, she tried her dad again. He answered, sounding groggy, said he'd been out late bowling. They exchanged a few snippets of small talk and he promised to call back later.

Her cupboard was bare, so, donning a floppy hat and her largest pair of sunglasses, celebrity style, she headed out to the local market. On her grocery list: beer, bread, sliced cheddar, a carton of milk, carrots and a case of Dr. Pepper. She squeezed the F150 between a Rolls and a Ferrari. It was a shady spot for Shane and she didn't have to worry about door dings. Old money and nouveau rich, both, would be careful opening their doors.

The Rancho del Zorro market, though conveniently located in the center of town, was small and pricey with narrow aisles. Frequented mainly by housekeepers and nannies, the elderly looking to get out and about, or the bored out-of-their skull trophy wives, the store rarely had a crowd. The best thing about it was that people left you alone. Fully engrossed in their own lives, they hardly bothered with anyone else's.

She'd grown up in a university town where wealth was concentrated in intellect, not bank accounts. She looked at the people here with a kind of reverse snobbery. It wasn't fair to them, and it was likely she was wrong in many cases, but she equated most of these people with superficiality and deceit and shifted the burden of proof to them to show her wrong. So far, the only person here who'd done that was Luke.

Inside the store, she rounded an end-cap and there stood Piper, looking like she'd bitten into something nasty. "I need meds for my stomach. Any ideas?" She cocked her head at Randi. "What's up with the disguise?"

She picked a bottle of wild berry Maalox for Piper and ignored the question of her appearance. Maybe Piper didn't watch the news. "Maalox works for me, and the taste isn't bad." She got a bottle for herself for good measure. "You're not feeling well?"

"It's been a shitty week." Piper twisted the top and cracked the medicine open. She poked a finger through the protective foil, tilted it back and gave it a swig.

"Agreed. How's our Something Special?"

"So far so good."

A Hispanic nanny, pushing a cart with white kids hanging over the sides and fighting over a piece of candy, squeezed past them. Piper waited until they'd moved out of earshot. "I intercepted a message for Houston last night. Thought you might be interested."

"What kind of message?"

Piper capped the Maalox and put it in the basket. "Blair's Horse Transport. About a pickup scheduled for Friday night."

"The night Stacey was killed?"

Piper nodded. "It was scheduled, then cancelled."

Randi took her sunglasses off. "That's weird. Lucky Jack has plenty of rigs. The only reason you wouldn't ask Houston to haul your horse would be if you didn't want him to know you weren't coming back."

"What I said in the lab. Stacey was going to screw him over."

Danny had overheard Jaydee saying neither Stacey nor her horse would leave the ranch alive. The way the evidence was adding up, Jaydee'd been true to his word.

Twenty-One

"YOU NEED TO COME down here." Kira sounded wor- ried.

"Why?" Randi braked for a slow-moving van with Arizona plates pulling away from the market.

"It's Houston. He comes in for lunch and orders a burger, right? Then he sits there staring off into space, not eating. Josh walks by with four shots. Houston gets up and helps himself to two of them right off the tray. Slams 'em down while Josh is standing there in shock."

"Seriously? I can't believe that."

"I wouldn't have either, if I hadn't seen it with my own eyes. But I'm not done. There's more. After he pounded the shots, he mumbled something to Josh, knocked his chair over, didn't bother to pick it up and left without a word."

"Did he pay?"

"He left a fifty for an eight dollar ticket, not counting the shots he swiped."

"Where's he now?"

"Heading toward the beach. I can see him through the

window. He's staring at the sky, not even looking where he's stepping. Something's wrong. I'd go after him but I'm swamped. I'd send a busboy, but Houston isn't exactly being sociable. He'd probably go off on my guy and I'd never see him again. I'm short-handed as it is."

The groceries were in the back. A right-hand turn would take her home; a left would lead her to the coast. This was Houston they were talking about. He'd never been anything but good to her. She flicked the turn signal down. The milk would have to wait.

Randi snapped Shane's leash to his collar and shielded her eyes from the sun. It didn't take long to find Houston. People intending to come to the beach wore swimsuits, shorts, flip-flops. Those who went as an afterthought came in jeans, boots and a Stetson. She caught up with him as he pulled long and hard on a cigarette. Smoking wasn't allowed in Del Mar, even outside. He'd stopped short of the water beside a woman with a herd of children using her legs as maypoles. The woman looked at Houston like he was a crazy guy out for her brood, held out her arms and corralled her kids.

Shane trotted to Houston's side and nuzzled his hand. Small talk might break the ice, get Houston to talk about what was going through his brain, but the only thing she could think of was to ask if he'd seen her on TV last night and she couldn't get the words out. He'd let her know if he had.

"Nice day," she said.

He gave a nod indicating he'd heard and started walking. She trailed behind, kelp popping beneath her shoes. Shane ran along the edge of the water, chasing first a flock of sandpipers, then a yellow lab with a tennis ball clutched in its jaws.

Houston squinted. "Kira send you?"

Randi jogged to catch up. "She's never known you to leave food on your plate."

"She's a mother hen with the best of them, isn't she?"

"It's why we love her, isn't it? It's all part of her charm." She parroted Luke. "Her strength and her weakness."

Beads of sweat clung to Houston's temples. He wiped them away with his sleeve. "One way to look at it, I guess."

Other than sweating despite the cool breeze, Houston seemed fairly normal. Maybe he'd calmed down after causing a scene at Kira's place. They walked the beach in silence until Randi felt comfortable enough to ask if he'd ever met a big redhead named Fitz. Like McWynn said, murder for financial gain was always an attractive motive, and anybody could have slipped into the barn unnoticed that night.

"No."

"Never seen a guy like that around the ranch?"

Like he hadn't heard the question, Houston veered off toward a rock near the base of the bluff and climbed it with surprising agility. No easy feat in cowboy boots. He settled on its table-like surface, pulled out another cigarette and stuck it between his lips.

Randi scrambled up the boulder after him, calling for Shane to follow, which he did, but halfway up he started backsliding, toenails clawing for purchase. Houston grabbed hold of Shane's collar and pulled him on top of the rock. All four feet stable, Shane shook his fur, spraying them with sand and salt water. *Take that, humans.*

Randi brushed the sand off Houston's sleeves. "Sorry."

Houston rubbed Shane's chest. "He's just doing what comes naturally. He's a good dog."

"The best."

"Helen and I had one like him once. I like big dogs. She's got those damn terriers and all they do is bark at anything that moves. She says they get rid of rodents. Far as I'm concerned, *they are* the rodents."

"Speaking of the ranch," which they hadn't been really, but close enough, "Helen told me you've had some lowball offers." She wanted to ask if the money was enough to cover Jaydee's gambling debt, but that might douse the conversation.

"We're not selling. It'd kill Helen. She had a rough childhood in the city. Her parents got evicted and the three of them lived on the street. I'm talking the alleyways of Chicago. Scarred her for life. Nope, that ranch is her church." He took the cigarette from his mouth.

The silence sat between them until Houston ground out the cigarette and tucked the butt in his pocket. "You ever think about taking a walk?"

"Right now? You ready to go back?" She braced her hands against the boulder, ready to launch herself onto the sand.

"No. A one-way walk. I mean hit the beach and head south. All the way to Rosarito. I'd park myself in a hammock with a lobster burrito in one hand and a Carta Blanca in the other."

She dried her hands on her jeans and thought again about the bloodstains Houston had seen. "Sounds good, but I prefer Tecate, in a can with lime and salt. And I'd go with you, but McWynn would slap the cuffs on me soon as I hit the border."

Houston didn't seem to be listening. "Mexico isn't what it used to be. Drugs and guns are too easy to come by these days. It's a shame. Go down there now, you might lose your head. There was a time that meant you got too drunk. Now, it's literal."

A crab skittered across a shallow indentation in the rock. Trips across the border had been one of her and Jaydee's favorite jaunts. "I heard you have a gun now."

Houston gave her knee a paternal pat. "Don't worry. I keep it hidden."

"You were the only anti-gun cowboy I'd ever met. How come you changed your mind?"

"Bought it when we shipped Rebel here from Brazil. Some people down there didn't want to see him leave the country."

"How come? You didn't steal him, did you?"

"I can't talk about Rebel."

"Why not?"

Houston looked out over the water. "I like you, Randi. It's unfortunate Jaydee treated you the way he did. If there was any way I could fix what he did to you, I would. That boy's always ridden hell for leather and lived for the moment. It's not the way I wanted him to turn out, but as parents, we can't always choose that sort of thing." He spat over the side of the boulder. "Matter of fact, you can go your entire life thinking you know someone, then find out you haven't a goddamn clue."

Tide was coming in. Soon it would be slapping against the rock. Houston was right about Jaydee, and his words helped soothe her wounded pride, but why couldn't he talk about Rebel?

Houston picked at a chunk of moss wedged in a crevice in the boulder, and when it broke free, he chucked it into the surf. Shane's haunches quivered. Randi laced her fingers through his collar and he panted hot breath in her ear.

"Funny thing is, I thought all this trouble was being brought on us by some outside evil. Now I'm starting to realize things may be closer to home than I'd like to believe." He frowned. "I don't like where that leads."

The waves moved closer with each break. Sea spray misted Randi's face. If she were the betting kind, she'd wager the farm she and Houston had the same killer on their minds.

Luke's vet manual sat heavy in Randi's lap. Diarrhea, pneumonia, septicemia and E. coli—all causes of death in foals.

"Kick him!" Helen's voice came through the F150's open window. Randi looked up from the book to find Houston's wife perched on the top rail of the arena fence. "He's not an egg! He's not gonna break!"

The boy thumped the horse with his heels, but his mount would have paid more attention to a horsefly than to the kid's useless legs. Randi smiled. Helen's group horseback riding lesson reminded her of her own childhood. Every week she couldn't wait for Saturday morning to roll around. Not even a foot of snow could keep her from the barn. For an entire day she was in heaven. Grooming, tacking up, riding, cooling out, brushing and putting away her horse, leaving him with a carrot and a pat on the nose—it was always over far too soon.

The boy's horse shuffled into a jog. "There you go," Helen said. "Now keep him there. Don't you let him break to a walk unless you tell him he can. He may be bigger, but you're the boss. Remember that."

Randi returned to the manual. She'd become obsessed with finding out had happened to those two colts, refusing to accept it was just "one of those things."

On the seat beside her, Shane's legs twitched and he alternated growls with whimpers. She reached over and tucked his stuffed monkey next to his head until his dreaming noises morphed into steady breathing.

Three of Helen's Jack Russell terriers were tied to a post at the base of a tree, the others held captive in a wire dog crate. One of the penned dogs must have done something to antagonize one of the tied-up ones, because a furious racket ensued. Within seconds, a few yips and yelps turned into a bench-clearing brawl, with snarls and yowls and screams like the dogs were going to kill each other, causing a lanky brown horse with a tall skinny girl on his back to bolt to a dead run. The girl lost her balance and, hanging sideways in the saddle, let out a bloodcurdling shriek.

Shane kicked Abu to the floor, bolted upright and pricked his ears at the window. Even the raucous Jack Russells shut up.

"Megan!" Helen yelled. "Stop him!"

The horse turned the corner and doubled its speed, running the straightaway, hooves pounding the ground, neck stretched out and ears back. Megan clung to the bay's ribcage, but without leverage on the reins, she had no way to stop him. If she didn't right herself in the saddle soon, she'd fall off and be trampled under the horse's churning feet.

The other kids had wisely pulled up their mounts and parked them along the rail. Four-legged time bombs waiting to explode—all of them. Randi sat helpless in the driver's seat. If she got out of the truck, the creak and shadow of the door opening had the potential to be a match on gasoline, and then there'd be a whole arena full of bolting horses and screaming children.

Helen picked up the megaphone she never used. "Whoa!" Her voice blasted like a foghorn.

The runaway horse screeched to a halt. Megan still hung at the horse's middle, looking like she wasn't sure if she should climb back on or drop to her feet. Silence fell over the ring as Helen made her way to the pair in the center of the ring. The girl slid off to land wobbly-legged onto the dirt.

With the kid out of immediate danger, Randi got out of her truck and joined Helen in the ring. Helen put her hand on Megan's shoulder. "You know what you gotta do. I don't have to tell you."

The girl's face said she'd rather do anything but get back on that horse.

"Be tough. You're a cowgirl, aren't you?"

Megan bit her lip but accepted a leg-up from Helen anyway.

It wasn't the kid's fault. Helen should have left her dogs in the barn, or in the house. She knew better. Clearly, something had her distracted.

Helen waited until Megan reached the others waiting at the rail before she turned to Randi. "I used to believe everyone was teachable. These days I'm not so sure." She propped her hands on her hips. "Houston calls me the ultimate optimist when it comes to getting these kids to ride like winners. I've still got a lot of work to do around here. Not giving up yet." Helen's steely gaze faded as her eyes fixed on a car coming down the driveway. She took hold of Randi's arm and squeezed. "Go tell that damn detective I've got nothing more to say to him."

Helen had picked the wrong messenger. Randi wasn't going to tell "that damn detective" anything, because she had no intention of being seen.

Twenty-Two

MCWYNN'S CAR SLOWED AS it rolled past the arena. Randi froze under the detective's stare like a deer in the headlights. If she didn't move, maybe she'd be invisible. The sedan stopped, waited, then turned left. It chugged up the steep road to the Hills' house where it disappeared around the back. She envisioned the worst. Jaydee had called a meeting with McWynn to expose how she was still in love with him. He had proof. She'd spent the night.

Trying not to worry—nothing she could do about it—she left Helen to her class and returned to her F150 to bury herself in the vet manual and resume her search for a cause of death that showed no signs.

She lost track of time until Luke popped his head in the window. Shane stood up, slapping his tail against the seat. He scrambled over the divider and pressed his meaty paws on top of her thighs in his haste to get to Luke.

He tilted his head toward the ridge. "That cop's up there."

"I know. I saw him."

"Marty will be back in town Sunday night."

"Marty?"

"My attorney friend. I told you about him at dinner, before we went to Rickert's party, remember?"

"Oh. Right."

"I've emailed him a statement with the basics so he can get started on your case."

"Case?"

"Yes, your case, Randi. You've seen the news, haven't you?"

Oh God. This was serious. Far more serious than she wanted to acknowledge. "So you witnessed my fifteen seconds of infamy? That's what Kira called it."

"I saw it." He pulled the driver's door open. "Scoot."

She lifted the center console and slid toward Shane. Luke folded himself behind the wheel, sandwiching her in the middle and making it impossible for her not to be aware of his warmth and the pleasant way he smelled.

He propped an elbow on the steering wheel. "All the automatic waterers in the barn were shut off last night."

"On purpose?" Last week, before everything took a turn for the worse, she would have assumed something like that would be an accident. Now she wasn't so sure.

"Hard to tell. A groom discovered it this morning. The horses were thirsty, but everything got turned back on before it became a problem."

"I hope Houston hurries up and gets those cameras installed."

"He's got a guy coming out this weekend."

"It's Thursday. He should put a rush on it. A lot could happen between now and then. Look how many 'accidents' have occurred this week since I found the first colt."

"Agreed."

Shane picked up his paw and thumped it on top of the manual.

"Is that one of my old vet school books?"

She removed Shane's foot. He licked her hand as she brushed aside the remnants of dirt. "I found it at the office. Mind if I borrow it?"

"Not at all. You don't have to ask."

She tapped the cover with her fingernail. "I just thought of an article in a veterinary journal I read a while back. A crop of thoroughbred babies died unexpectedly one year. At first they had no idea why."

Luke fixed his gaze out the windshield. "I remember that. It was traced to the pastures the mares grazed in. Something to do with the weather that led to high cyanide levels in the leaves of..." He snapped his fingers.

"Cherry trees."

"Exactly. When caterpillars ate the leaves, they left cyanide-laced poop on the grass."

"The grass poisoned the mares' milk. It didn't hurt them, but it killed their foals, which got me to thinking of the oleander somebody slipped into Sydney's bucket."

Luke shook his head. "Oleander would kill the mares before it got to the foals."

"Yeah, I guess you're right, but Tim Tyler brought up the atropine I give Zany when he was going nuts about his vet bill. I can't help but wonder if—"

"Randi—"

"Tyler even admitted he used atropine in a movie once."

"You can't compare these mares to the thoroughbreds. Those horses consumed the cyanide-laced leaves over a period of time. A one-shot deal wouldn't do the trick and, again, too large of a dose would kill the mares."

"But it's possible."

"Anything's possible. The problem is, it would have to be given slowly and in small doses by someone who had knowledge of poisonous substances and with the opportunity to deliver them."

"So you're saying..."

"I'm saying, Tim Tyler is not our man."

She crossed her arms. She almost wanted Tyler to be guilty of murder. He was cruel to animals and not very nice to humans either.

"You want to peg Tyler as a killer because you're upset by what he did to you—and rightly so—and because there's a rumor going around he wants to turn this ranch into a condo kingdom, but coming at it from obscure angles isn't going to get us anywhere."

She smoothed the fur on the top of Shane's head. "Of the colts that died, were either of them insured?"

Luke was quiet for a second. "It's inconsequential."

"Why?"

"I have to sign off on a newborn's health for the policy to be in force." He shifted on the seat and reached for the door handle. He pulled it open and stuck one foot out of the truck. "Neither of those colts made it to their first checkup."

The scent of orange blossoms wafted through the open window above Randi's kitchen sink. Finches in the jacaranda flitted from branch to branch, going about their business with single-minded purpose. Luke said that by June the tree's bare limbs would be overcome with a plethora of lavender blossoms and that afterward the blooms would drop and surround the trunk with a carpet of purple.

She'd become attached to this little house and its yard full of wild things. A deck with a hot tub and a three-stall barn out back, and the place would be perfect. Curious how things became dearer to your heart when the threat loomed that they might not be around much longer, and choosing to leave was a far cry from being *forced* to go. As her father was fond of saying, "You never miss the water till the well runs dry."

From outside, Shane half-purred, half-howled his "let me in and feed me dinner" plea. Right on schedule. Randi opened the back door and he leapt into the kitchen like his tail was on fire.

She took out a frying pan, slathered the bottom with butter, collected two pieces of sourdough and a couple sections of cheddar, then sliced an avocado. Comfort food. While the cheese was melting, she served up Shane's dog chow but left the bowl on top of the counter until her sandwich finished grilling. Shane eyed his meal as if to make sure it didn't get up and run away. Every few seconds a drop of drool fell to the floor.

Her dog wasn't much for mealtime conversation. Still, as a dining companion, he was more interesting than plenty of guys she'd gone out with, ones who were either too full of themselves or completely lacking in self-confidence. She hadn't found any-one in the middle. Such a man might not exist. She flipped the grilled cheese and reconsidered. Luke was the only guy she felt comfortable around who was at ease with himself at the same time. She never worried he might think something she said was out of line or that she'd ask a question he'd think was silly.

When her sandwich turned a crisp, golden brown, she put Shane's dog bowl on the floor. He dug in, tail wagging with gus-to. She finished eating shortly after he did, washed the grilled cheese down with a can of Dr. Pepper and took her plate to the sink.

No room in the dish drainer. She'd let things stack up this past week. Domestic chores didn't seem important the way they used to, so she left the stuff where it was but forced herself to sort through the growing pile of mail. Catalogs and junk mail were filed into the recycle bin. The new bills were piled on her desk next to the old ones.

Scooping an armful of dirty clothes from the floor, she put them in the washer, topping off the load with the last of her favorite lavender-scented laundry soap. Turning away from the clothes, she noticed the message light on her phone. *Blink, blink, blink...*

She pushed the button. Her father's brief, unnecessary state-ment of who he was and request to call him back was followed by a fumbling hang-up that took longer than it should have. Worrisome. The second message was from Karen Thornton, the editor at *HorseWorld*, who wanted to know how the artificial insemination article was coming along. Karen's voice was sharp enough to cut rope as she explained why she was getting nervous. Randi hadn't checked in lately and she'd gone out on a limb for her in the first place.

She had to get back to Karen, but it was her dad's call she returned first. He didn't pick up. He'd wanted to come to her aid and she'd denied him. If he'd started drinking again she'd blame herself, which was ridiculous, but old habits died hard.

She left a voice mail for Karen, promising to have something substantial emailed to her in a day or two. She hung up, hoping she'd told the truth. Heading for the computer she worked until her brain screamed *Uncle* and it was impossible to tell the cream from the curd.

At the faraway wail of a siren, Shane lifted his nose to the ceiling and let out a stream of mournful howls. His toenails made a clacking noise as he crossed the room headed for his bed, still muttering about the sirens. He scratched, circled three times, then flopped down, making himself into a compact furry doggy donut.

She glanced at the clock. Eight-fifteen and she could barely keep her eyes open. Was this what her life had come to? Twenty-nine years old, single, up shit creek with the cops thinking she committed murder and hittin' the hay before nine? Pretty pathetic. Shedding her clothes, she left them where they fell on the floor, crawled up the ladder to her bunk, curled herself into a ball and pulled the blanket over her head.

Horseback. A cloudless night sky. She touched her steed lightly with her heels and with mind-boggling speed and power he responded to her cue. Two bodies. One mind. There was nothing they couldn't do.

She woke with her chest slick with sweat. The clock read 12:37. Coyotes yipped in the distance. She flipped her pillow over to the cold side and tried to fall back to sleep. She'd give it ten more minutes, then she'd climb down and proofread her work. If she couldn't sleep, she could at least be productive. The article was *almost* finished.

In the meantime, she let her mind wander back to her dream. Her subconscious was trying to tell her something. The fact was, a woman could handle a thousand pounds of flighty, powerful horseflesh as well as a man. A woman could load a trailer, hitch it up to a truck and maneuver the rig, down the interstate or over a winding mountain pass. A woman could take a horse over a course of stadium jumps higher than her head, thunder 'round a cloverleaf pattern of barrels with pinpoint precision at a blistering gallop, or master the technical intricacies of a dressage pattern or a Western trail course with as much expertise as anybody with a pair of balls.

When it came to horses, men and women played on a level field.

Luke had been right. She'd been so focused on Tim Tyler as an evildoer, she'd pigeonholed him into the role of murderer. Then she'd pegged Jaydee because it was convenient and she hated him. In being so myopic, she'd overlooked something very important. Women were just as competent as men—for better and for *worse*.

Piper had unlimited access to everything at Lucky Jack. Piper didn't approve of the way Stacey was jerking Houston around over money. She believed Stacey didn't deserve a stallion as fine as Rebel. Not only that, but she despised Stacey's spoiled-princess attitude and how she thought she abused the power of her purse.

Piper knew how to handle horses, and wouldn't get her head kicked in while cutting their tails off. She also had the means and opportunity to contaminate Sydney's feed, set horses free on the sly, and shut off the water in the barn. Piper was convinced Stacey was about to cut off Houston's major source of income via Rebel's stud fees. Piper was as capable as they came, but was she capable of murder?

Twenty-Three

PIPER BENT DOWN TO unhook a blanket strap from beneath a horse's belly. "I'd be enjoying my coffee and bagel right now, warming myself in the sun, if I wasn't stuck doing Roberto's job. I don't mind helping Houston, but when Jaydee gives the orders, it kind of rubs me the wrong way." She slid the blanket over the horse's neck and gave Randi a direct look. "Know what I mean?"

"You bet I do." Randi zipped her jacket and shoved her hands in the pockets. The stable felt damn cold this hour of the morning, but she'd come early because last night's ruminations about Piper being a killer refused to leave her alone. Things felt different in the light of day. Dark-minded thoughts took on a brighter perspective. Piper didn't look the part, but plenty of murderers didn't. Stacey was killed on the next aisle down. Was it possible to be so physically close to where you'd recently murdered someone and act calm about it? Perhaps it depended on whether your life was better now, or worse, because of your actions.

Piper propped a hand on her hip. "Jaydee texted me with an

order to un-blanket."

"Where is he?" Hopefully far, far away.

"Who knows? A bar, somebody's bed, a poker room? The jerk didn't even have the guts to call me and ask me to do this in person. I'm busy. Got plenty of my own shit to do around here."

Piper left the stall with a bang and slid the adjoining door open, exposing a horse Randi had never seen before. The red roan gelding's color reminded her of rose petals floating in icy milk.

"He's new." Piper's scowl turned to a smile. "Came in from Chico on consignment. The girl used him for team penning, but she's off at college now and the family can't keep the horse *and* foot the tuition bill. That's their story, at any rate."

"Nice." The horse was a beauty. "So, hey, listen... I'm trying to finish up my article. Got a few loose ends. Can you help me out?"

"Long as I can talk and work at the same time. What kind of ends you got?"

"Frozen semen."

"What about it?" Piper hung the roan's blanket on the dowel outside the stall, swiping the clinging shavings off with her hand. "We don't ship frozen."

"Right, but if you did, how would you go about it? How would you package it?"

Piper crossed the barn aisle and slid inside another stall. "With straws."

"Straws? Bendable striped things?"

"Hardly. They're made of polyethylene."

"You said frozen required a special storage container."

"The straws go in liquid nitrogen tanks." Piper waved her hand. "Since you're standing there, would you mind taking off the black mare's blanket?"

Randi faced the stall of the horse Piper referred to. She'd forgotten the mare's real name. Everyone called her Lady Godiva because she hated having anything touch her body–halter, bridle, saddle, even raindrops–and, worst of all, her blanket, including when it was coming off. Most horses put two and two together, but not this one. She opened the door. Lady Godiva shot her a warning look and pinned her ears. Was this punishment for asking questions Piper didn't want to answer?

Horse teeth clamping down on your flesh didn't feel good, but neither did an elbow to the muzzle. Randi stood straight and tall, sending vibes that, despite being the smaller of the two, she wasn't gonna take any crap. When she was sure she and Lady Godiva had come to an understanding, she unhooked the buckles and eased the blanket off her twitching skin. Easy as pie. She gave the mare a pat on the shoulder and closed the door.

Randi folded the blanket over the bar. "How did Stacey come to own a stallion like Rebel in the first place?"

"You don't know?"

"Nobody ever told me."

"It was after she met Jaydee, but before they got married."

Married. The image of Stacey's face, wide and innocent the first time she introduced herself as Jaydee's wife, overlapped the mental picture of her dead in Rebel's stall. Both were unforgettable.

"You okay?" Piper peered out the bars lining the upper part of the enclosure she was working in. "You don't look so good."

"I'm fine." She plopped herself on a tack trunk in the barn aisle and stuck her legs out. "Go on."

"Stacey's lifelong dream was to own a horse people would take one look at and be blown away by. She had an ego about it. She wanted a stallion everybody and their brother would want to breed their mares to. And, of course, price wasn't an issue."

"Then what?"

"Stacey set her sights on Rebel after she saw him win the National Cutting Horse Association Championship Futurity. Can't say I blame her. Not only is he gorgeous, the horse is smart. Quick on his feet, like a cat. All you have to do is stay out of the way and let him get on with his job."

Piper came from the stall with that dreamy look in her eyes horse people got when they talked about one they felt was exceptional. "He can be a little arrogant in the ring, but I think that's a good thing. Got to show the cows who's in charge, you know? It's like, could you be Hugh Jackman and *not* think you're pretty damn cool?"

"Did Stacey feel the same way?"

"Cutting's in vogue with celebs. Stacey fancied herself running with the Hollywood crowd, and Houston's always had his eye on Rebel's bloodlines. He's big into lineage, you know."

"Is that why he keeps that fetus in a jar?"

Piper laughed. "I suppose."

"I broke it the night Stacey was killed, and the last time I was in Houston's office it was on top of the filing cabinet, good as new. I guess it's safe to tell him it was me."

Piper froze. "Don't say a word about it."

"Why not? At the very least I need to offer to pay for the new jar."

"Houston doesn't know it broke."

"Weird. The cops never saw the glass, either. Somebody cleaned it up. You?"

Piper dipped her head. "Houston called me out here after he found you with Stacey's body."

She didn't like the way that sounded, or the way Piper said it. "When I saw the mess in his office, I took care of it."

"Thanks." A regular Cerberus, Piper was.

"No problem. I fix things for Houston so he doesn't have to deal with them. Comes with the territory."

Did that include Stacey?

"Anyway, where was I?" Piper asked. "Oh yeah, after Rebel won the cutting horse title in the States, a cattleman in Brazil bought him, shipped him off to South America. The plan was to use Rebel to strengthen the breeding stock of the Brazilian horses. Get a leg up on the competition, so to speak. The guy's vision was for his Quarter Horses to become the best in the world. He had a chip on his shoulder for some reason and really wanted to kick our American butts. Rebel became a national hero down there. Not only with the gauchos, but with kids, old people, everybody. They made T-shirts with his picture, banners, all sorts of crapola. I remember reading about it and I made fun of it, but it was actually kind of cool."

"Why would the Brazilian guy sell Rebel if his new country was so enamored with him? Especially since Stacey was an American."

"He didn't sell him to an American."

"You just said he did."

"Right, but at the time, he didn't know it."

"You've lost me." Was Piper being cryptic on purpose, or did all her stories unfold like jigsaw puzzles?

"Houston did some digging and discovered Rebel's owner was in a boatload of financial shit. Trouble with some South American thugs. Even though he was totally strapped for cash, the guy had emphatically stated Rebel would never leave Brazil. Houston came up with an idea." Piper picked at something in her teeth, which seemed to derail her train of thought. "Maybe I shouldn't be telling you this. I don't want to get Houston into trouble."

"Come on, Piper. You can't start a story like that and not finish it. Besides, I respect Houston as much as you do."

Piper stared at the rafters. "All right, but you didn't hear this from me."

"Understood."

"Houston had connections. He'd done a couple of horse deals down there and he and this other guy had gotten to be buddies. His friend pulled some strings and Houston was able to hire a shill to do the deal."

"I get it. Houston's connections, Stacey's money. Pull a fast one on the guy and together, get the horse the two of them had been drooling over. Thus the partnership."

"Exactly." Piper sat on the trunk opposite Randi and hooked her fingers around her knee. "Rebel's owner didn't find out the shill had turned around and sold the best cutting stallion they'd ever laid their hands on to an American, much less to a California girl, until it was too late. It was great for Lucky Jack, and the highlight of my career as a breeding manager, to get a horse like Rebel, but..."

"But what?"

"Truthfully, the way Houston and Stacey went about it wasn't the greatest. Not illegal, but stupid all the same. Stacey's idea, of course. Those guys aren't the type of people you want to piss off."

Which was why Houston bought the gun. "You think they came up here and killed Stacey for revenge?"

Piper carved half-moons in the dirt with her boot heels. "The thought crossed my mind."

"Why wouldn't they take Rebel while they were at it?" A chill wind gusted down the barn aisle. "Why not kill Houston, too, if retribution was what they were after?"

"Don't think I haven't wondered that. You're asking a lot of questions. I don't have all the answers." Piper stood and brushed the dirt from her butt. "Let's get out of here and into the sun." She plucked her jacket off the wall hook and headed for the door. "I've got to make a run to Luke's clinic for some supplies anyway."

Randi tagged along. She wasn't finished with Piper. "Any idea what Stacey was doing in Rebel's stall Friday night? Was she waiting for the horse transport to pick him up? Then what?"

Piper shrugged. "Beats me. She was so prissy, right? But I swear to God she would have slept in the stall with Rebel if she could have."

"Jaydee mentioned that."

"Yeah? Did he tell you Stacey wouldn't give Rebel or Matt up, even when Jaydee told her to?"

They'd reached Piper's Corolla parked near one of the barns. Randi braced a hand on the hood. "Are you telling me the rumors about Stacey and Matt are true? And Jaydee *knew* about Matt?"

"He figured it out when Stacey told him she was moving to Matt's ranch near Indio in the desert." Piper fished for her keys. "Jaydee said that if she thought she was taking Rebel with her, she was dead wrong."

"How do you know?"

"I overheard their fight. So did Danny. We were in the lab. The lovebirds were in the breeding barn."

Piper had confirmed what Danny said.

"You should have told the detective."

"Why? He's got own ideas about who did it." Piper seemed eager to get away all of a sudden. Unlocking the door of the Corolla, she slid behind the wheel. "Anyway, I don't trust cops. I figure the sooner they leave the ranch alone, the better it'll be for Houston." She started the car.

Randi gripped the side-view mirror. As if that would keep Piper from leaving. "Stacey's dead. Someone is responsible. You've got to tell them what you just told me."

"Sorry." Piper put the Corolla in reverse and looked over her shoulder in preparation to back up. "You're on your own with that one."

Twenty-Four

THE TOYOTA ROLLED OUT of sight. Randi blew warm air on her hands. Had Piper shared Stacey's plans to leave with Rebel to take the attention off herself as a suspect? Or was it valid proof of Jaydee's guilt?

She skirted a stand of sycamores on her way to the paddocks and came upon Jaydee's Ram in front of the main barn, engine ticking as it cooled.

Circling the Dodge like it was an alien spaceship, she noted the broken headlight from Stefan's iron gate. No sign of Jaydee. She gave the handle a tug and the door swung open. He wasn't big on locking things.

Inside the cab a strand of braided horsehair hung from the rearview mirror. The dashboard shone like it'd just been wiped with Armor All. No fast food wrappers or any other trash in sight. The backseat was a different story, littered with papers and all sorts other junk Jaydee had tossed there. He was a pack-rat, forever losing things that turned up in the back of his car. His wallet, textbooks, phone numbers and wads of cash. The reason for that ridiculous car chase could very well be buried under all the debris. Maybe what he'd been frantically searching for was under his nose the whole time. A long shot, but she had a few minutes and Jaydee wasn't around, so...

Would she know "it" if she saw it? She crawled onto the backseat, pushing aside a pile of sweatshirts, a couple belts, a handful of baseball caps, a roll of toilet paper, two more foosballs, and couple of plastic bags and a shank snaffle. What was the deal with the foosballs? Had he turned to gambling on that game too?

The remainder of Jaydee's clutter consisted of ranch catalogs and invoices for feed and supplies. She brushed away one of the pieces of junk mail and, lo and behold, a pile of room key cards rained down upon the floorboards.

A door slammed high on the ridge.

Crouching, she peered out the window to see Jaydee trotting down the winding path from his house in a black long-sleeved shirt and matching slacks. He might have dressed the part, but he had a spring in his step that didn't seem apropos for a grieving widower. If he was heading out, he'd reach his truck in under a minute. She grabbed a handful of the key cards from the floor, shoved them in her jacket pocket and scooted out of the Dodge. Ducking behind the nearest hedge, about four feet tall, she made a peephole through the thick leaves where Jaydee couldn't see her.

She didn't have to wait long. When he got to the Dodge, Jaydee pulled out his keys and climbed inside. He took out his wallet and inspected the contents then opened the glove compartment and removed a flask. He drank, wiped his mouth and traded the flask for a cigarette case. A match flared. No Camel or Marlboro. This was handmade, long and skinny. He held the smoke as long as possible before spewing a skunky-smelling cloud.

He punched some numbers into his cell. "Hey. Is it a go?" A pause. Randi strained to hear the rest of what he was saying, pressing her head against a thorny branch. "That's bullshit, man. You're ripping me off... yeah... well... that's your opinion...

whatever. Meet me in fifteen." Jaydee disconnected and slid from the truck, slamming the door so hard the Dodge rocked on its wheels. He pinched the end of the joint, stuffed it in his pocket and started back the way he'd come, shuffling back up to the house. The spring had left his step.

Randi waited until he'd closed the front door before moving into the clear. Who was ripping Jaydee off? Fitz? Tim Tyler? How? For what?

The squeak of the garage door drew her eyes to the rear of Jaydee's house. A few seconds later a car emerged. A low-slung flash of sliver, followed by a plume of dust, sped down the drive-way. Stacey's new Mercedes SL.

Randi sprinted for her truck. She'd have to hurry to catch the SL. She jumped in and gunned it, praying no dogs, rabbits or chickens were out meandering as she hurtled down the drive-way, catching the Mercedes the instant before it turned onto El Camino. She followed as far back as she could without losing him, but the road was practically deserted. He'd see her tailing him if he bothered to look in his rearview mirror, but she wasn't all that worried. Jaydee had never been one to look back.

Thirteen miles north on I-5, Jaydee took the last exit before Camp Pendleton's one hundred twenty-five thousand-acre buffer between San Diego and Orange County. The Marine Corps base encompassed prime Southern California real estate, where wildlife and habitat protection was one of their top concerns. Thank God for a few good men.

The off-ramp coiled around in a hairpin turn and, at the bottom, in the shadow of the freeway overpass, sat a brown stucco building with a red tile roof. Above a dark-paneled doublewide door, spelled out in cursive white bulb lights—the chasing kind— was the word *Stingray*.

Jaydee drove the Mercedes to the left. Randi headed right. Hooking her purse over her shoulder, she went around the back of the building. There were no windows on this side, just a narrow strip of dirt littered with broken bottles and cigarette butts. A weed-covered embankment rose sharply beside her, and the traffic from the interstate roared above her head, the ground shaking beneath her feet each time a heavy semi passed by.

She reached the edge of the building and braced a hand on the stucco, slowly tilting her upper body to peer around the corner. Jaydee sat behind the wheel of the SL. She jerked her head behind the wall and waited. The sound of Merle Haggard punched the air. Jaydee had always been a fan of what he called outlaw country. Fitting.

She hid behind the wall for a song and a half, at which point Jaydee cut the music off and another car pulled beside him. Three doors slammed and the second car idled. There was some huffing and grumbling, then a man's voice said, "Get over it. You want to play, you gotta pay."

More protests and door slamming. Stacey's Mercedes fired up. Both cars reversed and pulled out of the lot, leaving her surrounded by silence. Jaydee had done some type of deal, in under three minutes flat, but what? She stepped around the corner, surprised to see Jaydee heading toward the Stingray's front entrance, shoving something in his back pocket. Where was the Mercedes?

She followed him inside. She'd imagined the Stingray to be a dive bar with a concrete floor, a stage set up in the far corner, rows of colored spots tracking along the ceiling and a haze of smoke drifting over the sparsely populated barstools. In contrast, the place reeked of disinfectant, had beige and brown textured carpeting and NO SMOKING signs posted everywhere. No stage, no spotlight, just a barricade of potted palms separating the entrance from a gaming room.

Jaydee took a seat at one of the tables, facing the opposite wall. Randi kept going past the game room into a café called the Rat Pack. Older men in faded jackets mixed with clean-cut military types sat at the tables. Not including the waitress, she was the only woman. She shouldn't have been surprised. What did she expect from a restaurant with a rodent in its name?

She parked herself in front of an ATM with a view of the game room and pretended to read the terms and conditions of withdrawing money while she waited for Jaydee's next move. The dealer tables were evenly spaced over the carpet. Blackjack, Three Card Poker, Pai Gow and EZ Baccarat—whatever that was. She could get through a night of Hearts, Crazy Eights and Old Maid, but that was the extent of her card-playing skills. And as far as gambling went, after she lost her roll of quarters in the slots, she was more than happy to call it a night.

Flatscreen TVs lined the walls, broadcasting bowling, billiards and professional card games. More ATMs bookended a bar at the back. A dealer, a tall woman with cropped steel-gray hair and a string of Mardi Gras beads round her neck, made her way to Jaydee's table.

Randi's stomach rumbled. Looked like Jaydee planned on staying put for a while, so she retreated into the café and took a seat in a cushy black Naugahyde chair. A photo of Frank Sinatra hung from the wall. Beside him a neon sign flashed, "Steak and Lobster $9.99."

All she'd put in her stomach this morning was coffee. Luke wouldn't approve. The floor looked clean and the counters were shiny, so she took a chance and ordered a scrambled egg sandwich on a croissant and another cup of coffee, turning her chair to watch the front door in case Jaydee bolted before she had a chance to eat. Although... transportation might be a problem. Jaydee wasn't the type to ride the bus.

The egg sandwich arrived. Chunks of pineapple, cantaloupe and honeydew on the side. Pretty good for three-fifty, and it didn't taste bad either. Apparently the Stingray figured the less you spent on food, the more you'd leave at the poker tables.

Twenty minutes after walking through the door, she'd finished her food and was in desperate need of a bathroom. Too much coffee and, between questioning Piper and chasing Jaydee, no time to go. The waitress pointed to the restroom on the opposite side of the casino floor. It was unfortunate, but unless she wanted to squat outside, she had no choice but to venture past Jaydee.

She dared a glance at him. Wasted worry. Jaydee hunched over his cards, clutching them like they told his future. The player sitting to his right, a grizzled man with his baseball cap on backwards, looked like he'd just come from the Turner Construction site on the other side of the freeway. Jaydee was dressed like he was playing hooky from Qualcomm. Construction-man scratched his crotch.

From her seat inside the bathroom stall, Randi expected to read names and numbers promising a good time, but the walls were immaculate, and the only thing on the door was a bolted down sign: DOES GAMBLING HAVE A HOLD ON YOU? IF YOU OR SOMEONE YOU KNOW HAS A GAMBLING PROBLEM... CALL 1-800-GAMBLER.

By the time she came out, Jaydee was gone and so was the crotch scratcher. What the hell? He couldn't have lost all his money *that fast,* could he?

The dealer's eyes met hers and formed a question: *Are you here to play or not?* It got her to thinking. She hatched a plan as she crossed to the table. A scheme like the one she had in mind ideally required more time to think it through, but the tall woman stared her down. She'd have to make it up as she went. A plaque read: $10 minimum. $20,000 maximum. She didn't have ten dollars in her purse, or twenty grand to her name, not that she had a clue how to play these games anyway, and they appeared way too complicated to fake it.

She smiled as she took Jaydee's still warm seat. "This is my first time here. I was expecting ringing slot machines and people throwing dice and spinning roulette wheels."

"It's not Indian land." The woman's name tag read *Marta.* "Technically, we're a card room, not a casino, but this property has an exemption—California-style gaming."

"An exemption? Sounds like code for shady money changing hands under the table." She laughed.

Marta didn't. "I just work here, hon."

"Oh, right. Just kidding."

"Did you want to play?"

"Well, I'm not sure." She swiveled to see the front door. "Those guys sitting here earlier, did they hit it big?"

"One did."

"And the other guy?"

"He got a phone call and left."

Crap. Which one was Jaydee? "Sharp dressers have all the luck, don't you think?"

"Not this time." Marta shuffled the cards.

A phone call. Somebody must have come for him. Who? Coco? All Jaydee had to do was snap his fingers and she'd come running.

"It's policy not to talk about customers. You know how to play Pai Gow?" Her eyes were razor sharp. Marta was a card dealer. Marta read people for a living.

"I'm actually here doing research for an article. I'm a journalist."

"Is that so? What's it about?"

"Addictions. I do a column for the paper. This week I'm covering gambling." She hated to lie. Not only was deceiving people wrong, she was really bad at it. At least the journalist part was the truth.

"What paper?"

"The *North Coast Times*." It was the first one that popped into her head, and by the time Marta could validate it, she'd be long gone. "Would you like the number of my editor? Or my business card?"

"No." Marta paused. "I trust you."

Guilt. The topping on the cake. "I was hoping you'd talk to me. If anybody comes in, we'll stop and I'll disappear."

Marta reshuffled as she checked the room. Everyone in the building, save for the two of them, was in the café. She made a call. "How long? Okay." She hung up. "You've got ten minutes till the boss comes back."

"Great. Thank you. Okay, let's see..." Where to start?

"You need some paper? A pen?"

"I have a good memory." Right, mind like a steel trap. This was how lying got you into trouble. "My angle is to get inside the brain of the compulsive gambler. I don't know if you run across those types."

"I get all types in here, and my late husband was a GA counselor. His kid brother had it bad. He's still doing time."

If Randi had a tail, it'd be wagging.

"We worked the Strip together till he died. Two years ago, I came out here on my own."

"Really? I'm a recent transplant myself. How do you like it?"

"It's a different planet from Vegas, but most places are." Marta fingered the beads round her neck, pulling the strand of purple even with the green and red. "I'm not used to how early things shut down, but it's nice to get away from the crowds. How about you?"

"Jury's still out."

Marta looked clear through her. "What else do you want to know?"

"How do people get hooked?"

"Don't you have vices?"

"Definitely. I'm not real great at picking men and sometimes I drink too much. At least both of those include a few thrills, but losing money? I don't get that at all."

"Gambling's an escape, hon, like booze or drugs. They win a few times and they get the bug. Before they know it, when they're at the table, or the track, or in front of the machines, they're in the zone. It's an intense chemical experience. A fireworks show in the brain."

"Are certain people predisposed?"

"My theory," Marta put a hand on her hip, "and keep me anonymous—I see my name in the papers and I'll hunt you down—is that some people have the seed, but you can't become an alcoholic before you take your first drink. They start out slow, win a little and get cocky. It's a thrill, but instead of cutting their losses, they keep at it. After a while they lose perspective, forget when to hold 'em and when to fold 'em, as Kenny Rogers says. Most of the time alcohol is involved. Sometimes drugs. It loosens them up."

"Even in the middle of the day?" Jaydee had started his party about eight this morning.

"Clock time becomes a non-issue to people with a problem. Hours, days, they all run together, and when the money runs out, they hit the ATM and start over again. Personal bank accounts are easy to drain and the first thing to go."

"What next?"

"Nonessentials: jewelry, clothing, antiques—whatever's been gathering dust. Then it's the things they *do* need: cars, houses, rent, food money. If there's a family involved, or a significant other, that's when it hits the fan. I had a guy come in here last month and start screaming at his girlfriend sitting at my table. He went to ride his Harley, found out she'd sold it two hours prior. Practically dragged her out of here by her hair. Manager called the cops on him."

"Yipes." *Yipes?* Good one. An intelligent journalistic remark. Luckily Marta was on a roll.

"The addict doesn't just wreck his, or her, own life, they take anybody that cares about them down with them."

"After they run out of stuff to sell, then what?"

"Beg, borrow, steal. First it's from those dumb enough to lend them money. Myself and my late husband included. My brother-in-law told elaborate stories about how he got screwed by so-and-so and needed more time to pay it back, which he never did. When he ran out of people to borrow from, he started to steal. From there it was a giant spiral downward." Marta squared up the cards and cut the deck. "Addicts will do whatever they have to do to get their hands on more money, even if it means ending up homeless on the street or doing time behind bars."

"Is there anything you can do?"

"For my brother-in-law, no. In here, a couple people have hinted they need help. I slip them the number of a GA member, a guy who was my husband's friend. If my boss knew, he'd fire me in a heartbeat—never mind the signs the gaming commission makes him put up in the bathrooms."

"Your secret's safe with me." Randi collected her purse and dug for her keys. "This has been most helpful, Marta. Thank you so much. You've been great, but I gotta run back to my desk before I forget what you've told me."

"You got it, hon. One more thing. The guy you're looking for, Mr. Sharp Dresser?"

Randi feigned surprise.

"I saw you eyeing him when you came in the place. He's got it bad. Set your sights on a man with some stability and you'll be a lot better off."

Twenty-Five

"BLUEBERRY MUFFIN?" KIRA ASKED from across the bar.

"No. Thanks though."

"They're from the bakery down the street. Just arrived. Fresh as a Frenchman."

"Cute." She smiled. "I'm not hungry."

"Blueberries are good for you."

"All right, all right, I'll take a muffin, but keep the Jägermeister capped."

"That reminds me. I came up with a new drink. I call it a 'Mule Kick.'"

"Sounds painful."

"On the contrary. It's quite smooth. Two shots of espresso, one of Baileys Irish Cream and a splash of vodka. I top it with a chocolate mint leaf."

"How do you know it's smooth? You don't even taste it."

"I combine the nonalcoholic stuff first, and if that works, I rely on memory. Want to try one? Perfect for a morning pick-me-up."

"Nope. Pass. I appreciate the offer, though."

"Suit yourself." Kira reached into a pastry case and handed her a small plate overflowing with blueberry muffin.

Randi took a bite; it melted in her mouth. "I just watched Jaydee sell Stacey's new Mercedes outside of this place called the Stingray. You heard of it?"

"Yeah. It's a card room up the coast. What happened?"

She told Kira about tailing Jaydee, following him inside and her discussion with Marta afterward.

Kira smoothed her ponytail. "She's right. Nobody beats the house. Not in the long run. Why do you think that Wynn guy lives in his penthouse suite with a bed full of babes? You won't find him hunched over the craps table crying into his Kamchatka and spilling ashes on the carpet like the rest of the poor slobs. There's a reason for that."

Randi dug into the pocket of her sweatshirt and spilled a handful of the card keys onto the bar. "I found these in Jaydee's truck."

Kira narrowed her eyes. "*In* his truck? What were you doing in his truck? Were you two in the backseat?"

"Of course not. It was *without* his knowledge or permission."

"Well, then, that changes things." Kira fanned the pile of cards with her fingers. "Luxor, Bellagio, Venetian." She shook her head. "I don't get it. How's Jaydee making that kind of cash? Not training horses. We know that much." She pointed to the napkin. "Whatcha writing?"

"Just making some notes." She flipped the napkin so Kira wouldn't have to read upside down. "People with motives. Weak or strong, no matter: Houston, Piper, Tim Tyler, Jaydee, Matt Watson, Fitz and unknown Brazilian thugs."

Kira gave it a glance. "Why Houston? Granted he was acting bizarrely out of character the other day, but still..."

"He and Stacey came to an agreement on how to divide the profits from Rebel's stud fees. Nothing was in writing. Stacey took advantage of their relationship to change the terms in her favor. After that, things went downhill between them." She couldn't tell Kira about Houston and Helen's financial woes. It was hard to find fault with Kira, but she did have a problem keeping her lip zipped.

Kira held a wineglass up to the light checking for water spots. "Keep going. Who's next on the list?"

"Matt and Stacey. Affair or friends? Helen says affair, as you and Piper do, but Matt says friends."

"I know what I saw."

"Anyone who got a look at me hanging all over Jaydee at the Triton could easily have drawn the same conclusion, and we both know nothing could be further from the truth."

Kira shook her head. "Stacey wasn't drunk when she and Matt were making cozy in the booth, nor was she drugged. Not to toot my own horn or anything, but I'm hardly ever wrong about relationships. If I had known you in college, I could have saved you a lot of heartache."

"Hindsight."

"Doesn't it bug you that you don't know if you slept with Jaydee or not?"

"Are you kidding? It's driving me crazy, but what am I going to do? Ask him?"

"Good point. He'd brag till he was blue in the face, even if he was making it up." Kira poured a glass of water and propped a lemon wedge on the lip. "What about all the other weird stuff going down at the ranch?"

Randi doodled some M-shaped seagulls along the edge of the napkin. "The two dead colts. Mysteries, both of them. Then we have the tail cuttings and the water shut-off. Not to mention the poison leaves in Sydney's feed and Zany running down the middle of El Camino Real." She shifted on the stool. Something in the bar mirror caught her eye. Leaning over, she motioned for Kira's ear. "Those cops," she whispered. "How long have they been sitting there?"

"About five minutes. Came in right after you did."

"*Right* after?"

"Shortly, yeah."

"How long have they been looking at me?"

Kira took a step back, checked the police and cocked her head. "Don't you think you're being a little paranoid? You can't see where they're looking. They're wearing sunglasses."

"It's not that bright in here."

"This is SoCal, babe. Wearing sunglasses may or may not have anything to do with the sun."

In addition to mirrored glasses, both policemen wore fitted britches and gleaming knee-high boots. Motorcycle cops. Kira was wrong. Their heads were turned in her direction. They'd heard about her at the station, seen her on TV and had orders to follow her and catch her hooking up with Jaydee. She wasn't being paranoid.

Ten minutes later, the cops got up and left. Kira gave Randi her "I told you so" look and Randi smiled, paid the bill and said goodbye. She figured if she was going to make any headway on what happened to Stacey, she needed to talk to the horse transport company. A pickup had been scheduled for last Friday, but it didn't happen. The transport was cancelled. By who? Jaydee? Did he head straight to Rebel's stall to take care of Stacey? Would that better his financial situation and fill his pockets for his gambling addiction?

Blair's Horse Transport was in the "barrio." Not a real *barrio*. No gang members on the corners or anything like that. North County's version equaled blocks of Mexican restaurants bordered by industrial warehouses. That was as hardcore as it got.

The transport company sat at the end of a long brick row. A truck yard filled the rear with vans and trailers not in use. The loading docks were empty and the retractable metal doors were closed tight. Through the office's glass panel, beneath the words BLAIR'S TRANSPORT, a desk and some cabinets were visible. A bell jingled when Randi opened the door.

A woman with hair piled high on her head, glasses hanging from a chain and a string of pearls around her neck collected her glasses from her chest and put them on. The plaque on her desk said PATTY. Straight out of the *Far Side* comic strip. "May I help you?"

"I hope so. Someone from Lucky Jack scheduled a horse to be picked up Friday night. A stallion, I believe." She sat in the nearest chair. The office smelled musty and every visible surface had a light coating of dust. "Apparently it was cancelled that same night. I'm looking for the name of the person that made that call. Any way I can find out?"

Patty pushed off the balls of her feet and rolled her chair to a wall-sized map of Southern California. She put a finger on a purple section. "That's Stuart's area. He might know."

"Can I talk to him?"

Patty shook her head. "Vacation."

"When will he be back?"

"Tuesday."

"Can you pull the job up on your computer? Or do you have a file? It's important I find out who called off the deal."

"That's where the girl got killed, right?"

"Yes."

Patty tapped her keyboard. "Sorry. System's still down. Been that way for forty-five minutes."

"Does Stuart have a cell? Can you give me the number?"

She considered the request for longer than Randi thought polite, but eventually she jotted down a number and handed over a sticky note. "I gotta warn you, he doesn't like to be bothered when he's not working."

"Thank you." Randi stood up and tucked the number into her pocket. She pushed through the door, jingling the bell again. Patty wasn't the most helpful secretary in the world, but she'd earned some good karma in the end.

Stuart didn't answer. She left him a detailed message, hoping he could deliver the goods before it was too late.

Twenty-Six

FRIDAY'S MAIL CAME EARLY. A brown envelope curled into a U-shape filled the box. Postmarked San Diego. No return address. Randi ripped it open as she climbed the porch steps. An eight-by-ten glossy. The glare of the flash reflected like a fireball off Jaydee's Dodge. One leg in the cab, one leg out, she held the magnum of J. Roget champagne neck down to prove it was empty. Arms intertwined with Jaydee's, she grinned like a simpleton.

Slamming the front door with her foot, she pulled out a chair and sat down hard. Dumbfounded, she stared at the photo for a good ten seconds before her brain kicked into gear. Who did this? Was this the only copy? If not, how many were out there? She glanced up the driveway at Luke's mailbox. Had he gotten one?

Oh God—the cops.

There was no way to know if McWynn had his hands on this, but Luke's box was a short walk away. She was giving serious thought to going through his mail, but before she could get up the guts, he appeared at the top of the driveway, heading her way. She shoved the photo in the junk drawer and scampered to the bathroom to run a brush through the tangled mop on her head. She was swigging mouthwash when he knocked. Shane spun in circles with excitement as Luke stepped through the door. She avoided eye contact. Seemed like the first thing Luke did each day was check her demeanor and overall well-being by looking into her eyes. "Want some coffee?" she asked.

"Everything okay?"

"Yep. Fine." She went into the kitchen.

"Coffee sounds great." Luke pulled out a chair. "Thanks." He scratched a crusty spot on the table with his thumbnail.

Neither spoke until the coffeemaker beeped. She filled the mugs, poured a generous splash of milk in hers and added a sugar-in-the-raw to Luke's cup. "It's hot. Might want to give it a minute."

"Thanks for the warning." His breath made tiny ripples across the surface.

Why was he here? Had he seen the picture? Doubtful. He wouldn't be acting all friendly if he had. She took the seat across from him and picked a neutral topic to get a conversation rolling. "Heard from your kids?"

"I got an email from Ursula last week."

Every time he said his ex-wife's name, a purple-skinned octopus with ruby lips and a thatch of white hair popped into Randi's head. What would Luke think if he could read her mind?

"She says ever since Mason turned fifteen he's been giving her a hard time. Like someone flipped a switch. Sweet little boy to hell on wheels."

"Testosterone."

"'Fraid so."

"What about Jen?"

"Showing interest in high heels and boys. Too soon, if you ask me."

Randi sipped her coffee. "I don't have much experience with the male teenager, but as for your girl, buy her a horse. The sooner the better."

"Great idea, but Urs wouldn't go for it."

"Horses are good for girls."

"No argument there, but they also remind her of me."

"She's the one who wanted the divorce—right?"

"Doesn't mean she doesn't blame me."

"Well, from what you've said, you two are like night and day."

"I should have caught a clue when she started handing out house keys to every handyman in Montana." He put a hand on the back of his neck. "They were handy, all right."

"You were twenty. No one should get married at twenty."

"I think it could have worked—with the right person." He twisted the band around his wrist. The silver caught the sunlight and reflected off the wall.

"I've always meant to ask where you got that. It's very unique."

"Came from my brother."

Luke had never mentioned a sibling.

"He's dead."

"Oh. I'm so sorry." She couldn't have known, but that didn't make her feel any less like a fool.

He shrugged. "It's okay. You didn't know."

Questions loomed, but Luke looked so sad she couldn't bring herself to ask. Turned out she didn't have to.

"Car accident. He lived in New Mexico. This bracelet was his. Used to belong to a Zuni uncle of ours on my mother's side."

"What was your brother like?"

"He took after our father." Luke smiled. "He got the Scandinavian genes. Light hair, blue eyes, fair skin, like yours. It's funny. I always wanted to look like him, and he wanted to look like me. Dark and mysterious, he used to say."

"It looks good on you."

"The silver band or the mystery?"

"Both."

The corners of his mouth turned up as he lifted the mug to his lips. His cell rang and his hand jerked, causing a wave of coffee to slosh to the floor. He glanced at the screen, face flashing with recognition. "Huh. Whadda ya know?"

He ignored the spill and the ringing continued.

"Aren't you going to answer it?"

"Nah. She'll leave a message."

"A client?" Why had she asked? None of her business.

"Barbra."

Randi reached for a kitchen towel and wiped up the coffee, scrubbing harder than necessary. Luke was single, attractive, kind and great with animals. Why wouldn't Barbra be calling? Why did she let it get to her? Luke was her boss, not her boyfriend.

He bent down. "Here, let me get that. You don't have to clean up after me."

"It's done." She scooped up the towel, balled it up and tossed it in the general direction of the sink. "Does Barbra practice soring?" Her heart beat faster, and her voice went up a notch. "I hear it's what the Saddlebred people do. At least the ones who value winning more than the horse's welfare." She felt like a puppet controlled by an evil puppeteer. Somebody else was voicing these thoughts, not her.

Luke gave her a funny look. "Who told you that?"

Piper had. She shrugged. "How does she get that super-high leg action? Metal spikes? Chains? Chemicals?" *Good Lord, shut up!*

"Randi... you're out of line."

Her skin grew hot. She paced the floor and forced herself to think about something else.

"Barbra's good to her horses. Her favorite gelding colicked last week, remember? She went for the surgery option without hesitation. Hung out for the entire procedure. What have you got against her?"

"Nothing." She hung her head. How embarrassing. She wanted to crawl in a hole. Even Shane coiled his body into a tight husky-like ball and tucked his nose beneath his tail, hiding his eyes.

Luke slapped his thighs, braced his hands and stood up. "Thanks for the coffee. I should be going."

She enjoyed his company and wasn't ready for him to leave, but since she'd ruined the moment with her catty comments, she couldn't think of how to ask him to stay without sounding like an idiot.

He walked up the driveway, checked his mailbox and retrieved the contents. Rifling through the stack, he looked over his shoulder at her bungalow then disappeared behind his massive wooden door. She never did find out what he'd come for.

Friday night at Kira's restaurant, on the hunt for Matt Watson, Randi surveyed the crowd and wished she'd made an effort to upgrade her outfit. Lipstick and earrings wouldn't have killed her. She just didn't have the energy to deal with things that used to seem important.

Bodies were jammed in every nook and cranny. Strong perfume went straight to her head and a high-energy buzz of conversation floated above the mass of people. All these happy, laughing, partying souls without a care in the world. It seemed like forever since she'd been one of them.

Matt sat at the bar. A female posse in short skirts, cleavage-baring tops and impossibly high heels formed a semicircle around him, eyeballing him like a cowboy would look at a slab of prime rib and a beer after a long, hard day in the saddle.

One of the girls was Coco.

Matt made eye contact and waved Randi over. Feeling like the chosen one—despite her grubby clothing—she lifted her chin and shouldered her way through the crowd to the bar. Coco gave her a hard stare and put down her drink. "*You* again." She grabbed the arm of one of her friends and pulled her away. Coco and her girl-gang retreated, bouncing off each other's shoulders and leaving Coco's drink behind.

"Wow." Matt raised his eyebrows. "I'm surprised she didn't

bare her fangs and bite." Despite the carefree lilt in his voice, the shadows under Matt's eyes proved he was long past due for a good night's sleep. He had on stonewashed jeans and an oversized Pendleton shirt-jacket. His hair was wet and instead of surf wax, he smelled of smoke.

"I'm not Coco's favorite person."

"That's obvious. What'd you do to her?"

"Nothing. She's in tight with the two people I'd like to see drop off the face of the Earth, that's all."

"Let me guess. Jaydee and—?"

"Tim Tyler. They're her 'buddies,' she says. Part of me wants to corner her and pick her brain. The other part wants to corner her and pull her hair."

"A chick fight, huh? Interesting. What're you drinking?"

She motioned to the bar, where Kira had already set out a bottle of Negra Modelo, lime wedge perched on the lip. Kira slid it across the surface. "I'm making her a cheeseburger, whether she likes it or not. She looks low on iron."

Randi rolled her eyes.

Kira ignored her. "How 'bout you, Matt? The *North Coast Times* gave my burger four stars. High praise from the fishwrap."

"No thanks. I'm taking a break. No meat of any kind for a while."

Kira seemed surprised. "No meat?"

"Nope. I will take a drink though."

"Sure thing. What's your pleasure?"

"Strongest you've got."

"That would be the Five Horsemen. Ever heard of them?"

"You mean the *Four* Horsemen?"

"Sort of. Served in a glass, they're Jack, Jim, Johnny and José."

"That's four."

Randi cleared her throat. "Kira adds Jägermeister to the mix."

Matt held up a hand. "Sold. I'll take it."

Kira caught Randi's eye and they shared a look. The Horsemen equaled loose lips even better than Kira's Mustang Mai Tai.

"Gotcha." Kira smiled through her freshly lipsticked lips then got down to the business of mixing his poison. When she finished, she handed Matt his drink. "Careful. Those guys pack a powerful punch. Especially when they're hanging out in the same glass."

"¡Salud!" Matt took a generous slug. He elbowed Randi and motioned toward the television mounted in the corner above the bar. "Hey, there's the jerk who attacked you."

Tyler's face filled the screen. The camera pulled back to show him arguing with a beautiful woman on a bridge. The wind shoved her filmy red dress between her thighs. Randi's stomach tightened at the sight of him. "Must be an old movie. He doesn't look that good anymore."

"He came at you hard that day. Why?"

"He was mad about his bill. He wants Zany in the show ring. Otherwise, he's threatening to sell him at auction."

"Wow, I've heard of angry customers, but he was way out of line."

"Thank God you came along when you did." She poked the lime down into her beer bottle, remembering the look in Matt's eye when he held the hammer over Tyler's head. On the outside, Matt professed love, peace and harmony, like a hippie born too late. But she'd seen a fire in him, an inner rage that burned white hot.

He took another drink. "Word is Tim Tyler might be the next Clint Eastwood."

She gulped her beer. "Sure, and I'm the next Jane Smiley."

"No, it's true. A friend of mine told me. She's a teller at his bank. A big production company is working on an epic Western. Something along the lines of *Dances With Wolves, Part Two.*"

"I hope they don't put Tyler on a horse. Or if they do, we better hope PETA is standing by."

"My friend said he wants in in a big way, but the bigwigs say he needs to come up with a lot more cash."

"Are you kidding me? He's trying to buy the role? I knew he had a huge ego, but *come on.*" There it was. Right there. Developing Lucky Jack would give him the capital he needed to launch his comeback.

Matt shrugged. "Money talks." He backed himself off his stool. "Speaking of talking, there're too many people in here. Come with me for a minute." Matt took hold of her arm and, before she could protest, led the way through the EXIT door to the employee lot.

It was much quieter outside, but with just one streetlight shining, it was creepy in a "Let's take Pauley out back" wise-guy kinda way. Matt stopped at a patch of gravel behind the dumpsters.

She'd been hoping the booze would get him talking about Stacey so he'd confess the truth about their relationship, but he'd left his drink inside.

Matt picked up a handful of gravel and let it trickle out between his fingers. "Guess how I spent my afternoon?" The glare of the lone streetlight showed Matt's hair was greasy, not wet like she'd first thought. How long had it been since he'd showered?

"From the look on your face, I take it you weren't surfing Swami's?"

"Unfortunately not. The swell was killer today, too." Matt shook his head. "Nope, I was stuck at a station downtown. The cops don't get it. Like I said, anybody could have picked up that hammer. It's not like I lock my truck or anything."

"You're not worried you might get ripped off?"

"I'll let the man upstairs take care of thieves."

Then there was Jaydee, the atheist, who never locked his Dodge, who always said most people assumed things were locked in the first place, which meant you didn't have to actually follow through with doing it.

Matt patted his chest pocket. "I could use a smoke."

He must not have sworn off meat for health reasons. "Good luck. This is Del Mar, remember?"

"Yeah. The People's Republic, where you can't even smoke in the out-of-doors. Get real." He lit up anyway.

Randi leaned against the dumpster. "Mind if I ask you a personal question?"

"Is it about Stacey?"

"Yes."

He waited. "I think I've answered enough questions for one day."

"Believe me, Matt, I understand, but I'm not the cops. I'm just trying to get to the bottom of this thing."

He took a drag. "What the heck. Shoot."

"Was Stacey leaving Jaydee to be with you?"

Matt turned his head away, looking like Shane when she tried to give him a pill. If she buried it in a treat, he'd gobble it down.

"Stacey loved you. You know she did."

His Adam's apple rose and fell.

"She wanted a divorce, didn't she?"

No response.

"We all know how Jaydee can be, and if you and Stacey were friends, she would have confided in you."

"I'm not comfortable breaking her trust."

She didn't have the heart to say the obvious, that Stacey was dead and wouldn't care. "You're helping to nail her killer. Some people think it's me. We both know that's not true, and I really need your help."

Matt reached for something around his neck, the same way she reached for Pegasus. A cross. Why was he running around with a married woman? It didn't make sense.

"Stacey stumbled onto something last Friday. The day she was killed. Something she wasn't supposed to see."

"What was it?"

"I don't know." He dropped his cigarette and ground it into the gravel. "She was afraid. I know that much. She refused to talk about it."

"Did it have to do with Rebel?"

He shrugged.

"Why was she taking him from Lucky Jack?"

"How did you know that?"

"Blair's Transport."

Matt took a deep breath and exhaled slowly. "I told her to keep Rebel at my uncle's ranch in the desert until we could figure out what to do. She wanted to get him as far away from Jaydee as possible. The horse would have been safe there. Jaydee doesn't know about the place.

"Stacey thought Jaydee loved her at first, but later she came to realize he was using her. Big surprise, I know. She told me once that people always grabbed at her to save themselves. Jaydee wasn't the first. A couple years ago she helped out an old boyfriend and a loser uncle too. One fell into the bottle and the other had a gnarly meth habit.

"With Jaydee, like I told you the other day, it's all about the dough." Matt rubbed his thumb across his fingers. "Stacey said you could feed a third world country with what he burned through at the Indian casinos alone."

"He told the cops he was in Vegas when Stacey was murdered, so how could he have killed her?"

Matt shrugged. "It's an hour flight. No big deal."

"So you think Jaydee went to Vegas, came back, murdered Stacey, then flew back to Vegas?"

"I do."

She glanced at the cigarette on the ground. Two things in this world she couldn't stand: those who hurt animals and those who littered. "Helen told me that earlier on Saturday, when Stacey was late for Rebel's collection, she was out with you."

"She'd finally worked up the guts to leave." His expression turned defensive. Subtle, but unmistakable. "She wanted to talk about it."

"The way Helen put it, you were at the wheel and she couldn't see where Stacey's head was."

Matt said nothing. She'd condemned him from hearsay. If someone told him she'd crawled out of Jaydee's bedroom at six in the morning, what would he think? "Are you the one who told Stacey to renegotiate her agreement with Houston?"

"Absolutely. The deal was bogus. The Hill family was sucking her dry."

"You loved her back, didn't you."

He struck a match. It burned down to his fingers before he dropped that on the ground too. "I wanted her to be happy. Jaydee didn't appreciate her. She was too good for him."

Randi was trying to decide how she felt about that statement when the EXIT door flew open with a bang. Kira stuck her head out. "Burger's ready. Come get it before it gets cold."

"Guess we should do as she says." Randi bent down to pick up the match and cigarette butt.

"Wait." Matt grabbed her arm. "I haven't gotten to the reason I wanted to talk to you. Why I brought you out here in the first place." He let go of her arm and, by the look on his face, she had the sinking feeling she didn't want to hear what he had to say.

"I was down at the Double L yesterday, shoeing a couple of their warmbloods. I forget how the subject came up, but one of the owners happened to mention you and Jaydee had been seen hanging all over each other at the Triton." Matt looked confused. "I seriously hope that's not true."

Twenty-Seven

SATURDAY MORNING, RANDI JOINED Luke inside the corral of a shaggy black mare named Tilly. "Hey there. What's going on with her?"

Luke crossed his arms. "How about you tell me?"

Tilly plunged her nose into the water bucket and sucked with noisy gulps. When she finished, she raised her muzzle and flapped her lips. Water streamed between her teeth and onto the dirt.

"For starters, she's a slob."

Luke laughed. "Excellent diagnosis."

Before her was a problem that had nothing to do with the noose tightening around her neck. If she could spend the entire day with horses—no Jaydee, no cops, no Tim Tyler and no condemning news reports—she could face the situation head-on rather than running scared.

Tilly walked without dropping her hip and with no hitch in her gait, despite a lump the size of a tangerine on her hock.

"Well... she's not lame." Easing between the bars, Randi put one hand on the mare's furry belly, palpating her hind leg with the other. "And she doesn't mind me touching it so, because of the swelling, I'd say it's capped. Knowing Tilly's personality, I bet it happened when she went to kick her neighbor, missed and smacked one of the corral rails instead."

Tilly swung her head toward the adjoining pen and flattened her ears at a flea-bitten gray cowering in the corner. Randi smiled. "She's a sweetheart to people but a hell-bitch to other horses."

"Very good. You're my best tech, you know."

"Luke... I'm your only tech."

"Well, so what? You're a good one. For your next trick, you're going to tell me how we're going to treat her capped hock."

"Bute, for sure. Then an ice pack and a corticosteroid injection?"

"Perfect. I'll handle the needle. You get the pills and the pack."

"Deal."

"We make a good team, you know."

She rubbed Tilly's neck, hating how her face flushed without warning, and praise from her boss seemed to bring it on like nobody's business.

"Before we get started, there's something else." The temperature of his voice dropped.

"What is it?" If Matt had heard about her and Jaydee being together, word had probably gotten around to Luke. The horse community was a hotbed for gossip.

"I spoke to your father."

She buried her fingers in Tilly's mane, watching Luke over the top of the mare's neck. "My dad? Why?"

"He's worried about you."

"How do you know?"

"He called me. About two this morning."

Oh God. "My mother always used to say nothing good happens after midnight. Was he drunk?"

She knew the answer. Luke didn't have to spell it out. Tears burned her eyes but she refused to let them fall. Damn, damn,

damn.

"Nothing you can do about it."

Untangling her fingers, she smoothed Tilly's mane. "I need to go. I have to see him. Soon as we know who killed Stacey and McWynn lets me leave, I'm getting on a plane." Luke was being so kind to her, she couldn't tell him she wasn't coming back.

He snapped a twig in half. Shane, waiting patiently outside the corral, perked his ears at the sound. "That's who I wanted to talk to you about. McWynn. He came by the office yesterday looking for you, but when he found out who I was, he started questioning me regarding the regularity of Zany's treatments. He wanted to know if you were telling the truth about needing to be here at the ranch the night Stacey was killed."

"What'd you tell him?"

"I backed you up, of course. It's not like I had to lie." Luke shoved his hands in his pockets. "Then he asked me if you'd been spending time with Jaydee."

The photograph. McWynn must have seen it. "Spending time?"

Luke took off his baseball cap and ruffled his hair. "As in clandestine dinners and sneaking over to his house. That sort of thing."

She inhaled. Pain shot between her ribs and she clutched her side. "What'd you tell him?"

Luke's eyes were steady on hers. "I said that scum-bucket is the last man you'd ever want to spend time with."

She held his gaze and concentrated on breathing slow and steady.

"What's wrong with your side?"

"An inopportune meeting with a tree branch. It's nothing."

Luke stepped forward, arm extended. "Let me see."

She was too embarrassed, felt too self-conscious to lift her shirt. His hand hung in the air as awkward as a refused handshake and that made her feel even worse.

A car rolled to a stop next to Tilly's corral. McWynn. The passenger window came down and he leaned across the seat.

"Morning."

"Detective," Luke said.

McWynn nodded. "Ms. Sterling, I have some things to discuss with you. In private. Can you come down to the station today?"

"Is that necessary?" Luke asked. "I've got her pretty well booked. With appointments, that is."

McWynn didn't look at Luke. "Then I'll come by your place this evening, how's that?"

"Fine." The lump of dread in her throat made more than a one-word answer impossible.

"Good. See you then." He made a u-turn and drove down the driveway.

"Thanks, Luke. For saying what you did."

"I've got your back, Randi." He reached for Tilly's withers and rubbed little circles with his fingers. The mare stretched her neck out long and low, closing her eyes as she relaxed under his touch.

For most of her adolescent life, Randi had wished she were a horse. Some things hadn't changed.

Twenty-Eight

NAIL SCISSORS, RANDI HAD discovered at Denver Tech, made an excellent tool for cutting away the old duct tape from a horse's injured and wrapped hoof. Small enough to maneuver, yet sharp enough to deal with tough, sticky material. She dug through her vet bag for the third time, outside the stall of the mare with the hoof wall separation, but couldn't find the scissors.

Her mind was on McWynn. Was he coming to her house to arrest her for real this time? They had the DNA results coming in, her prints were on the murder weapon, a photo of her hanging all over Jaydee was circulating, there were half a dozen people who'd say they saw them together, and Jaydee was doing nothing to squelch the talk. Probably fanning the flames. The way McWynn likely saw it, her goal was to get her lover back, along with the money and lifestyle she'd enjoyed seven years ago. Whatever it took to attain what was rightfully hers.

Would they haul her off in handcuffs, leaving Shane at the door with his head cocked and a puzzled look on his face?

She shook it off. Had to focus on the mare's injured foot.

Maybe Houston had some scissors. She left the barn and made the short trek to his office. Inside, she pulled out his chair and tugged on the drawer. It stuck, but when she gave it a serious yank, it jolted open, exposing a gun, its shape visible beneath a towel. Her stomach rolled itself into a knot. Was this what Houston considered "hidden?" At least the drawer contained a pair of scissors. She eased it closed and tried not to hyperventilate.

The fax machine next to the desk beeped twice and spat out a piece of paper. She craned her neck and stole a glance.

I agree to the terms for shipment of frozen semen of Hesa Rebel Man for the fee of $5,000. Alberto Silva Oliveira. His signature followed. The phone number on the top of the page was: 55-11-4394-2513.

Frozen? Was that a mistake? She fired up the computer and Googled international dialing codes. She found International Country Calling Codes and World Time Zones. A bubble sprouted from the earpiece end of the old-fashioned telephone: *Where are you calling from?* She chose United States from the drop-down menu. *Where are you calling to?* She typed in the number and, *to call from United States to Brazil...* appeared on the screen.

Brazil? Home of the cash-strapped-turned-pissed-off cattleman? Whether or not those people had anything to do with Stacey's death, it appeared they weren't finished with Rebel yet. Piper had stated more than once that Lucky Jack didn't deal in frozen semen, but Brazil was too far to ship cooled and the fax said frozen. Interesting. This was a contract, with terms this guy Oliveira had agreed upon. Surely he expected a signed reply. Somebody at the ranch knew about this deal. The question was, who?

She carried the paper to the copy machine, checked the door to make sure nobody was coming, made a duplicate, put the original back where she found it, folded the copy and tucked it into her pocket.

Downtown Rancho del Zorro consisted of charming over-priced boutiques, French or Italian bistros and two solid blocks of real estate offices. One could try on a ritzy outfit, eat a croissant or buy a country mansion. All of the above if you were super rich and it was a really good day.

Sandwiched between Zorro Properties and Café Soleil was Luke's veterinary headquarters. His truck functioned as a mobile office, and he had use of a large animal clinic/hospital on the outskirts of town, but he kept the brick and mortar space for his medical library, client files and supplies. Also, Randi suspected, so Mrs. Fowler, his aging widowed secretary, would have a job to pay her rent.

Randi came through the door. Luke, on the phone, had his back to her. He didn't turn around.

Mrs. Fowler, who doubled as a watchdog, gave her a stony glare. A minute later Luke hung up, but before Randi could say anything, Mrs. Fowler held up a finger, making it clear she, not Randi, was first in line for his attention. "Piper Powell needs a refill on Phenobarb for her Dobie's epilepsy," Mrs. Fowler told Luke. "She doesn't want the dog-sitter to run out while she's on vacation."

"Vacation?" Randi squeaked. Piper could go on vacation but she couldn't go home to Colorado to pull her dad out of the gutter? She hated to whine, but life truly wasn't fair.

"Yes. Vacation." Mrs. Fowler stared at her like she was brain-dead. "She's going to Brazil. I've always wanted to go there. I don't think I'll make it though. This office would fall to pieces if I left."

Brazil?

A coincidence? Highly unlikely. Did Piper plan on delivering Rebel's frozen semen in person? Did Houston know about this? Pieces were coming together but she didn't know how they fit. She touched the copy of the fax in her back pocket to make sure it was still there. She wasn't going to mention her discovery in front of Mrs. Fowler, who, like Kira, couldn't keep a secret to save her life.

Randi took a seat. "Luke... I was wondering... the control samples held back from each collection, do they contain enough sperm to impregnate a mare?"

Luke considered the question for half a second. "Could. Sure."

"So if I wanted to, I could skim off the control, freeze what I took, then ship it overseas whenever I filled an order and that way I wouldn't have to worry about shelf life?"

"It's possible, yes."

"What about the breeding report? Every mare bred to Rebel has to be logged in, right?"

Luke nodded. "Along with the date, method and location."

"When does it have to be done?"

"Not until the end of November. AQHA rules."

"What about the liquid nitrogen tanks used for storing frozen. Are they hard to come by?"

"No. You can buy them from any ranch supply catalog."

The Ford's tires rolled over the cobblestone parking lot of Jo-sé's Hideaway. It was Saturday night and the joint was jumpin'. Dusty work trucks, a few family vans and one bright red Ferrari. No empty parking spots and no white reverse lights.

About a month ago, Luke showed her a little turnout around the bend about a quarter mile down with a patch of earth big enough for a car and a half. From there it was short walk back to José's. She drove in at an angle and checked the clock. Five fifty. Ten more minutes until she was supposed to meet Kira, who'd called an hour ago craving restaurant food other than her own.

Holing up in her jammies, cracking a Negra Modelo and losing herself in a Kinsey Millhone mystery sounded like a much better plan, but Randi had agreed on dinner anyway. She'd told McWynn he could find her at home, but waiting for him was like waiting for a lynch mob. If he wanted her that bad, he'd have to work for it.

All the Hideaway's bar seats were full, so she found a place along the wall with a clear view of the front door. Rows of colorful piñatas swayed in the breeze. She smiled at a burro wearing a giant pair of turquoise sunglasses. Nearby, a band of strolling mariachis corralled an unsuspecting table, and four elderly Hispanics, resplendent in sequined black velour bolero jackets, belted out *Besa Me Mucho*.

A flash of movement near the front door caught her eye. For a second she thought it was Kira, but it turned out to be a food server carrying a tray of steaming Mexican *platos*. He stopped and set the tray down beside a man and a woman who didn't break eye contact to acknowledge him, or the food. The man murmured something to the woman. She ran her knuckles alongside his cheek, across his jaw and down his neck. He took her hand in his and smothered her fingertips with kisses.

Randi's stomach gurgled. Hunger. That's all it was. She'd be fine once she got some food.

Ten minutes later, Kira showed up, shrugging off a red leather jacket as she came through the door. The same hostess who had a thing for Luke led them to a booth.

"Sorry." Kira flicked her white-blonde hair off her shoulders. "Traffic was a bitch."

Randi ordered a Hornitos margarita on the rocks, with salt. Kira got her staple, a virgin Bloody Mary, extra spicy. Randi filled her in on recent events, beginning with the photo in her mailbox and ending with the news of Piper's upcoming trip to Brazil.

Kira started to ask questions, but the waiter appeared. He set down drinks and a basket of tortilla chips and removed his pad and a pencil from his apron pocket. Randi ordered an enchilada combo, chicken for Kira, cheese for her, with sour cream and rice and beans, to split.

Food items handled, Randi crossed her arms on the table. "Before you ask your questions, I need to bounce something off you."

Kira dunked a chip in the salsa. "Bounce away."

"What if Piper, who's in charge of preparing Rebel's sperm for shipment, skims enough off the control sample to make up a full dose?"

"How?"

"Easy. All she has to do is open the fridge, take the appropriate amount from the control, freeze and store it until she gets an overseas order and boom—off it goes."

"You think Piper is *stealing* Rebel's sperm? Houston would never stand for that."

"What if he doesn't know?"

"How could he not?"

"The control gets tossed from the lab after a few days when the sperm die, anyway. If Piper skimmed enough for a full dose while it was alive, froze it, then hid it, he'd never know."

"Why frozen?" Kira chuckled. "Funny how you're such an expert on semen these days."

"Yeah, hysterical. Cooled has a short shelf life. Frozen lasts indefinitely, so you don't have to worry about it dying and you can ship it anywhere, at any time. Piper herself told me how much the Brazilians wanted Rebel's bloodlines, and it would have to be frozen to travel that far."

"Hmm." Kira tapped her jaw. "I still can't see her doing that to Houston."

"That bothers me too, but maybe Piper doesn't see it as stealing. The control doesn't produce income. That's not its purpose. The only way she'd get herself into trouble would be if something went wrong on a previous buyer's end and Houston had to access the control within the time allowed. If he noticed it was light, and/or missing altogether, then he'd have reason to be suspicious."

"What about the legalities? The red tape?"

"As breeding manager, Piper has full authority to sign the forms."

"You have a point. People can rationalize anything. Especially if there are greenbacks involved. I'm sure Piper is eager to upgrade that piece-of-shit Corolla she drives, and she can work on her tan in Rio when she goes to pick up her cash." Kira finally chewed the chip she'd been dunking. "What about Stacey? See any ties to her death?"

"Stacey might've come into the barn late last Saturday night and caught Piper siphoning off the samples in the lab. Piper knew Stacey planned on taking Rebel away from Lucky Jack because she heard Stacey and Jaydee arguing. Now Piper has two problems. Stacey knows she's stealing and, at the same time, by taking Rebel away, she's removing Piper's source of cash. Piper calls Blair's and cancels Rebel's pickup, then she waits until Stacey goes to take Rebel from the stall and hits her over the head with Matt's hammer."

Kira folded her hands on the table. "What about Piper's prints?"

"She could've worn gloves."

"Do you have proof she's part of this supposed scheme?"

"Not yet. I'm still trying to reach the driver from Blair's to see if he'll give me the name of the person who called off Rebel's transport. I'm fairly sure whoever it was also killed Stacey, and if I can find a liquid nitrogen tank, that's at least enough evidence to take to Houston."

"What's this tank look like? How big?"

"From a stock description on the web, they're about two feet tall, fifteen inches in diameter and can hold approximately five hundred straws of frozen sperm. You could store something that size pretty much anywhere at the ranch."

Kira shook her head. "I know what you're thinking. Don't even consider it. People with deadly secrets will go to desperate lengths to keep them."

"I don't have a choice. McWynn is probably knocking on my door as we speak, ready to nail my butt unless I find out who *did* kill Stacey."

"I'm coming with you."

"I'm trying to be stealthy. No offense, but how can I do that with you around?"

Kira let out a sigh. "Well if you're going to risk your neck at least take a weapon with you."

"Like what? I don't do weapons. You know that."

"Take that Swiss Army thing your dad gave you for your birthday."

"With the cute little toothpick?"

Kira didn't think it was funny. "There's a knife in there. Find it. It's better than nothing. Bring your cell, and Shane too."

"I wasn't planning on going home first."

"If you go without a knife or your dog I'll call the cops on you myself."

When the food came, they ate without talking. The mariachis strolled past, strumming fast and furious, smiling with gold-rimmed teeth. A red-haired man, with the kind of voice that cut the air and could be heard over everyone else, sat across the room at the bar. Randi sat up straight. "Kira, look, I think I see that Fitz guy."

"Who?"

"You know, the one who came in your restaurant bragging about a fortuitous murder. Is that him?"

Kira craned her neck. "Well I'll be dammed. There he is. Fitz, in the flesh."

"From the way he's rolling around on that bar stool, he's already halfway into the bottle. Gives me an idea."

"Loose lips," Kira said.

"Great minds." Randi smoothed her hair. The margarita had infused her with a not-so-healthy dose of bravado. "Check it out. The seats on either side of him are empty. We can find out what he's really up to and maybe who's pulling strings behind the curtain, too. I can't go poking around Lucky Jack until later tonight anyway."

Kira pushed her plate to the center of the table. "Let's hit the ladies' room and spiffy ourselves up a bit. Fitz will be putty in our hands."

Twenty-Nine

They straddled the stools on either side of Fitz, sandwiching him in the middle. His thighs mashed Randi's. He wasn't necessarily overweight, just big—like a Samoan. Fitz, the Irish Samoan.

"Well, hel-lo-whoa-whoa." He smiled like he'd won the lottery. "To what do I owe the pleasure?"

Kira extended her hand and introduced herself.

"I remember. You're a hard one to forget." Fitz twisted his torso, hazy gaze settling on Randi's chest. "And you are?"

"Randi. Randi Sterling."

"Nice to meet you." Fitz slapped his hot, sweaty palm into hers, pumped it a couple of times, then pulled it away to plunge his finger into his drink. The liquid in Fitz's glass was the color of a dead lizard. "I'm celebrating tonight." He popped his finger into his mouth.

Randi lifted an imaginary glass. "Cheers."

"Care to join me?" Fitz tipped forward and pulled a fat wad of bills from his back pocket. "What're you drinking?" Peeling a Benjy off the roll, he tossed it on the bar.

"Negro Modelo, please."

"Ice tea for me," Kira said.

"Long Island?"

Kira shook her head. "Virgin doesn't exist in that brand."

Fitz eyeballed her with suspicion. "You don't partake? I don't believe it. There's no way you could make such a mean mai tai without having the pleasure of gulping it down your gullet."

Kira laughed. "Oh, don't you worry. I've drank more than my fair share over the years. When you start at age twelve, it runs its course fast."

Fitz slapped his thigh. Kira always told the truth about her past but nobody believed her.

"You live around here?" Randi asked.

"Nope. I hail from the City of Angels."

"Is that your car out front?" She tilted her head toward the Ferrari visible through the window.

"The four fifty-eight? It's one of them."

"Sweet ride."

He puffed his chest out. "Wanna go for a spin?"

"Later. First I want to learn more about you." She gave him a fawning smile. "Where in L.A. do you hail from?"

"Hollywood Hills."

"Wow." She stretched her eyes as wide as they would go. "That must be so exciting, rubbing elbows with the stars and all."

"Oh sure. I see Johnny Depp and his kids in the market all the time. Plus Cameron Diaz and I have the same hairdresser. Things like that. After a while you get used to it. Seen one, you've seen 'em all."

"Are you in the movie biz?"

Fitz straightened his spine. "Not directly. I'm in oceanfront condos. New projects, mainly."

"Whereabouts?"

"Malibu, Santa Monica, all the way on up the coast to Ventura."

She put on a puzzled expression. "I didn't know there was

anything left along the coastline to develop."

"I know how to fight to get what I want." Fitz nodded, eyes closing. "Oh, yeah. Anybody who goes up against the coastal commission learns how to work the system, let me tell ya."

"The Midas touch," Kira said. "Sounds like you've got it."

"You bet your sweet ass I do. Pardon my French."

"What brings you down to San Diego?"

"A partnership, dollface. Some people say partnerships are sinking ships. Not this one. This is the Niña, the Pinta and the Santa Maria, all rolled into one." Fitz showed his teeth, clearly pleased with himself.

Randi's cheeks ached from the strain of her unrelenting smile. "What's in your glass?"

Fitz stared into his drink. "Tonight, ladies, I'm dancin' with the green fairy."

"The green fairy?"

"Same as Picasso, Hemingway, Poe and Van Gogh. Ha. That rhymes."

"Absinthe." Kira whipped out a compact mirror to apply more lipstick. She took her time.

Fitz watched, fascinated.

Finished, Kira gave him her best pose. "Some say it makes you crazy, or brilliant, depending on how you look at it. Some say it's two sides of the same coin. Typically it's served by pouring cold water over a sugar cube on a slotted spoon."

The bartender, a wiry Asian who looked like he'd go Bruce Lee on anyone who gave him any flack, tossed a towel over his shoulder. "I'm fresh out of slotted spoons."

"Sugar?" Fitz snorted. "That's the pussy way. I drink mine straight."

"With balls of steel," the bartender said, "no doubt."

"They also say it's a hallucinogenic," Kira added. "Though you'd probably be dead if you drank enough to be seeing pink unicorns."

"Worse than tequila," Fitz agreed. "Or better, depending on how you look at it."

Just because Kira didn't imbibe didn't mean she didn't love to talk alcohol, and Fitz obviously loved to drink. Their conversation turned to wormwood, mescal, etc. etc. blah, blah, blah. Randi was impatient, wanted Fitz to spill his guts, but she trusted Kira had a method to her madness so she waited it out.

When the talk of spirits finally wound down, Randi put a hand on Fitz's arm. "Tell us what you're planning to build here in town. Oceanfront units?"

He blinked and swayed on his stool. "You ask a lot of questions."

"I've been thinking about getting into real estate. It seems so—" she pretended she was searching for the perfect word, "—I don't know—so *glamorous*." Her mother had gotten her real estate license and tried her hand at it after the divorce. Randi knew from her mother's complaints about people tooling her for months then buying from someone else, the biz wasn't as exotic as it seemed.

Fitz gave her hand a protective pat. "It's a nasty profession." He shook his head. "You've gotta get lucky."

As in Lucky Jack? Had he made a pun on purpose? "Are you lucky?"

"Me?" Fitz rolled his head, neck popping. "Hell, sweetheart, I've got a leprechaun in my pocket."

Kira chimed in. "This must be an important deal, for a successful L.A. developer like you to come south to our little town."

"It's a moneymaker."

"Any zoning battles for you to fight?"

"I already won."

"How'd you do it?" Randi did her best to channel a doe-eyed deer.

"I'm in thick with your city councilmen. Plus I've got lawyers on staff who can get around any restrictions the goddamn treehuggers throw at us."

"What's so special about this deal?"

"Well... like I said, I'm friendly with a certain celebrity." Fitz wobbled on the barstool. It creaked beneath his weight. "Helps to open doors. People hear a name associated with the project, they want in on it."

Randi's ears perked. "Whose name?"

"The ladies love him." Fitz slurred his words. "He gives us credibility. He's our face and our label. You know, someone the people can trust. Not only that, but they'll want to be just like him and live where he does. Bunch of sheep."

"So, who is it?"

"I wish I could say, blondie, but I've been sworn to secrecy."

"We won't tell a soul."

"Nope. Can't do it."

"Brad Pitt?"

Fitz shook his head. "Not telling."

"Matthew McConaughey?"

Fitz laughed but it wasn't a pleasant sound.

"Nicolas Cage?" Randi badgered. "Jake Gyllenhaal?"

"No, no, no. I'm not saying even if you guess, so don't bother wasting your breath."

"I know, I know!" Kira bounced up and down on her stool. Fitz couldn't have missed her jiggle. "That one guy. What's his name?" She waved her arm like a kid who couldn't wait to answer. "Tim Tyler!"

Forget Tim Tyler, Kira was the real actress around here.

Fitz's mouth grew hard. "I don't want to play this game anymore."

"What amenities will your condos have?" If Randi got him thinking about another aspect of the project, hopefully he'd forget Kira had just named his man. "Pools? Tennis?"

It worked. Fitz grabbed a napkin from the stack on the bar. "Full luxury. I'll draw it for you." He slapped both hands against his ribcage as if searching for a pen. Randi supplied him with one from her purse.

"Tennis courts." He grew more animated. "Pools and lots of parking. We're even going for a rooftop nightclub if we can pull a cabaret license." He scribbled on the paper, but he pushed too hard and the pen kept poking through. "Damn!" He crumpled the napkin and tossed it across the bar, missing the trash can by a good three feet. The bartender glared at him. Fitz shoved his empty glass to the edge of the counter. "*Uno mas, Señor.*"

"Last one, *Señor*. Then I'm cutting you off and calling you a cab."

Fitz made a face. "Yeah well, so what? You got some competition in the drink department, bub." He jerked his thumb toward Kira.

"I cut people off sooner than that," Kira said under her breath.

Randi hid her smile. "What is it about this deal, Fitz? What makes you so excited? I can see it in your eyes. You're on to something."

He shook his head like a stubborn toddler.

"Don't we look trustworthy?" Kira asked.

"Sweet as sugarplums, but I ain't saying shit."

Kira faked a pout.

It didn't take Fitz long to cave. "Okay. Okay. One little thing, that's all you're getting." He wagged his finger in front of Kira's nose. "The owners have to sell. We have a guaranteed profit sitting on the table, waiting for us to come and get it." He burped, filling the air with the aroma of fermented licorice. "Problem is, we're up against a pair of stubborn mules."

"I don't get it," Kira said. "Why would anybody *have* to sell?"

"Oh, sweetheart, you're killing me, sitting there like a vision of loveliness." Fitz put his hand on the bar, preparing to push himself off the stool. "I'm afraid I've said too much."

Randi knocked Kira's keys off the bar with her elbow. They clattered to the floor. Fitz made a move but Kira put a hand on his chest. "No, no. I've got it." She gave him a wink then slowly folded her body in half as she bent over, giving him a clear view of her Freya tattoo busting out above her thong as she collected her keys. She swung herself around and flashed her cleavage. Fitz wiped something off the bar with his palm. Drool?

"Tell you what," Kira put the keys to the Mustang in Randi's hand. "We'll both do a shot with you if you'll hang out and party with us."

Fitz seemed to be reeling from massive overstimulation. A few seconds later a Grinch-like grin spread from ear to ear. "Blondie, you said you don't drink. You're gonna break your hard and fast rule for little ol' me?"

Randi held her breath. Fitz had called Kira's bluff. Perhaps he wasn't as drunk as he seemed.

Kira flicked her hair so the ends brushed against Fitz's cheek. Randi could have sworn he trembled.

Kira winked. "Two more absinthes. Straight up."

The bartender opened his mouth to argue. Kira reached over the bar and whispered in his ear.

"Hey! What're ya talking to him for?"

"I told him not to worry about the cab. I'll make sure you get home safe and sound. My car may not be a Ferrari, but I'll give you a ride you'll never forget."

Randi held up her glass. "In that case, I have a special toast. Here's to Fitz. *Arriba.*" She gave the bartender a knowing smile. "*De bajo.*" Lowered the potent green potion until the glass almost touched the bar. "*Al centro.*" Brought it to the center until all three glasses clinked together. "*Y entro.*" It wasn't exactly right, but it was one of a handful of things she remembered from Spanish class.

Fitz threw his head back to finish the rest of his drink and, with his chin high in the air, couldn't see Kira pass the bartender her shot who, in turn, tossed it into the sink and handed the glass back to Kira—all in three seconds flat.

Kira set her empty shot glass down with a thunk, smacked her lips and slapped both hands on the bar. "Whoa! Now that's what I call a drink."

Randi went last. If there had been a flame nearby, her mouth would have erupted with fire. "Yuck!" Her face contorted as the absinthe burned a hole in her gut. "Nasty stuff, Fitz." She coughed. "Makes tequila taste like fruit punch."

Fitz put a hand on his belly and laughed like that was the funniest thing he'd ever heard. Recovered, he turned to Kira.

"Okay, blondie, let's hit the road. I've got something I want to show you."

"Sure, babe. One thing first though." She gave his cheek a playful pat. "Randi has my car keys and she's not going to give them up until you do."

"Huh?"

"Tell us how you work your magic. Spread the wealth."

"Seriously?"

"Deadly."

"But—"

Kira cut him off. "It'll be our little secret. Just the three of us."

Fitz looked annoyed. "Then can we go?"

"Anything for you."

"Okay, fine. None of it will matter soon anyway." Fitz appeared to be doing his best to pull himself together so he could get the hell out of Dodge and be alone with Kira.

Randi almost felt sorry for him. He was going to be deeply disappointed if he expected to get Kira in the sack.

"You listening?" he asked.

"Intently. If I'm going to get into real estate, I want to learn from the master."

If Fitz had an inkling he was being played, he was past the point of caring. "Okay." He lowered his voice, hiccupped. "This doesn't work for everybody, but the key is to pinpoint the target's weakness. For instance, I give a guy envelopes stuffed with cash, plane tickets to Vegas and the best suites money can buy. You see, he has this little problem."

Randi piped up. "Suites at the Bellagio?"

Fitz nodded. "His favorite."

"So what you're saying is..." It wasn't easy to keep her tone light and bimbo-happy so Fitz wouldn't shut down. "...you're kind of like a drug dealer, stringing a junkie along?"

"A drug dealer? No, but sometimes the result justifies the deed. Businesspeople understand that." Fitz blew his nose into a hankie and stuffed it in his pocket, enjoying his soapbox. "Remember that, ladies. It's one of life's toughest lessons. There ain't no such thing as a free lunch."

"Meaning?"

Fitz looked at Randi like she was as dumb as a doornail. "The guy does things for us—unpleasant things—to drive down the value of the property. Then he gets his rewards."

"What kind of things?"

Fitz gave another hiccup and held up his index finger, but didn't answer the question. His face turned gray-ish green and he looked like he might puke. Instead, he checked his watch. "Stay tuned, girls. The grand finale is going down tonight. Tune in tomorrow and you'll read all about it."

Thirty

RANDI HITCHED HER PURSE strap over her shoulder as the fading taillights of Kira's Mustang cast a red glow on the road outside the Hideaway. The tinkle of voices from the restaurant waned, and the clock had yet to strike twelve, but *I go out walking, after midnight* played in her head to the tempo of her steps. Great horned owls hooted from a cluster of pines and the air was fresh with the smell of star jasmine.

The evil-tasting absinthe made her more confident, strolling along a dark rural road by herself, than was prudent. Still, a walk was a good way to burn off booze.

After a second girls' room rendezvous, she and Kira had come up with a plan. Kira would see that Fitz arrived at his hotel and would deliver him into the hands of a competent employee, but that's where her obligation ended. Then she'd drive to Randi's place and they'd go to Lucky Jack together. Randi had to admit, despite her original protests, and the fact that Kira had a hard time keeping quiet, she liked the idea of company. The last time she'd gone to the ranch in the middle of the night by herself had not been a gratifying experience.

A car roared by, headlights glaring off the trees. The sound receded, the car disappeared and darkness fell again, leaving her alone to sort through everything Fitz had said.

Assuming he was telling the truth, Jaydee had been the one to taint Sydney's feed with poisonous leaves, cut the outcasts' tails, shut off the water supply and let a handful of horses out of their corrals, allowing Zany to almost get killed on El Camino Real. Matt had been right, gambling had taken over Jaydee's life and his mind along with it. She sped up, clogs loud on the pavement. Click, clack, click, clack. The faster she went, the more nervous she got, like she was already running from something. She half expected someone to leap out at her from the bushes. Fifty yards down the street her cell phone shattered the silence.

It was Luke. "Are you sitting down?"

"No. I'm walking. Is something wrong?"

"Houston just called. There's been a third colt."

Her ankle rolled and she almost went down. "Rebel's?" she panted, limping, but kept on going.

"Yes, but not the one with the face marking. Not the one you're so attached to. This guy is a big strapping fellow."

"*Is?*" Luke had made a mistake. "You mean *was*?"

"No. I mean *is*. When Houston found him, he had a faint pulse and was hanging on by a thread. He put him in the trailer and he's bringing him to the clinic. I'm heading there now."

"What about the roan mare? The one due to foal tonight? I'm worried about her."

"She's not in labor yet, far as I can tell. Problem is, I can't reach Piper. She's not answering her phone."

"That's weird. She's usually pretty accessible."

"Where are you? Can you get out to the ranch and check on the roan?"

"Of course." Best to leave her current whereabouts, and the conversation with Fitz, along with her plans for finding the tank she believed would contain Rebel's frozen semen, out of the conversation. Luke didn't need to be worrying about her on top of trying to save the colt. "I have to make a quick stop to pick up

Shane, then I'm on my way." And she could kill two birds...

The phone call had taken her attention off the road and for a moment she was completely disoriented. Mist crawled through the trees and something rustled in the brush. Her buzz had evaporated, eaten up by adrenaline.

Seemed like she should have made it to her truck already. It hadn't taken this long to walk *to* José's, had it? She picked up a wobbly jog, wishing she wasn't wearing clogs, digging for her keys in her purse as she went. Pens, tampons, chapstick and, at last, the plastic square of her remote lock. Finger cocked and ready on the alarm button, she rounded the bend and, much to her relief, came upon her fortress of black steel. In sight. Almost there. She pressed the unlock button and heard the latch release. She wrenched the door wide, jumped in and stuck the key in the ignition.

Fitz had mentioned a "grand finale," and she couldn't shake the feeling her Something Special, the colt she'd watched being born and promised to keep safe, had a starring role.

Rain tapped the roof of the truck the entire way home. Luke's exterior lights were on; the inside was dark. She dug the pads of her fingertips into Pegasus's wings. If anyone could save the colt Houston was bringing in, it would be Luke. She'd seen him perform miracles on horses others thought were goners.

Halfway between Luke's house and her bungalow, the rain quit being polite. Fingernail-sized drops beat fast and furious as she pulled in beneath the carport. She ran as fast as she could for the front porch and still got soaked. A business card was wedged into the door. She hesitated, staring at McWynn's name before she plucked the card out and stepped inside. She shook the water from her hair and threw her keys on the table. They skittered off and clattered to the floor. Her heart skipped a beat. Shane wasn't on his dog bed.

Sometimes, when he heard thunder, he curled himself into

a ball in the shower stall, but a quick check of the bathroom showed he wasn't there. Wait a second. The kitchen door was open partway. Most times, if she knew she'd be out late—unlike the night she met Jaydee at The Triton—she left it like that so he could come and go as he pleased. She hadn't done that tonight. Not to mention, he hated getting wet. So why was it open?

Had McWynn taken her dog because she hadn't been home? No. Of course not. Ridiculous. Cops didn't kidnap people's dogs.

Flashlight in hand, she hurried down the back steps and plunged into the backyard. She patted down the shrubs lining the chain link fence, releasing the perfume of wet things. Water pattered the earth. Over and over she called for Shane, but his name was carried away by the wind. She dug through the thick foliage, fingers twisting among the leaves, sticks and mud.

Two weeks ago there'd been a news report of some sicko running around San Diego County tossing raw meat poisoned with strychnine over fenced backyards. Victims were found with their bodies twisted like pretzels, lying in pools of blood from their nose and mouths. Randi's jitters bubbled to panic. *If anything like that had happened to Shane...*

Thorns ripped her skin, reopening her wounds from fighting the brush when she chased Zany, but she didn't care. Some time later, soaked and shivering, she retreated into the bungalow where it was damp and dark and deathly still—nothing moved, nothing creaked, nothing barked, nothing squeaked and nothing breathed. Thunder rumbled and lightning lit the walls. She paced the length of the room, water dripping onto the floor, stopping briefly to stare at her ghost-like skin smudged with grime in the mirror. She never should have left Shane alone.

Thirty-One

MOONLIGHT TOSSED A REFLECTION off the pavement stretching in front of the F150's headlights. Alone in her truck late at night, especially without Shane riding shotgun, Randi questioned the sanity of returning to the place where she'd found Stacey dead. The killer always returned to the scene of the crime, one way or another, wasn't that what they said? To cover tracks, hide evidence or for some other macabre reason beyond the scope of everyday reasoning.

Some*one* had killed Stacey. Some*thing* had killed those two colts and now, possibly, a third. She could be putting herself in serious danger, but Luke had asked her to check on the pregnant roan, and she needed to find a liquid nitrogen tank. She had a feeling the Brazilian's contract for frozen semen was connected to Stacey's murder, same as the call to Blair's Horse Transport, she just hadn't figured out how.

She'd left a note punched through the nail in the door for Kira, explaining why she couldn't wait, that she had to see to the mare, and asking her to please hang out in case Shane came back. Kira would be pissed but she'd also understand.

The Ford lurched from the pavement of El Camino Real onto Lucky Jack's driveway. The cattle guard rumbled beneath the tires. Shane always sat up and perked his ears at this point, but she couldn't let her mind take her down that road. Not yet. As much as it went against every fiber of her being, finding Shane had to wait.

Along the ridge, Jaydee's half of the house sat dark, but a lamp shone from inside Houston and Helen's bedroom. If, God forbid, she ran into any unforeseen circumstances, this time she wouldn't hesitate to call for help.

She pulled the truck behind an unkempt hedgerow, switched off the headlights and got out. Though she was here at Luke's request, she'd rather fly under the radar. The rain had stopped as suddenly as it had come. Same with the wind. The mild scent of horse manure mixed with pungent sage filled the air.

The moon hung in the sky like a circle of paper, its image rippling in a fresh puddle. A distant band of coyotes let loose a boisterous round of high-pitched yips. From the looks of things, it was an everyday night at Lucky Jack Performance Horses. The Swiss Army knife sat in her windbreaker pocket along with a penlight, and her cell phone pressed comfortingly against her back pocket. This time she was prepared. The only thing missing was her dog.

In her Nikes, instead of those damn clogs, she covered the remaining half of the driveway at a good clip, and except for the horses clustered in pastures on either side of her and the croaking chorus of an entire nation of frogs, she appeared to be alone. Still, she couldn't help turning around every couple of steps to make sure she wasn't being followed.

She found Something Special napping, with his mama standing guard. He slept with his front legs curled, hind limbs stretched out to the side, little ribcage rising and falling in perfect rhythm. She had to make sure it stayed that way.

Minutes later, she ducked inside the birthing enclosure on the backside of the barn, relieved to find the unborn foal still tucked inside the roan mare's belly. Safe. For now. Where was

Piper? Why hadn't she answered Luke's calls? Her Toyota wasn't in the lot, but sometimes she parked behind the broodmare pasture on the other side of the ranch. Maybe she was busy in the lab, perhaps helping herself to one of Rebel's control samples, or getting it ready to freeze for shipment to Brazil, and couldn't be bothered to answer her phone.

Randi gave the roan a quick once-over. A dainty beauty with delicate ears, the veins along the mare's neck stood out, and an inspection of her underbelly showed she was running a miniscule bit of milk. She wasn't cranking her head around to stare at her flanks or raising her tail in discomfort, so contractions likely hadn't started. Once her water broke and the second-stage labor began, delivery would happen fast.

Randi left the mom-to-be and pushed open the door to the main barn, grateful the aisle was flooded with light. The stall inhabitants paid her minimal attention as she walked by, a flick of an ear here, a swish of a tail there, necks drooping and eyes half closed. The reassuring rush of an automatic waterer surged through the barn, and across the way, the persistent hum of the refrigerator made her feel everything was going to be okay. Piper's absence would be explained by something mundane, the roan would have a healthy foal and both it and her Something Special would live full-length lives filled with warm sunshine and the glory of thunderous show ring applause.

She rubbed her arms—shouldn't let her guard down. Her brain ping-ponged back and forth between fear and reason, refusing to settle for very long on either side of the fence, as she walked the breezeway to the breeding barn. The light was on in the lab but the door was locked. She tried Piper's cell and, to her surprise, heard it ringing inside the lab. She knocked, peered inside the brick-sized window. Rattled the knob. Knocked again.

Leaning against the door, she remembered—years ago, another lifetime it seemed—Jaydee had mentioned as they stumbled, laughing, into a vacant stall, that Houston hid a spare key to the lab in the barn's kitchen. That way, if she got too freaked out, they could always go behind closed, locked doors. Although, he'd added, holing up would take all the fun out of it. At the time, she'd agreed, thinking the stall was the most daring and risqué place she'd ever done it. Now it all seemed idiotic, and not very comfortable either. Not to mention the splinters.

After all these years, could the key still be there?

Backtracking to the kitchen, she started with the cabinet drawers, easing them open one by one. Contents: duct tape, bandages, pliers, wire cutters and rat turds the size of pine nuts. No matter how refined a barn was, no matter how clean it was kept, rodents always found somewhere to live and something to eat.

She took a step back and surveyed the kitchen. For a man, Houston was organized. Where would a methodical guy hide a key? She checked the top of the fridge, lifted the floor mat below the sink, peered behind the microwave and rearranged a row of bowls in the cupboard. No key.

At the edge of her vision, a shadow scampered by. Or did it? A shiver shimmied down her tailbone as she imagined a killer tiptoeing up behind her back, hoisting a hammer above her head and...

Focus!

One of the drawers on the opposite side contained several rolls of colored wraps—polo wraps—used to protect horses' legs, but this section appeared different from the others. There was something about the way these parcels of stretchy fleece were arranged, not all hodgepodge like in the other drawers. Five wide and five deep, spaced equidistant apart. Logical. Organized. She picked up the first roll. Nothing. The second. Again, nothing. Underneath the sixth leg wrap, a red one, was a hoof pick. Attached to the hoof pick was a wire, and attached to the wire was a key.

A fluorescent glow flickered the length of the lab. The narrow confines of the space made Randi want to bolt. Instead, she locked herself in.

Piper's cell lay on the counter. One mystery solved. Piper hadn't answered Luke's calls because somehow she and her phone had gotten separated. Next to the phone sat the cylindrical Equitainer. The container for cooled, not frozen, semen. White letters ran up the side: *Rush. Fragile. Biological Materials.* On the top it read: *Warning. Do not open until vet is present and ready to inseminate.* She undid the latch and found a plastic cup bordered by coolant cans. The cup held a baby bottle liner secured with a rubber band. Carefully, she lifted it out. Fifty cc's, about a quarter of a cup, with today's date and Rebel's name on it. A control sample. A microscopic frenzy of approximately one billion high-priced sperm chowing down on the extender fluid at this very second.

Did Piper intend to transfer a portion of this sample to those poly-straws she told her about? If skimming was what she was up to, the tank containing the straws of frozen semen were likely here in the lab.

A door slammed in the breeding barn. Hurrying to the small window high in the lab's door, she peered through the glass. The big room was dark. Who was out there? Piper? Jaydee? If she left now, she'd be an obvious target with nowhere to hide, but she didn't like the prospect of being cornered in the lab, either. She had no excuse at the ready for what she was up to.

A couple of plastic gardening cans blocked the closet at the rear of the lab. Might be a good place to stow away for a minute if need be. She moved the cans out of the way, and as they scraped along the floor, a moan came from inside the closet. *What the hell?*

"Hello?" She tried the knob. Locked. Of course. This was getting old. "Is somebody in there?"

She tried the lab's door key, but the fit wasn't even close. She'd picked locks as a kid. It wasn't hard. Stick a bobby pin inside the hole and wiggle it around. She didn't have a bobby pin, but, thanks to Kira, she had a Swiss Army knife and the knife had a toothpick.

Mentally crossing her fingers, she stuck the slender white stick inside the hole and wiggled it around. It caught, then slipped again. Damn it! She took a deep breath and steadied her hand. This time, jabbing the toothpick in as far as it would go, she heard a click. She eased the door open. A crack of light split the tiny space.

Crammed beside the toilet, knees to her chest, hands behind her back, bound and gagged, was Piper. Her eyes, huge with fear and confusion, darted over Randi's face. In the corner of the closet was a metal tank with the letters LN2 stenciled in yellow along the side. Liquid nitrogen.

"Don't worry. I'll get you out of here." She switched toothpick for knife and wedged the blade between the stretchy fleece and Piper's neck. "Hold still." She pierced the material, working it in a sawing motion until finally the polo wrap gave way. She flung the strip of material aside. "Who did this to you?"

Piper shook her head, spluttered and coughed, sounding like she was on the verge of throwing up.

"Can you stand so I can get to the rope around your hands?"

Piper stared past her. Her eyes narrowed. Her nostrils flared. Someone else was in the lab.

A flame-like heat unfurled along Randi's skin. Her mind screamed *Turn around! Run!* but she couldn't move. Next came the whooshing sound of lungs expanding, followed by a forceful exhale. She covered her head and ducked, but not in time. A searing pain crashed through her skull and everything went black.

Thirty-Two

RANDI'S HEAD FELT LIKE it'd been run over by a truck; brown spots formed along the edges of her vision. Her hands were tied behind her back and her ankles lashed together. No gag though, and for that she was grateful. From the smell of dust, the press of cold porcelain against her spine and the thin line of light beneath the door, she figured she was in the same closet where she'd found Piper and the liquid nitrogen tank. Piper was gone; the tank was not.

Her legs were crammed underneath her butt, so by stretching her fingers, she could almost touch the ropes binding her ankles. If she could free her legs, she might be able to escape. Teeth clacking from the cold, she clenched her jaws and, imagining her fingers were spider legs, groped for the bonds. Her hands were like stone and the rope tying her feet like a strand of cement. She dug into the middle of the knots, ignoring the stabbing spines of the cord and the protests of her aching, frozen fingers.

The roan mare was going to give birth any time now, if she hadn't already. Piper, wherever she was, was in no shape to protect the newborn foal, and now, as it turned out, neither was she. Fitz had said the "grand finale" was going down tonight. Whatever it was, someone was going to die.

She worked the ropes with renewed energy. Worked them and worked them and worked them, refusing to give up. When her fingers cramped so bad she couldn't take it anymore and the brown spots became solid and closed in around her eyes, she felt a teensy bit of give.

Twisting her wrists so the tip of her forefinger cozied up against one of the knots, she finally got a second finger between the rope and her skin, but as soon as she felt an opening she got excited, tensed up, and her fingers slipped the wrong way. The whole mess tightened and there went her freedom. Damn it! Her shoulders caved, dropping her hand to the concrete floor. Now what? Dirt, dirt and more dirt. Because she had nothing better to do, she let her fingers roam. Nestled under the bottom of the liquid nitrogen tank was something small and cylindrical with a pointed end. A screw? A nail? Whatever, it had a point, in more ways than one.

She stabbed her anklebone at least a dozen times, praying her tetanus booster was current, although lockjaw was at the bottom of her worry list right now. Especially since her icicle-like fingers were about to snap right off but, to her surprise, after countless jabs, one of the ropes broke apart instead. She stifled a cry, stretching her legs as much as she could, which wasn't far, but using mini scissor-kicks the rope finally inched its way free and unwound from her ankles.

She struggled to stand inside the cramped closet. Without her arms to brace against the wall, she lost her balance and flopped onto the toilet seat, landing hard on her butt bone, the only part of her body that, until now, hadn't hurt. She thumped her joined hands against her back pocket. Her phone was gone. Not that she could use it with her hands tied, anyway.

Rising shakily from the toilet, she maneuvered so her back faced the closet door. After fumbling for a while, she managed to grip the doorknob long enough to turn it till it opened. She slid back first into the lab, blinking in the glaring brightness. Way too exposed. If whoever did this peeked through the window high in the door, that would be that. Maybe this time they'd finish her off for good.

Piper's cell phone and the Equitainer were still on the counter. A twitch, used to subdue horses by twisting the noose end around their upper lip, lay on the floor. This one was the old-fashioned kind, a piece of wood, about a foot long with a loop of chain, the noose, protruding from one end. Barbaric-looking compared to its replacement, two lightweight aluminum tubes in a V shape. This thing was a relic, and this artifact had been used on her head not long ago. There was blood on the end to prove it.

She got down on her knees to pick up the twitch, and, after a lot of huffing and puffing, managed to shove half of the wooden part down the back of her jeans. She couldn't use the twitch with her hands tied, but the feel of the round piece of wood pressing against her skin was reassuring, nonetheless. Next, she sidled to the counter, stood on her tiptoes and inched her way around until she could grasp Piper's phone behind her back. The plan was to stuff it in her pocket, in case she was somehow able to free her hands and call for help, but her arm jerked in the process and the phone crashed to the floor. The battery broke apart and ricocheted off a nearby wall, spinning to a halt beneath a cabinet. Useless to her now. No way could she collect the parts and put them back together.

A high-pitched neigh bounced off the walls of the breeding room. She scrambled to the door and dared a peek out the window. Jaydee stood along the far wall. In his hand was a lead rope. At the other end, Rebel tossed his head, danced in place and swished his tail. Why had Jaydee brought the stallion to the breeding barn in the middle of the night?

He was talking to someone but she couldn't see who or make out his words. She pressed her ear against the doorjamb. "Stacey's piece of shit little sister..." Jaydee's voice trailed off. "She'll never get this horse. I'll make damn sure of it."

"Oh yeah?" *Piper*. "How do you plan on doing that?"

Back at the window, hoping for a better angle, Randi gave a little hop and banged her forehead against the glass. Oops. She jerked away. They had to have heard. Silence fell over the barn. She waited for the door to fly open, for Jaydee to come storming in, face twisted and red, spit flying from his mouth.

Her heart slammed against her chest, but the door stayed closed. Finally, Piper spoke. Then came more hoof stomping and Jaydee yelling at Rebel to knock it off, followed by the snap of a whip.

One more try at the window. Jaydee was in the corner now. He couldn't see the door of the lab from where he stood. If he stayed put she could sneak out of the lab undetected.

Using the same behind-the-body-door-opening technique, a bit improved by the practice, she slipped from the lab, tiptoed down the steps and hid behind the half-wall of the wash-rack. The brick partition was old and there were chinks in it for her to peer through, but it was only about four feet high. If Jaydee came looking, he'd find her in no time flat. Piper lay curled on her side, trussed up like a Thanksgiving turkey, next to three large feed barrels. Piper's eyes found hers. She mouthed the word *help*.

"Hey, Piper, nice little scheme you conjured up," Jaydee called from the other end of the room. "Too bad you're going to have to kiss your fast cash goodbye."

Scheme. Fast cash. Had she been right about Piper?

"From what I hear," Jaydee continued, "they've got a waiting list in Brazil longer than my dick."

Rebel snorted and there was a rapid-fire ringing of hoof-beats as he swung his haunches in a circle. Jaydee jerked the rope, then tied the stallion tighter to the iron ring in the wall.

"What do you want this place to be, Jaydee, besides overrun with tasteless condos—maybe another goddamn Home Depot?"

"Shut up. Or I'll gag you again, and this time it'll be around your throat."

"Your parents will be homeless. On the street. This ranch is their life. How can you do this to them?"

"What are you? Innocent?"

"I didn't do it for it for me. My plan was to save Lucky Jack, you idiot. That money was for damage control, damage you've done for your own inane selfish reasons."

"Yeah, well, if your motives were so goddamn altruistic, why didn't you tell Houston you were skimming from my wife's horse?"

"He would never have approved of me depleting the control samples, or selling back to the Brazilians. You know that. The difference is, I'd rather tread the line of black and white than have the ranch go under. At least my way there might be something to fight for."

Jaydee fell silent.

"Do the right thing. Untie me and put Rebel back in his stall."

"Not on your life. Whatever happens to this horse, his blood is on your hands now. That's what you get when you tamper with supply and demand."

"You disgusting creep. What you're doing is nothing short of murder."

Jaydee laughed. "Tell your sob story to a jury. Unless they're the goddamn animal rights morons, they're not going to give a rat's ass. We're talking livestock, Piper. Not pets. Sometimes I think you forget that simple fact."

"You're a chicken-shit." Piper rocked herself back and forth. "You ought to be ashamed." Her voice cracked with emotion. "You're nothing but an unfeeling beast of a man. A heartless cold-blooded murderer of innocent animals."

Thirty-Three

DESPISING JAYDEE HAD BEEN a long time coming. Now, no longer postponed by a misguided sense of romantic nostalgia, the sight of him made Randi sick. How had he done it? No trace of poison, no deadly cuts or bumps? Not a scratch anywhere on the foals' bodies? What was he, some kind of deadly Dementor?

Jaydee untied Rebel and gathered the lead rope. Whatever Jaydee had in store for him, Rebel didn't like it. He squealed and crow-hopped, lashing out with a hind leg. Muscles bunched, he flexed sideways and, with a rebellious twist of his head, ripped the rope from Jaydee's hands. He took off at a gallop, beelining toward the breeding dummy at the other end of the room, lead rope bouncing behind him like drops of water in a hot pan.

Jaydee dashed for the lab, taking all three stairs in one giant leap. Randi ducked as low as she could go behind the half-wall.

At the other end of the room, Rebel rose up and came down hard on top of the dummy mare at the same time Jaydee burst from the lab, the AV clutched under his arm. "Whoa! Whoa!"

Rebel had reached the dummy. A Mack truck couldn't stop

him now.

"Randi!" Piper whispered. "Cut me loose! There's a pair of scissors in the lab. Check the drawers!"

Couldn't Piper see her hands were tied? What was she thinking?

"Just get them! You can do it."

As long as Jaydee stayed put, struggling to hold the AV in place, and as long as Rebel stayed on top of the dummy, Rebel's body blocked Jaydee's line of sight, but any second now, Rebel would be done and back himself off the mounting dummy, giving Jaydee a clear shot.

Randi left the relative safety of the wash-rack, anticipating the roar of Jaydee's voice as she went trip, trip, tripping up the steps and into the lab. She made it unseen, but there were too many drawers. Her fingers shook as she fumbled behind her back. The drawers rattled, making a racket Jaydee couldn't miss. Somehow, thirty seconds later, the cold metal of scissors brushed her hand.

Jaydee's head was turned toward Rebel. She snuck from the lab and knelt beside Piper, who was scooting into position to work her ropes against the blades when Jaydee howled like Rebel had kicked him in the stomach.

Unfortunately, Rebel hadn't.

Randi was shocked at how fast Jaydee moved. Dropping the scissors, she leapt to her feet and ran for the sliding door leading to the breezeway. Jaydee chased her, his steps heavy with fury. Ten more yards to go, not far, but the door was open only about a foot—not wide enough. In the instant it took Randi to half-halt and twist sideways, Jaydee hooked his foot around her ankle and with no arms to break her fall, she hit hard. Her shoulder slammed into the ground, knocking the breath from her lungs.

Before she knew it, Jaydee was on top of her, crushing her body with his. He slapped the back of her head. "How did you get loose?" He reeked of booze. "How did you get out of the closet?"

"Get... off... me." She tasted blood; her lips were rubbery from where her teeth had sunk in.

Jaydee pressed his palms into her shoulders and rocked himself back until he sat on her butt. "Never mind how you got out. Now you're going to have to be a good girl and do what I tell you. Not easy for you."

She bucked and squirmed in a fruitless attempt to unseat him. He dug his fingers down the back of her pants and grabbed the twitch. "Don't move, or I'll bash your head in. You should have stayed put. This is none of your business."

She braced for a blow, for the feel of the twitch slamming into her skull but, to her surprise, Jaydee's muscles went slack and, for a moment, except for the sound of his breathing, the room was quiet. Even Rebel, free to roam with nobody on the other end of his lead rope, stood ground-tied, ears up, eyes fixed on Jaydee. Everybody was waiting for the crazy man's next move.

Jaydee shifted his weight, forcing a grunt from Randi. A pebble pierced her cheek and she was surprised by the intensity of the pain, considering everything else. Jaydee didn't give her long to ponder it. He spun around on her butt, grinding her hipbones into the dirt, until he sat facing her feet, and grabbed hold of her ankles.

Without her legs, she was totally screwed. She kicked as hard as she could until he had to shift his grip and lost his hold for a split second. She landed two good, solid blows to his chest. Reaching behind him, he smacked her head again. She reeled from the pain and swallowed blood. Tears streamed down her face and onto the floor.

She winced as he wrapped her ankles tight with something that crinkled like plastic. Two swift jerks later, he tied a knot and leapt to his feet. He'd won. Now her hands *and* her feet were tied *again*. She pictured him throwing his hands in the air like a rodeo contestant in a calf-tying contest.

She couldn't see where he was going but heard his boots cross the room. Rebel's hoofbeats were followed immediately by the clang of a metal bar. Jaydee must have confined Rebel in the cattle chute. With only a few inches of room on each side, he wouldn't be able to move.

"You got the collection, Jaydee," Piper called out. "Leave Rebel alone. Let him go."

Rolling to her side, Randi huffed and puffed and squirmed until she could see what Jaydee was doing. Not an easy feat with her hands behind her back and her two legs bound into one. Running his fingers down the captive stallion's head, Jaydee traced the mark of the Flying V. "Whoa there, big guy." He reached into his jacket and pulled out a ping-pong ball. He held it up to one of Rebel's nostrils as if measuring for size. Then he took out a second one.

Thirty-Four

ITCAME TO HER in a rush of horror. When she was twelve her mother had read a story from the newspaper, at the breakfast table, of a man convicted of killing racehorses by putting ping-pong balls up their nostrils. Horses couldn't breathe through their mouths, and without a distinguishable cause of death, the owners had collected fat insurance checks and the killer got a hefty cut.

Foosballs were smaller than ping-pong balls, and foals' nostrils were smaller than those of adult horses. The morning Jaydee had chased her and Kira down in his truck, he'd been searching for that stupid ball she kicked under his bed. He must have thought she was onto him and believed she'd taken the foosball as proof, but Luke had said the foals weren't insured, so Jaydee had killed them for a different reason. The reason didn't matter at this point; all that mattered was stopping him from suffocating Rebel.

"Hey, Jaydee." Hard to sound conversational when your voice shook, but if she could buy some time, maybe Luke or Houston would show up. Somebody. *Anybody*. Even McWynn.

She'd be thrilled to see him right now. "Who took the picture of us at the Triton?"

"Some guy I found in the parking lot. I thought you'd like a memento of our time together."

Like a hole in the head. "So you mailed me one. How kind. Thanks. Who else got a copy?"

Jaydee ignored her. "I cared for you, Randi. Believe it or not. I do have some regrets about the way things turned out."

"Some regrets? Are you kidding me? I put my entire life on hold for you, uprooted myself, left my dad, my friends and my home. No explanation from you 'about the way things turned out.' You don't treat people like that, Jaydee."

Amazing how many words could flow lying sideways on the ground. Each time her mouth moved, more blood pooled on the inside of her cheek. "I actually defended you. I told people you weren't a killer."

"You wouldn't understand what happened with Stacey, and I don't have time to fill you in."

"You couldn't take two seconds to pick up the phone before I left Colorado to tell me, 'Never mind, I married someone else?'"

"I thought about it."

"Is there a *but* coming?"

"You were my insurance."

"Insurance? Against what?"

"Women like it if they feel there's someone waiting in the wings. Fear of loss is a powerful motivator. Stacey was more apt stay married to me with you around."

"You're sick. Just plain sick. I can't believe I ever saw anything good in you."

"I said I was sorry. What more do you want?"

"You're sorry, all right. You're whole life is sorry, and trying to pin Stacey's murder on me is the icing on your sorry cake."

Jaydee lowered his hand. He'd quit what he was doing to pay attention to her. It was worth the toll his confession took on her self-esteem.

"It's not what you think, but it doesn't matter because time's run out." He held one of the ping-pong balls up to the light. "Everybody's time is up."

What was he doing? Checking for cracks? She had to stall him some more. "What happened that night? After we left the Triton and went back to your place?"

"What do you think happened?"

"I think you drugged me."

"Oh, please. Spare me your drama, Ran. You wanted to be bad. And yeah, I slipped you a little something. I thought it would make you more fun. It used to work with Stacey. She didn't mind. You're a lightweight. I should have only given you half." His hand closed around the ping-pong ball and he met her eyes. "If it makes you feel any better, nothing happened. I'm not a rapist."

Randi didn't let her relief diminish her anger. "Got it. Not a rapist. Just a murderer."

"What are you talking about?" Jaydee looked surprised. "I didn't kill Stacey."

"Then who did?"

Raising the ping-pong ball, he stroked it along the stallion's cheek.

If she could keep him talking, Piper might be able to pull free of her ropes. Maybe she'd gotten hold of the scissors. "Listen, if you tell Houston and Helen what's going on with that Fitz guy, they'll help you get it straightened out. They're your family."

"My family? Are you kidding? What do you know about my family?"

"I know they've always done their best for you." She lifted her cheek a quarter-inch off the ground, wanted to make sure he heard her. "And now you're destroying—"

"Shut up!" Piper hissed. She was a good twenty feet away, but her eyes burned. "Why are you wasting time? Jaydee's going to suffocate Rebel and you're making chitchat? What the hell?"

Jaydee jerked his chin. "Is that what you think this is about, Ran? Family? No, no, no. It's not about Fitz or Tyler, either. They have no clue as to what I actually have planned. I'm not reading from their script tonight. What's going down right now is way more brilliant than any harebrained scheme those dumbasses ever dreamed of."

"Oh, yeah?" Keep him going, keep him talking. "Brilliant? How brilliant?"

"Jesus!" Piper rocked back and forth so hard she banged her head on the wall. "Do *something*."

Jaydee spun on his heels. "When Rebel's dead and I get to the roan's foal out there—and the colt you're all smitten with—let's not forget that one." He waited a beat; his tone grew dark. "I heard you already named it."

She'd never seen him look so ugly. "I don't know what you're talking about."

"Bullshit. Listen to me. The semen I just collected will be the last of Rebel's line, and a dead horse won't do Stacey's little sister a damn bit of good, no matter what Stacey's goddamn last will and testament says."

"What about the mares already in foal?" Piper raised her voice. "Huh? Did you think of that, asshole?"

"I'll take care of that when the time comes." Calm and collected, he was more frightening than when he was mad. "I'm not a fool. I took the frozen straws from the tank and now I've got Rebel's final dose in the AV. Never mind what she claims, Piper never shipped to Brazil. She's holding out for more money. Those South American fools have nothing. I hold all the cards, all the sperm they're drooling over, and they'll pay whatever I ask."

"You'll never get away with it."

"On the contrary, Rebel's death will be logged as unfortunately premature, but natural. I'll be set for life and never have to think about money again. Then I can tell Tyler and his goon to go fuck themselves."

"What about us?"

Piper needn't have asked. It was clear by the smirk on Jaydee's face he wouldn't be sending them on their merry way.

"When I finish with the horses, I'll take care of you two. Killing Randi wasn't part of my plan. An unfortunate mishap, really. You, Piper, I won't mind so much."

Piper made a squeaking noise.

"After that, I'm catching a flight out of here. I'll be in Brazil before anybody even thinks to look for me, and I don't ever plan on coming back."

That was it then. Jaydee's big gamble. The last of Rebel's sperm. Win or lose, he was gonna get high. "Those colts you killed were babies." Randi's voice shook. "Do you do everything Tyler and Fitz tell you to? Is there no end to your greed? To your addiction?"

"Come on, Ran, they're just horses. Service nags. Christ, what's the big deal? That's one thing you and I never saw eye-to-eye on. Think about it. In some countries they even eat them."

"Tip of the iceberg on our differences, Jaydee. What you'll never understand is that the horse you're about to kill has more integrity than you'll ever have."

Rebel raised his neck, eyes wide, ears pricked.

Jaydee collected the soft part of the stallion's muzzle below his nostrils, grabbing only enough flesh to twist. "It's okay, boy." He pinched the fold of Rebel's nose, then looping the chain of the twitch around his skin, he cranked the wooden handle and tightened the noose.

The whites of Rebel's eyes showed, but he wouldn't move his head now. He defecated, loud splats on the cement. Jaydee eased the ping-pong ball into Rebel's nostril. The slit of his nose was just wide enough with the chain pulling downward to force the sphere into his airway.

Randi's heart thudded against her ribcage. How long would it take for Rebel to suffocate once both balls were in place? Five minutes? Four?

She approximated the distance between her and Jaydee. He was a good five, six horse-lengths away from her, his back turned to hold Rebel's head steady with the twitch. Talking wasn't working anymore. Only one thing would. She couldn't pull the trigger, but she'd had more than enough practice at aiming. Unless she wanted Jaydee to be the only one leaving the breeding barn alive tonight, she had no choice but to call his bluff.

Balancing on bruised knees and a throbbing forehead, she blocked out the pain and see-sawed back and forth until she was able to heave herself into a stinkbug position, head on the ground, butt in the air. Vomit climbed her throat. She closed her eyes and saw the colts as they fought for their lives, Jaydee straddling their little shoulder blades, foosballs positioned just right to stop their breathing.

What gave him the right to decide what lived and breathed and what didn't? Who told him he could play God? Rage welled inside her. She harnessed her fury and launched herself upward with everything she had. The force of her forward movement made whatever Jaydee'd lashed around her ankles loosen about half an inch. She looked down. He'd bound her feet with plastic grocery bag. He must have used the last of his rope the first time he'd tied her ankles together. Why all the bags?

She hobbled down the breezeway as fast as her baby steps would carry her toward Houston's gun.

Thirty-Five

ONE VERY LARGE PROBLEM with her plan. She couldn't hold a gun with her hands tied behind her back. She had enough trouble with them *untied*.

Panicked hoofbeats reverberated from the rafters of the breeding room along the breezeway and all the way to the main barn. Jaydee would have the second ball up Rebel's nose by now, and the more he struggled, the more he fought, the quicker he'd use up his air. If she didn't move fast, the stallion would be dead by the time she got to Houston's office.

But she couldn't move fast. She shuffled through the pass-thru kitchen. The plastic bag bit her Achilles tendons with every step. Shoulda worn her boots. Ignoring the pain, she searched for something sharp to tear through the bonds around her wrists. Had to take care of them, first. Nothing, nothing, nothing! She whirled in frustration. Her hip smashed into the counter, she lost her balance and toppling like a tree she fell to the ground. Dirt coated her lips and granules of grit crunched between her teeth. She rolled on her back and stared at the rafters like a helpless turtle.

It was over. Jaydee was going to kill one of the world's most magnificent horses, then he'd kill Piper, then he'd kill her.

She closed her eyes hoping for an answer. When she opened them, a wall-mounted bottle cap remover with a hood-like lip, tucked a few inches beneath the edge of the counter, filled her vision like a gift from God.

She struggled to her feet. Hunching her back, she bounced up and down, jamming her wrists against the ridged metal. It tore at her skin. At last a piece of it caught the plastic. She pulled, leaning all her weight in the opposite direction. Finally, something snapped. She mashed her fingers together, and knuckle-to-knuckle, palm-to-palm, rubbed them back and forth until the restraints fell away.

Now for her feet. She needed a tool that could tear through the plastic around her ankles, but time was running out. Rebel was going to die, if he wasn't dead already. Inside the sink, of all places, she spotted a hoof pick. Gripping the counter with one hand, she stabbed the hooked metal end into the thinnest part of the plastic around her feet. Her ankles bled but the bag finally ripped apart, and she ran like hell out of the barn to Houston's office.

Watch, this will be the one night in twenty he locked the door.

He hadn't.

She hit the light. On top of Houston's desk was a sticky note. In bold black letters it read: *STUART FROM BLAIR'S HORSE TRANSPORT*. Below it read: *Called for Randi.* A wheezing noise, like she'd stepped on a rubber ducky, sprang from her throat. The name of the person who'd cancelled the pickup and stopped Rebel from leaving Lucky Jack wasn't who she expected it to be.

She pulled the drawer open, flung the towel off, took the gun from its holster and sped from the office. Pointing the barrel away from her body, she ran down the barn aisle, hung a right at the kitchen, flew down the breezeway and charged into the breeding barn. Rebel was still confined to the chute and Jaydee had one of his damn plastic grocery bags over the horse's nose. Terror filled Rebel's eyes. Jaydee held the chain tight.

"Shoot him!" Piper's scream bounced off the walls.

The gun slipped through her fingers like it weighed a hundred pounds. Sweat ran down her forehead and into her eyes. Her knees shook.

Jaydee laughed. "No way. She'll never do it. Not if her life depends on it. If she can't blow away a paper man, how can she shoot a real one?"

Rebel's eyes had closed and his head began to nod. His knees buckled as he went down.

"Do something!" Piper's bound-up body wobbled back and forth.

The gun was a Glock 9mm, the same kind she shot at the range. She *had* this. A bizarre sense of calm settled over her and, to her surprise, her pounding heart slowed. She widened her stance, lined up the sights with her target and squeezed the trigger.

The thunder of the shot blasted her ears, the kickback far stronger than she'd expected, and the ejected shell, flying over her shoulder, made her flinch, but she held her ground. Jaydee slid behind Rebel as the horse sank, legs folding underneath him.

She hadn't hit Jaydee. He still had hold of the twitch. She hadn't stopped him from suffocating Rebel.

"Get the control!" Piper bellowed.

It took her a second before she understood what Piper meant. Nothing to do with getting a grip. "There's one more, Jaydee! It's in the Equitainer." The control Piper was preparing to skim from. "In the lab. You don't have the last dose from Rebel. You lost."

He stuck his head out from Rebel's side, indecision plastered all over his face. Rebel was on his knees.

Randi lowered the gun and took three steps, faking a dash to beat him to the control sample. Jaydee fell for it, dropped the twitch and raced for the lab. Rebel jerked his head up and staggered to his feet. The plastic bag floated away, and the ping-pong balls shot from his nostrils to bounce across the floor with an absurd sounding ping... ping... ping.

Jaydee flung himself up the steps. Randi raised the pistol, took aim and fired.

Rebel, panicked by the noise, scrambled like an ice skater trying to save himself from a fall, metal shoes scraping the concrete as he threw his body against the bars of the chute. The cemented posts squeaked in protest but held firm. Jaydee fell and rolled along the floor, crying out as he clutched a blood-soaked thigh.

She set the gun on top of one of the feed barrels and backed away from it, wiping her palms against her jeans. "You were right about one thing, Jaydee. I can't shoot a real man, but I can shoot you."

"*Randi.*" Piper's eyes bulged.

"Yeah, I know." She had to pull herself together, untie Piper and get help for Jaydee. She wasn't like him. She didn't understand him, definitely didn't love him anymore, but she wouldn't let him die. "I'll set you free, then I'll call him an ambulance."

"No." Piper shook her head. "Look."

Randi followed Piper's gaze to the breeding room door where, blending into the wooden wall, not moving, not speaking, Stacey's killer stood. The name on the sticky note. The woman who complained she always got stuck with the dirty work, the woman would do anything to save her beloved property, including stopping Stacey from taking away the horse that held the future of Lucky Jack in his million-dollar genes.

"Bury me out at Coffin Bone Canyon," she'd said over whis-key-coffee that day in her kitchen, "'cause I'll die before I give up this ranch."

Their eyes met. And here she'd gone and put the gun down. "Why, Helen? Why'd you do it?"

Helen moved fast for a woman her age, and before Randi knew it, she was once again on the wrong end of a gun. Once in a lifetime was too much. Twice was unthinkable.

"No choice." Helen's hand was rock steady. "I did what had to be done. That's what I always do."

"Mom." Jaydee winced as he sucked air in through his teeth. He'd found a polo wrap somewhere and was busy binding his leg. "I've got you covered. There's no way they'll pin it on you. Not with all the distractions I've provided. Leave Randi alone."

Strange thing for him to say when he'd planned on shooting her, but Helen didn't seem to listen anyway. She kept the weapon trained on Randi's head.

"I didn't set out to kill Stacey, but when I found she planned on leaving you and taking our Rebel... I tried to reason with her but she wouldn't listen. We started to argue. She hit me first. Slugged me on the lip, so I grabbed a hammer."

Randi's stomach twisted. It'd had about all it could handle tonight. "Matt's hammer. Convenient for framing him."

"No." Helen stuck her chin out, defiant. "Not true. It was only later I realized it might work in my favor. I just wanted to scare her. She didn't back down like I thought she would. She told me to mind my own damn business, but she didn't get it. Everything that happens at this ranch is my business."

"So you killed her because she wouldn't back down?"

"She spit on me. Nobody spits on me. It made me so mad I swung the hammer at her shoulder—her *shoulder*—but she ducked and..." Helen shook her head and stared at the floor. "Piece by piece, she was going to ruin us. It was only a matter of time. Somebody had to stop her. I didn't mean for it to go that far, but you can't change history."

Helen looked up, her eyes hard, all traces of emotion gone. "As for you, we're family here, and family sticks together, no matter what."

She breathed a sigh of relief. Helen had included her in her circle. She wasn't going to shoot her after all.

"You and Piper are the odd men out." Helen put her finger on the trigger. "I'm sorry."

Oh no. No, no, no. This couldn't be happening. Her life was *not* going to end here, in this barn. No way, no how. Her instructor always said a moving target was much harder to hit than a stationary one so, keeping the line of feed barrels in sight, she ran as fast as she could and ducked behind the first one like she was sliding into home plate. The blast boomed and a bullet whizzed past her head.

After the gunshot came an odd, hollow silence. Helen seemed frozen to the spot. Why didn't she fire again? Tears streamed down Piper's cheeks. Rebel pawed the ground then lifted his head, ears perked toward the doorway. Someone else was here.

"What in the Sam Hell is going on?"

Helen lowered the gun. Her hands must have been sweaty because she lost her grasp and the pistol clattered to the floor. With a sob, she ran to Houston and flung herself into his arms.

"It's over." Houston put his hand on Helen's back, comforting her and holding her steady but not pulling her in close. "Now we've got to make things right."

Thirty-Six

RANDI SQUEEZED HER EYES shut. It hurt to think. It hurt to move.

Something sizzled on the stove, and she could have sworn she smelled brewing coffee, but she was in bed, so how could that be? Her free arm dangled over the edge of the mattress and her fingertips brushed the floor. *Floor*? Her fingers couldn't touch the ground from her top bunk.

She remembered now. She'd tried to climb the ladder last night and had given up halfway. Too tired, too sore, too everything. Kira, bless her heart, had tucked her into the bottom bunk before she delivered the crushing news Shane hadn't come home. Randi'd cried herself to sleep. Alive, in one piece, yet without her dog, she'd never be complete. A weight settled heavy on her heart. She tried to move but could hardly muster enough energy to wiggle her fingers.

Something thumped the wall and a cold, wet nose pressed against her hand. Her eyes flew open. *Shane*! She threw her arms around his neck and tumbled off the bed, not caring how bad it hurt. He smothered her with doggy kisses, forcing her to shield her face with her arm. Beneath the crook of her elbow, Luke was in her kitchen, spatula in hand.

"Well, I'll be damned. What are you doing here?"

"Good morning to you, too." He had on jeans and a pale green button-down shirt and stood in front of a frying pan. "For starters, I've got cakes on the griddle."

John Denver's voice popped into her head. *Life ain't nothin' but a funny, funny riddle...*

"You hungry? Blueberry or banana? What's your pleasure?"

She tugged her T-shirt over her bare knees. "Blueberry, please."

"I knocked, but you didn't answer, so Shane and I let ourselves in. Hope you don't mind."

She wanted to leap up and throw her arms around him like she did to Shane, but her aching head didn't agree and her teeth felt gross. It was safe to assume the same about her breath, so she sat on the bed instead, basking in her elation. "Where did you find him?"

"I didn't. He found me."

"What do you mean?"

Luke waved the spatula. "Remember the microchip?"

"Of course. You made me inject it. First time I ever had to do it to one of my own."

"That's how the animal shelter knew to reach me."

"*Animal shelter?*"

"You were right about Tim Tyler, but at least he stashed your dog somewhere safe."

"Why'd he take him in the first place?"

"Jaydee's idea." Luke retrieved two mugs from the cupboard and poured the coffee. "He thought you'd focus only on finding Shane, leaving him free to do his thing. I guess he knew you were onto him."

"I'd love to say it was due to superior sleuthing, but it was more like superior dumb luck."

"Hey," Luke nodded at the book beside her bed. "Even private eye Kinsey Millhone gets some good fortune thrown her way every now and again." He motioned with his hand. "Come on. Take a seat. Montana-style flapjacks coming up. I made one for Shane, too." He tilted the pan so she could see. "Supposed to be a dog head. Looks more like a moth."

"A for effort. He won't care." She picked her robe off a pile on the floor, put it on, tied the sash and made her way stiffly to the table.

Luke pulled out a chair. "This place has closets, you know."

She smiled. "It does?"

"For hanging things. I had it made special that way."

"Funny."

"Turns out you don't have to meet my attorney friend Marty after all. How does it feel to be free?"

"Better than I could have imagined. Worth every cut and bruise on my body." She put her head in her hands. "I can't believe what Jaydee did. To me, to those colts, to his family."

"Greed and addiction aren't a good mix, and a disease is a disease. Be it M.S. or alcoholism or pathological gambling. Not that I'm condoning his actions."

"How did you know what went down last night? How'd you get all the answers?"

"Once I was sure the colt Houston brought in was stabilized, I went to Lucky Jack. Houston told me everything that happened, and Jaydee put his two cents in before the cops took him and Helen away. You know the rest of the story." Luke collected two plates from the dish drainer and set them next to the frying pan.

"I don't remember you being there. How come?'

"You'd already left with Kira. Houston asked her to drive you home. You don't remember that either?"

"No. How come?"

"Short-term memory loss. Could be the trauma, or a slight concussion. I need to check out that lump on your head."

She wasn't ready for that yet. "How'd Houston get a hold of her? She was here, waiting for Shane."

"He didn't call her. She called the ranch—looking for you."

"Oh."

"She left you something." Luke pointed to her desk. A square green bottle with a note attached to the stag's head label. Jäger-meister. A heart had been drawn in pink.

"She's a piece of work, isn't she?"

Luke set a plate of steaming pancakes on the table. A blob of butter spilled down the sides. "That she is, and a good friend to you, no doubt, but she should have taken you straight to the hospital. I would have."

She shook her head. "You know how emergency rooms are. I'd still be sitting in a plastic chair waiting to be seen instead of looking forward to digging into this delicious homemade break-fast."

Not much he could say to that. They both knew it wasn't far from the truth. She cut into the pancakes and shoved a bite into her mouth. "Did Houston and Helen know Jaydee was taking bribes from Tim Tyler to do those awful things?"

"I think they were sticking their heads in the sand."

"Houston knew something was up. He told me so on the beach. And Helen was probably concentrating all her efforts on covering up what she'd done." She was talking with her mouth full. She couldn't eat fast enough. If Luke noticed her pigginess, he was polite enough not to say so.

Luke leaned against the stove and crossed his arms. "Hous-ton didn't know anything for certain until late yesterday. He'd left his cigarettes in one of the tack rooms, and when he went back to get them, he caught Jaydee trying to suffocate another foal. Jaydee ran off and Houston got busy trying to save the colt. Then he brought it to me. Want some orange juice?"

"Grapefruit, please. What about Helen? I can't fathom how she could do such a thing. I've always admired her. There was a time I wanted to be just like her. Strong and loyal, convicted in my beliefs and comfortable in my own skin."

Luke opened the refrigerator and took out the juice. "We all have good *and* evil in us. Things aren't as black and white as people like to believe."

"Helen was offended by Stacey running around with Matt, I know that much. Whether they were having an affair or not is still a big question mark. Matt said he loved Stacey. That's all he'd admit to."

"Another tricky business."

"What is?"

Luke put the glass down. "Sometimes relationships don't have a great sense of timing." He came around the table. "Now, back to your head."

She waved her hand. "It's no worse than a migraine."

"Let me see." He skimmed his fingers over her skull. He checked her ears then lifted her hair and felt the back of her neck. "It's a good-sized lump, but I don't think anything's fractured."

She smiled. "I'm going to wear that sucker like a badge."

"Oh really? Miz Annie Oakley?"

"I like the sound of that, and despite the fact I was shaking like a leaf, firing Houston's gun was one of the most liberating things I've ever done." She laughed. "I never thought I'd say this, but NRA, here I come."

Luke raised his eyebrows. "Tell me something, did you aim for Jaydee's leg, or are you just a bad shot?"

"Ha, ha. The bullet went right where I told it to. I've wished him dead on numerous occasions, but that doesn't mean I could kill him."

"Too bad." Luke smiled.

She set her fork beside her plate. "What about Roberto?"

"Back in Mexico. For real this time."

"What's the story?"

"Unfortunately for him, he saw everything that happened the night Stacey was killed. Helen gave him some hush money and told him to go to back home, but he was all torn up inside and couldn't do it."

"Conflicting loyalties. So he went off the deep end and into a binge?"

Luke nodded. "When you called Helen from the Triton and

told her where he was, she found him on the street and drove him straight across the border. He's not legal."

"Will he be back?"

"I think they all try to come back. It's anybody's guess if he'll make it."

"Wow." She ran a hand through her hair. "I feel terrible."

"It's not your fault. You did what you thought was right for him at the time."

"Still..." Another uneasy thought tapped at her brain. "What's going to happen to the ranch?"

"Houston will do everything he can to keep it. Time will tell. Marty says Helen's likely looking at second-degree murder if they can prove it wasn't premeditated."

"What's the sentence for that?"

"Sixteen to life."

"And Jaydee?"

"He broke a handful of laws. We'll see what he gets charged with. I hope they throw the book at him."

"What about Tim Tyler?"

"I'm sure he'll hire some celebrity legal team, so who knows where he'll end up when the dust settles. I spoke with him this morning about Zany."

"And?"

"I offered him a twenty-five percent 'loyal client' discount off his bill, under the condition he allows you to continue Zany's treatment until we find out what's going to happen to Lucky Jack. He jumped at it. If he ever hassles you again, his fees double."

Sunshine streamed through the window. Shane lay curled on the floor, Abu at his side.

No running back to Colorado. Her wounds would scab and eventually scar. The damage would never go away, but she could learn to live with it. "I'll help, any way I can." Unless Kira told him, Luke would never know she'd planned on leaving.

"I'm sure Houston would appreciate your support." Luke wiped his hands on a dishtowel hanging from the oven door.

"About that head of yours, I think you're okay for now, but call me if the pain gets out of control or if you start feeling sick to your stomach."

"You're leaving?"

"I have a pre-purchase exam at nine-thirty." He checked his watch. "Gotta run."

"But... you didn't eat."

"It's okay. Throw the pancakes in the freezer. They'll keep."

She followed him to the door, her euphoria draining, leaving her hollow inside.

Luke pivoted on the porch. "Oh, by the way, the roan mare gave birth to a healthy colt. He's safe, and so is your Flying V baby. And Rebel, of course. Thanks to you."

She leaned against the doorway. "It's what anyone would have done."

"No. Not anyone. You saved that horse, Randi. You deserve the credit."

She shook her head. "Rebel saved *me*. In more ways than one. And as for you, I owe you big time for finding Shane and bringing him home."

"Yes, you do." His eyes sparked. "Don't worry, though. I've got a way you can pay off your entire debt in one easy night."

She drew her head back. He couldn't possibly mean... he wouldn't think—she loved her dog and all but—

"Dinner and a movie. I'll pick you up at six and we'll celebrate the first day of the rest of your life. Pardon the cliché. I know they make you writers cringe." Luke raised his eyebrows. "Hey, speaking of writing... ?"

"Couple more hours, then I'm sending my article off."

Shane's toenails clacked across the wood like he planned on following Luke out the door. She blocked him with her legs, but he plunged his nose between her knees, loosening the sash and parting her robe. He wagged his tail then went back to his bed and curled up with his stuffed monkey.

Luke took a giant step backward, grinning like a fool, without breaking eye contact until the morning shadow from the roofline fell across his face. "Six o'clock. Sharp."

"I'll be ready." She started to close the door, but Luke called her name and she pulled it open again.

"I almost forgot. Check your email."

She didn't watch him walk up the driveway like she usually did, but padded straight to her computer and opened her in-box. Luke had sent her an airline ticket to Denver, along with a voucher for a week's paid vacation plus free dog-sitting.

"Wow." She looked at Shane. "That's the nicest thing any-body's ever done for me. Maybe I should forget he's my boss for a while. Take a chance. What do you think?"

Shane lifted his head and opened his mouth in a wide pant-ing smile. If she didn't know better, she could have sworn he winked.

The Surf & Stirrup
Drink Recipes

RATTLESNAKE CIDER:
The perfect mix of sugar and spice. This mug of everything nice will warm you up after an evening of grunion hunting on the beach or a chilly desert night spent stargazing.
1 C hot apple cider
Shot of Fireball whiskey
Dash of Tabasco
Serve in a mug and top with whipped cream

COWBOY COOL-AID:
Chill out with a cowboy cool-aid after a run on the beach or a hot day in the saddle.
1 C Pacifico or Corona
1/2 C lemonade
Dash of cayenne pepper
Pour over ice in pint glass and salt rim

SHANE'S SLUSHY MONKEY:
Perfect for dessert or just skip dinner and get right to it.
1 scoop Chunky Monkey ice cream (Ben & Jerry's)
1/2 C milk
2 shots Bailey's Irish Cream
1 shot vodka
Crushed ice
Blend. Top with whipped cream and chocolate syrup.

REBEL'S YELL:

1 oyster
1 t spicy cocktail sauce
1 t lemon juice
1 t minced jalapeño
1 pinch diced cilantro
1 shot tequila

Shuck oyster and add to shot glass. Top with spicy cocktail sauce. Add the lemon juice, jalapeño, cilantro and tequila. Stir together and shoot!

MUSTANG MAI TAI:

1 lime, juiced
1 shot Gran Marnier
2 shots rum
1/2 shot Jägermeister

Shake ingredients with crushed ice. Pour into a highball glass. Garnish with lime wedge.

SURF'S UP:

2 shots Jägermeister
Crushed ice
Whipped orange juice
Sprig of chocolate mint leaf

Pour Jägermeister over ice. Top with whipped orange juice and sprig of chocolate mint.

FIVE HORSEMEN:

1 shot Jose Cuervo
1 shot Jack Daniels
1 shot Jim Beam
1 shot Johnny Walker
1 shot Jägermeister

Pour contents in shaker over ice and shake well. Pour into glass.

TEQUILA SUNSET:

1 shot tequila
Orange/pineapple juice
½ shot blackberry brandy
Cherry
Pour tequila into glass with ice. Fill with orange/pineapple juice and stir well. Add brandy. Top with cherry.

MULE KICK:

2 shots espresso (or black coffee)
1 shot Baileys Irish Cream
1 shot vodka
Mint leaf
Pour coffee into mug. Add Bailey's and vodka. Stir lightly and top with mint leaf.

ACKNOWLEDGMENTS

Special thanks to Sandy Arledge of Sandy Arledge Quarter Horses, for her infinite wisdom of all things equine, Kevin Dickson, ranch manager Vessels Stallion Farm, Michael Steppe, DVM, and the staff at Chino Hills Equine Hospital, and Audrey Pavia for guiding me through the complications of equine recurrent uveitis.

CPSIA information can be obtained at www.ICGtesting.com
Printed in the USA
BVOW03s1129030114

340849BV00004B/211/P

9 781938 467844